MARRED

SUE COLETTA

Tirgearr Publishing

Published by Tirgearr Publishing
Ireland
www.tirgearrpublishing.com

ISBN 978-1-910234-23-5

A CIP catalogue record for this book is
available from the British Library.

10 9 8 7 6 5 4 3 2 1

DEDICATION

To my husband, my love and best friend, Bob.

Without your support and encouragement this book would not be possible. I told you, honey, dreams really do come true.

I love you with all my heart and soul.

Q

ACKNOWLEDGEMENTS

To my many author friends who don't hesitate to lend an ear, offer advice and encouragement…a heartfelt thank you. I'm blessed to have you in my life. I'd also like to acknowledge my Tirgearr family. I feel fortunate to work with such a talented team. To my blog community—you rock! It never ceases to amazes me the lengths the writing community will go to support one another. To all of you, I send huge hugs and appreciation. Lastly, but certainly not least, a quick shout-out to my family: Dad, Bob, Bobby, Kathy, Berlyn, and Scarlet. You mean everything to me.

Prologue

Saturday, September 20, 2003

Even the weather betrayed me. Aqua-blue sky, not a cloud in sight. Niko and I sat in silence during the two-and-a-half hour trip north. Next week offered a new beginning, a chance to leave Boston and never look back.

I lowered the back passenger window. A light breeze ruffled farmland acres, and a full, round sun shined, burned, blazed as though this was an ordinary day. The limousine tires hit cracked asphalt, the road worn from a brutal New Hampshire winter. Birds whistled serenades. Preteens played basketball within the confines of school grounds. Young, adolescent voices carried in the crisp morning air, rustling hues of burnt orange, scarlet, and burgundy through autumn leaves. Mountains stood proudly as if they could protect us. Here, perhaps, but not in Boston, where my nightmare began eight days and six hours ago.

We drove by the Minot Sleeper Library, and my gaze narrowed on the patrons. A middle-aged woman clutched my latest novel close to her heart like a coveted treasure. Scorching heat jagged up my chest. Soon she'd enjoy my words while I endured the harshest committal.

Didn't she know? Couldn't she feel my pain, my anguish? Pure evil enveloped my life and then spit me out like bitterness on a delicate palate, leaving me reeling in torment.

The hearse carrying our dreams, our endless devotion, veered right through tall, iron gates and followed a winding road to the back of the cemetery.

My fingers curled around the armrest, and I shifted my sight to Niko.

Splayed hands on his knees, he turned only his head and offered a weak, faint smile. "You okay?" His voice was barely above a whisper.

To demonstrate what I thought of his stupid question, I shot him a cutting glare.

Palms up, Niko opened his arms. "What? I only asked if you were okay."

"Seriously?" I said. "How could anyone be okay with this?"

Two funeral employees in dark suits dragged a tiny coffin from the back of the hearse. Stark white, the casket rode in their hands as the men marched over burnt, dead grass. Lowering the coffin onto two bands, they stepped away. My baby lingered above the mouth of an awaiting grave—displaying my shame, announcing my cowardice.

"We've gotta go." Niko's words churned the sickening feeling deep in my gut.

I peered through the side window, the cemetery dark and gloomy through tinted glass. The world now appeared as it should, mourning along with me.

Niko said, "Babe?"

The limo driver opened my door and startled me. He reminded me of a prison guard, hands clasped behind his back, eyes focused straight ahead. Behind him, rows and rows of ghosts, shattered lives buried deep with nothing left but a headstone to mark their existence. In the distance, an emerging sea of blue soldiered toward the grave—Niko's fellow detectives, the ones who did nothing.

I twisted toward my husband, and a stabbing pain stole my breath. I bit my upper lip, waiting for the pang to subside. "Why are *they* here?"

"To pay their respects, Sage. Look, if you wanna blame someone—"

"Don't," I warned.

My crutches in hand, he dashed around the back of the limo to my door. Jaw clenched, I sneered at my new mode of transportation and steadied my balance with the toe of my splinted leg. I dropped my chin to my chest. Dammit. Why didn't I fight? Why didn't I *do* something, anything?

With a supportive arm around my waist, Niko coaxed me toward the gravesite. I passed him one of the crutches and rested my head against his strong chest. If only he could sweep me away, so I didn't have to face this devastation.

I squeezed my eyes closed. I couldn't look, couldn't witness the finality. It wasn't fair. I had no memories to savor. No first touch, no tiny fist gripping my finger. No first steps, first word. I never had the chance to admire a newborn's searching eyes, gazing at the world as a wondrous place. Instead, I had the harsh reality that wicked men roamed free, leaving destruction in their wake.

I had nothing, except the faint recall of precious feet kicking my insides, yearning to break free and experience life. My baby's lungs never had the chance to expand with oxygen-infused air. He would never know the magic of Christmas, or admire glorious lights dancing on tree limbs. My boy would not have the honor of placing a brilliant star on the top branch as his daddy lifted him so his delicate hands could reach.

For God sake, he didn't even have a name. The headstone was marked only with, "Baby Quintano." This was so cruel. Why did we have to endure such torture? There wasn't much I wouldn't do for my unborn son. But this? Dear God, not this.

Bob Jordan, the funeral director, recited the opening remarks. I cocked an ear, my grip tightening around the crutch. I slid my gaze toward Niko. Did he notice slight nuances in Bob's pitch, the unspoken truth I insisted he conceal?

Beneath gauze bandages, sweat seeped through the multitude of stitches zigzagging across my forearms. Pain throbbed from a dislocated knee, and broken ribs labored my breath—my injuries refusing to allow a moment of repose. Thanks to a mass murderer who slipped through Niko's grasp, tranquility no longer existed.

Tears brimmed in my husband's red-rimmed eyes and he offered me a reassuring squeeze. "It's almost over, babe."

I swallowed, averted my gaze. I didn't deserve his kindness, his love.

We huddled together opposite six Boston detectives in department dress blues. Cold stares in my direction, foreheads rippled in accusation.

Bob Jordan asked if we wanted to speak. Niko swept my hair out of my face, but I kept my head down, staring at the ground.

"I think we're all set," he said, tears hitching his voice.

Bob gave a slight nod and cranked a handle that lowered our child into the maw of nevermore. Hot tears slipped down the sides of my face, salt biting jagged wounds on my cheek, upper lip, and neck. The cemetery became eerily quiet. Soft gasps and muffled cries from my heart fracturing beyond repair pierced a cool September wind.

Inside I screamed, "No! Don't take our baby! Please, stop! I can't survive this!" Verbally, as usual, I remained silent.

As we rode through the cemetery gates, I swiveled to peer out the back windshield, a piercing ache deep in my empty womb. If only, somehow, this was just a bad dream.

Chapter One

Monday, July 17, 2006 1:30 p.m.

I used to believe people were inherently good, if only at their core. I saw the brokenness of the homeless. I respected the overachiever in the football star hoping for Daddy's approval even if he'd never get it. I saw the heart of sinners, the souls of lovers. Shattered dreams of an abandoned child. I saw good in evil, spirit in the unholy. I understood the complexities of love, marriage, life. Hell, I welcomed the challenge. I had hopes, dreams and affirmations. I did.

Then, that all changed. My views shattered, or my eyes finally opened.

That's what Niko said, though devastation also filled his eyes. No longer did he think of me as his optimistic wife who loved life. I missed our blissful marriage. I missed our baby. I missed my blindfold. If only I could put it back on. Most of all, I missed…me.

Living on autopilot was the only way I could survive.

After my third shower of the day, I hobbled down the stairs, clutching a load of laundry. White-hot pain shot to my right knee and folded me in half. The basket of clothes tumbled to the floor—socks, T-shirts, jeans, shorts, and Niko's sheriff's uniform strewn about the living room.

I fell back against the stairs, twined my arms around the railing, and stared at the white lines on my forearms. I straightened, and a thick scar on my jugular tugged at the skin. After three never-ending years, hours and hours of counseling, one small reminder—scars from the knife—and I relived that night in Boston.

The phone startled me when it rang.

I didn't want to answer, but for the Sheriff's wife that wasn't an option. "Hello?"

"Who's this?" A man's voice, distorted, disguised.

"Who's this? You called me."

"I think I have the wrong number."

A dial tone sounded.

That was weird. I shrugged it off and reloaded the clothes in the basket. When I headed down the hall, the phone rang a second time. I'd had it with this guy. "Hello," I answered, firm and harsh.

"Sheriff Quintano, please." Same voice.

"Didn't you just call here?"

"Sheriff Quintano, please."

"He's not home. He's at work. Who *is* this?"

The line went dead.

"Jerk!" I slammed the handset in the cradle, and a chill sheathed my arms in goose bumps. I'd announced to a stranger that I was alone in the house.

The cordless phone's musical trill resonated through the hall. Ruger and Colt jolted to their paws and took notice. I winced, not wanting to answer.

Third ring.

I rushed over. "I told you he's not home. What do you want? Why are you calling back?"

"Do you want to live forever?"

A cold sweat broke across my back. "What'd you say?" *This cannot be happening. Not again. Unless... evil followed us here.*

"Do you want to live forever?"

He found me. How? We were so careful. Niko and I hadn't left a forwarding address. Our phone number wasn't listed in the book. Neighbors asked where we were moving, and we refused to disclose any details. If questioned, I said north and left it at that. We escaped clean and faded into obscurity. Yet, he called.

I dropped the handset in the cradle, disconnecting from the past.

Adrenaline masked my pain, and I sprinted from room to room, closed and secured all the windows and double-checked the locks on the front and back doors, bolted upstairs, and pressed my foot on the sliders' security bar. Colt and Ruger watched me zip around the house, not knowing what was wrong. Ruger gave up and laid his head on crossed paws while Colt bounded over and stayed on my heels.

When I returned to the kitchen table, the phone rang again. My gaze locked on the handset, and I froze. Colt's face ping-ponged between me and the phone. He put the pieces together in his mind, trotted over, and knocked the receiver off the cradle, gently clasped the handset in his lips and carried it to me. By using his training to aid me, he was trying to help, but at that moment, it was the last thing I wanted him to do.

I didn't speak.

The man panted like Ruger after an exhausting game of fetch. I slapped a hand over my mouth and held back screams, refusing to give him the satisfaction of terrifying me. I also couldn't hang up. His breath held me hostage. My fingers lost feeling around the handset, knuckles white from lack of blood flow. Unable to move, I was in his thrall.

"Do you want to live forever?"

I gaped left, right. He could be outside my home hiding in the bushes. If I didn't respond, he might come inside. Perhaps he'd stalked me for days, weeks, months. Maybe he'd always been here. Out of reach, in the shadows. Watching. Waiting. Planning.

Why, oh, why was this happening again?

Razor-sharp pain shot to my right knee, ribs, arms, and stomach, his haunting question conjuring the injuries from the fateful night. I cringed. "What do you want?"

His demon-like cackle shot through my core like a poison-tipped arrow.

If only Niko had killed him that night…if his guts had splattered my living room walls, dousing me in his death…if he'd taken his last breath and his evil soul plummeted to hell…perhaps then I could breathe without his ghostly fingers around my throat.

How did he survive?

Niko had emerged outside the sliders and shot through one

of the doors. The bullet struck the masked man in the shoulder. Glass shattered everywhere. The dogs barreled inside and over to me, whimpering, licking the blood off my face. They were so preoccupied with tending to my wounds; the intruder got a shot off before he fell.

The bullet struck Niko in the shoulder, and he flew backward and landed in the garden I'd made around the apple tree. It had taken me days to edge the garden in slanted bricks. When Niko fell, those bricks drove into his spine and incapacitated him long enough for the assailant to scramble to his feet and flee.

But not before he hovered over me and offered one last warning. *"I'll see you soon, Sage Quintano."*

That night he cackled too, as though he foresaw this day. After the attack, I hid for weeks, months. I lost track of how long I made myself a prisoner in my home. January slowed my heart rhythm to a manageable pace. Niko said that was when I healed. Not true. I'd never be the same. He'd stolen my child, my soul, my very being. The person I once was—outgoing, funny, adventurous—no longer existed. With his wrath and venomous, malevolent acts, he'd marred me for life.

For that, he should pay.

Deep in his throat, he chortled, sounding like the devil incarnate.

I bolted into the living room. In the corner by the sofa a grandfather clock ticked, slow and loud like a dying patient's heartbeat. Disconnected from my tormentor, I thumbed the button for a dial tone. Niko's cell rang twice before I hung up. Because I hadn't shared the intimate details of the assault, if I explained how I knew this was the same man, there would be questions. Lots of questions. Questions I was unwilling to answer. If my husband heard the truth, he might leave.

I was trapped. Perfect prey. Nowhere to run; no place left to hide.

* * *

Two hours later, I was searching through old records. The moving van we'd rented in Boston, utility shut-off notices, a letter I wrote to the Boston Herald to stop the newspaper—every receipt from the weeks before the move to see if Niko or I had mistakenly given out our new address.

I found nothing.

A hospital bill caught my eye as I loaded the papers back in the box. In the corner of the bill was our phone number. This number. The woman in the billing department had demanded a way to contact us, and as I recovered at home, I overheard Niko rattle off the digits.

He glanced at me and mouthed, "It's fine. Don't worry."

Only now, it wasn't fine. This was how he'd found us. Found me.

Someone knocked at the front door, and Colt and Ruger howled. I whirled around, my heart sinking in my chest.

Another knock.

I approached the front entrance. One step. The other. I cracked open a peek-a-boo window at the top of the oak door.

I exhaled.

Our mailman, George, wore a smile that spread across his chubby face. "Need ya to sign fer this, Mrs. Quintano." He passed me a clipboard and a gold pen.

I signed my name on the line and passed it back. "Nice pen, George. Was it a gift from your wife?"

Small towns. Even though we'd only lived here a short while, we knew the key players—employees of the post office, police station, library, and supermarket. Hard not to. If the librarian heard me cough, she'd tell every patron to be wary of my cold. She couldn't help herself. All the more reason I offered a warm smile in public and nothing more.

"Yup. Betty found it at Carl's." Carl's Cool Stuff, our local antique/junk/pawn shop. "Ol' Carl sold it fer a buck. A buck! Ain't that a hoot? Real gold too." George shook his head. "Poor Carl. He's gettin' old." George was getting old, too. He forgot to hand me the priority mail envelope. "Whoops. Here ya go, Mrs. Quintano." He tipped his hat. "Ya have yerself a great day."

"You too, George."

I carried the envelope to the kitchen table, and a thrill zipped up my spine. I loved presents. The smudged return address made it impossible to tell who sent it, but I presumed Niko.

When we were first married, he sent me gifts all the time. He'd say, "Just because I love you." Or "Just because you make me happy." He called them his just because gifts.

I tore it open.

Inside the sleeve was a necklace I recognized immediately. As ten-year-olds, my sister and I saved our allowances to buy two necklaces, each with a silver-and-turquoise angel pendant. When put together they formed Gemini. Being identical twins—Chloe two minutes older and she never let me forget it—these necklaces professed our unity. A sacred bond we thought would endure through anything, no matter how old we got or what transpired in our lives.

I tossed it back in the mail sleeve.

We'd had words a few weeks ago over something stupid. I guess this was her way of saying she wanted nothing more to do with me. As I set the envelope on the kitchen counter, I couldn't imagine what had prompted Chloe to do this. But I intended to find out and dialed her number.

Her cell phone rang and rang. I called her landline and got her answering machine. "I got your message, Chlo, but I wish you'd reconsider. Call me back so we can talk about this. I'm so sorry. I should've never judged you. Please, Chlo, I miss you. I want my sister back." I sniffled. "Love you to the moon, 'round the world, and back again."

I waited to see if she answered. "Okay. I've said my piece. Call me." I was about to hang up when a man answered.

"Chloe isn't here."

I bit back the anger. "Joe?"

"Yeah."

"Tell Chloe her sister called…please."

"Yup," he said, but there was something in his tone that made me think otherwise. "This Sage?"

"Since you're sleeping with her, you ought to know." I dialed back the attitude in case he told Chloe. "Yes. It's Sage. Tell her I called…please."

"You can bet your sweet ass I'll do more than that."

"What's *that* supposed to mean?"

"Bye, Sage."

Before I could respond, he slammed down the phone, a crash that nearly broke my eardrum. As I re-cradled the handset, a familiar suspicion reared its ugly mug, a haunting question screaming through my senses—was Chloe safe?

Chapter Two

3:00 p.m.

Sheriff Niko Quintano drove down Bailey Road in Alexandria, wringing the steering wheel in his hands, upper lip twitching. A murderer roamed free in his sleepy community, muddying the lake's shoreline, stinking up the fresh pine scent, evil overshadowing glorious mountain ranges. Lack of violent crime was a large part of why he and Sage decided to move north. Niko was not as young as he used to be, and working round the clock to catch a scumbag who got his kicks slaughtering innocent lives was not what he had in mind for life after fifty.

He'd done his twenty-years at Boston PD—thirty, actually—and earned enough of a pension to support his family. He wasn't the type of man to sit around all day. Unlike his wife, who had the perfect excuse to do nothing and still refused to succumb to rheumatoid arthritis, his health was near perfect. Except for an ache in his left shoulder from where a bullet had sliced his rotator cuff.

When it rained or snowed, the old wound forced him to recall the night he almost lost Sage and to question himself. What, if anything, could he have done differently, when a serial killer decided to get even by torturing the one person he loved most in this world? No, dealing with a multiple murderer was not what he had in mind when they chose Alexandria from the other rural towns in the area. Far from it.

In the passenger seat, Deputy Frankie Campanelli stared out the window watching the world sail by. Swiveling toward him, she clicked off the stereo. "You look like you're a million miles away this morning. Is it cause of this?" She jabbed her chin toward a dirt road on the left, the latest murder site.

"I dunno. Just thinking about Sage. This morning we—" He paused, rephrased. "I thought things would be different here, is all."

"Hey, I get it." She flashed a flat hand. "Preachin' to the choir."

These murders must be getting to him. For a split second, he did a double-take as the sun illuminated reddish highlights in his deputy's raven hair and the breeze from the open window whisking her wispy bangs. He cleared his throat, erasing the image from his mind.

He hung a left onto a dirt road that climbed at a forty-five-degree angle, up a steep hill. "I'll never get used to these friggin' cliffs. Lookit this shit. Half the town's flat, the other half's like driving up the side of Mt. Rushmore."

"That's because we are, genius."

Niko banged a right at the top and Frankie took hold of the J-strap to keep from falling in his lap—thank God. "I meant a mountain," she said. "Mt. Rushmore's a mountain, right?"

"You're kidding, right?"

Gravel and ledge caused the Ford Police Interceptor to buck like a wild stallion, and he tightened his grip on the wheel as he set his sight back on the road. "The shocks are getting a great workout today."

Frankie stared out the windshield, no doubt resisting the urge to toss another wise remark his way. Why she showed some self-control wasn't clear.

At the peak, Niko swung in front of a deserted barn with natural siding, the clear coat peeling in narrow strips. Pine needles masked dead, straw-like grass. A heavily wooded lot surrounded the property with dense foliage, and Niko couldn't tell if the place was swarming with reporters yet. The faint scent of barbecue chicken lingered in the air from a smoldering campfire, smoke billowing through tree tops. Illegal, no doubt.

The press had probably camped out to snag a shot of the murder victim. Damn vultures. They could care less about the victims' families. A bunch of frickin' monkeys, the whole lot of them, climbing trees, lying flat behind brush. Anything for a story.

Squinting out the windshield, he slid the shifter into park. "Think the vultures are around?"

She threw her head back. "Hah! Probably. They don't give a rat's ass. But we usually spot a van on the main drag. Haven't seen one. You?"

"They probably paid the neighbor to stash it behind his house." He swatted the air. "Ah, who the hell knows with this crew? I'll tell ya, they'd never get away with this crap in Boston. But here…" There was no point in finishing. No amount of bitchin' would get them to stop. He was the sheriff, and he couldn't get them to back off. Frankie probably stopped listening, anyhow—her usual MO.

One hand on the door handle, he twisted at the waist. "This time, let's avoid the topic of Colebrook. There may be unfamiliar faces here, and I don't want them to get the wrong impression." Ever since Frankie transferred in from farther north, whenever someone asked about Colebrook, New Hampshire she used her favorite line to describe her quaint, rural hometown. "Where sheep are sheep and men are scared." Every time she did, Niko wanted to dive under the nearest desk and bury his face, mortified.

She rolled her lips. "Whatever. I'm only kiddin' around."

"That's fine when it's you and me. But cops who don't know you might not…appreciate…your humor like I do."

"Fine. Can we go?"

"What's the rush? You got a cow tippin' party to get to?"

Her mouth dropped open. "Sure, it's fine for you to use hillbilly humor, but not me."

Niko stuck his tongue out and exited the truck. Over the roof, he said, "Seriously. Let's keep it professional."

"Why do you always say that? Since when am I not professional?"

He raised one eyebrow and spun on his heels. Henry Reed, the officer who arrived first on scene, followed Niko and Frankie into the barn.

"Whadda we got?" asked Niko. "This our guy?"

At the mere mention of the crime scene, Reed turned a nice

shade of green. It was only a matter of time before he puked all over Niko's new Italian loafers that Sage bought him with the publisher's last advance. Eyes wide, the young officer slapped his mouth, cheeks puffed—a panicked stare, asking permission to leave.

"Go," he urged. "I can't have you contaminating the scene." As Reed bolted from the barn, Niko shook his head, muttering, "Damn rookies."

Raising his chin in greeting, he passed the Medical Examiner's assistant, Billy Michaels, the mayor's only son. He sniffed the air. Aramis cologne. That could only mean one thing. "Doc Gaines beat us here," he said to Frankie. "That's new."

The inside of the barn had a small loft that overlooked the first level. Decrepit wood walls crumbled over time, scattering pieces of timber across a faded wide-pine floor. Different size footprints ran back, forth, and diagonal, over the wood. With patrol strolling in and out at will, it was impossible to tell if the mutt left any prints of his own.

Decomposing flesh left a rank taste in his mouth, and the unmistakable scent of death filled his sinuses. He surveyed the empty room.

Where'd Frankie disappear to now?

His sight narrowed on the letter H painted in blood on the center pane of a side window, and his eyebrows drew together.

Frankie called his name. From where, wasn't clear.

No corpse was hanging from the rafters. Why would the mutt change his MO? Beneath the loft floor, an elaborate lacing of ropes stretched from a pulley system to a ten-inch wooden beam, halfway up the cathedral wall. Shredded ivory material dripped off stakes in a board, like pieces of raw meat, and zip ties dangled from the rope where the woman's feet must have been bound.

Now it made sense. "Where are you?" He figured Frankie was behind a massive wooden box, large enough to hold a body, toward the back of the main floor. But he couldn't see her or the ME.

Frankie rose to her feet—her shoulder length hair now clipped in a loose ponytail. With her olive complexion and radiant green eyes, some might call her a looker. Once she opened her mouth, however, the illusion was over.

As he approached the box, his mouth fell open. Beneath her Sheriff's Department windbreaker, Frankie was wearing skin-tight black jeans, a fiery-red T-shirt with a deep neckline, and a leather vest. Not exactly what he had in mind for his deputies. He wasn't strict with the dress code. Hell, even he despised the uniform. The only time he insisted was when they worked a crime scene or testified in court. Otherwise, all he asked was that they presented themselves as professionals. Leave it to Frankie to be the nonconformist. He gave it a shot anyway. "Where's your uniform?"

"How can anyone look good in that thing?" Her five-inch heels clicked around the front of the box, the sound muffled from disposable booties. *Tap, tap, tap* coiled through the barn.

Niko pulled his jaw closed and strode over to the ME, squatting next to a dead woman, behind the box. "What happened?"

Frankie hovered over his shoulder. "Freaky, right?"

Niko glanced back. She was a little too close for his liking.

"Lookit how her hands ripped right down the middle," she remarked. "That had to hurt, huh? Ooh, there's somethin' else." She hip-checked the ME out of the way and yanked down the front of the woman's gown. "She's still got her tits. Whassup with that?"

"This isn't right. Why wouldn't he—" With a slight shake of the head, he waved his hand in front of his face, erasing his comment. "This isn't right. He doesn't make mistakes. He knows exactly where to drive in those spikes. He wouldn't be careless enough to clip them right after the fingers. Last time, he drilled straight through the palm. And it worked. So why change it? Something's not right here."

Frankie pointed out, "Maybe he was in a hurry. Maybe someone was comin'. Maybe he knew her. It could be any one of a gazillion things."

"I suppose." He scrutinized the victim's injuries. "What'd we withhold from the press last time?"

She touched the back of her hand to Niko's forehead. "You

all right? You're the one who said we should say she was murdered and not give specifics. So that's what we did. We didn't tell 'em shit." She lowered her voice. "Frickin' vultures."

When he parted his lips to respond, she wedged her fingers under the center of her bra, wiggling, adjusting the cups. "This thing's been riding up on me all day."

He shielded the side of his eyes with his hand, and a flush crept across his cheeks.

"So," Frankie called him back, "what're you thinkin', partner? Copycat?"

"Nah." In the hopes of erasing the last two seconds from his mind, he cleared his throat. "You'd have to be a sick pup to copy this guy. Besides, how would someone know the signature? No. This is our guy, all right. He got sloppy. We figure out why, we'll be all that much closer to catching him." He paused. "Oh, right. Someone said there's a witness? Where's he?"

"Childs has him in the cruiser. Why? You think he saw somethin'? It's my understanding he only found the vic."

The Medical Examiner, Dr. Christian Gaines, a brilliant black man who must spend half his salary on Aramis cologne, straightened the dead woman's face. Black Xs stitched over the eyes and mouth appeared as though the killer was trying to erase her features.

See no evil; speak no evil? Nah. Too easy.

Deep indentations left red rings around her wrists and ankles from being handcuffed and shackled for hours before death, identical to the first victim, Shelly Winters. Long blonde hair clumped with dried blood matted crimson strands to the sides of her face.

Tiny freckles speckled her nose and high cheekbones, and for a flash, she reminded him of Sage at that age. He erased it from his mind. The last thing he needed was to emotionally relate. If he did, he'd never be able to investigate with a clear head. Stitch holes had trickles of dried blood, but the rest of her face was washed clean. Contusions and abrasions scarred her arms, and cigarette burns scabbed the soles of her feet.

Frankie gasped. "Whoa. She's way younger than the first one. What's she, Doc, 'bout eighteen?"

Gaines cut the stitching around the girl's mouth and examined her teeth. "As you are aware, I do not specialize in odontology. That said, if you are looking for my opinion, I would say…" He leaned in. "Approximately eighteen years of age, yes."

"What's with this box?" Expecting a hollow sound, Niko knocked on the top.

Thud.

The echo caved his stomach. "We know what's in here?" he asked Gaines.

"I am afraid I must apologize. My assistant opened it. He does not know any better, Sheriff."

"Wearing gloves?"

"Pardon?"

"Gloves?"

"When he raised the lid? Sorry, no." Without warning, Gaines hollered over his shoulder, and right into Niko's ear. "Billy, front and center."

To clear the ringing, he fingered his ear.

The mayor's son rushed over. Shamefaced, Billy shuddered in front of Gaines, and Niko thought for sure the kid was either going to cry or piss his pants. Before Gaines could admonish him, he spun toward Niko. "I'm so sorry, Sheriff. I didn't know it was evidence, I swear."

"Look, kid. I know you're new." He took a breath, controlled the urge to berate the boy. He couldn't take the chance of Daddy making his job more difficult. As it was, he had enough trouble keeping Frankie in line. Besides, one look at Gaines told him Billy would get a tongue lashing, albeit probably the best-mannered he'd ever heard.

He clamped a hand on Billy's shoulder, squeezed light but firm. "From now on, when you enter a crime scene don't… touch…anything. Nothing. Concentrate on your duties and do *not* let your curiosity get the better of you. Am I clear?"

"Yes, sir." Billy frowned, hung his head.

"I'm gonna have to print you. Make yourself available."

"Print me?" His bright-blue eyes flashed wide, cleft chin trembling. "Am I under arrest?"

With a loud exhale, Niko shook his head—fast becoming his usual response. "I need to exclude your prints from the others. If the perp touched this box…which I'm sure he did—"

"He did, Sheriff."

Upper lip curled, Niko eyed him like a rabid dog.

"He did, Sheriff. I swear. What's inside ain't pretty."

"Step aside." He folded his gloved fingers around a wrought-iron handle on the top of the box and raised the lid. "Whoa." He let go. The lid slammed shut. "That sick bastard." He chanced another peek inside. "There's got to be at least ten jars in here." Forehead furrowing, his gaze ran the inside of the barn. "Are we in *his* house?"

"He drained them," Gaines said, unbidden. "Did I not mention that?"

"No, Doc. You didn't mention that. I didn't see it in your report, either." A large vein in Niko's neck pulsed. "What the hell? A little heads up next time?"

His wife was a big proponent of meditation, always raving about the stress-reducing benefits. He closed his eyes, breathed in…out…

The Sheriff's face burned as though he was gazing down at the fringes of hell. Damn him. With Gaines' background, he should know better. For a number of years, Gaines had worked in Manchester. The city of Manchester, New Hampshire was the furthest thing from a small hick town. Murder ran rampant. Niko didn't care if the doctor had twenty bodies on his table. Without giving him the facts, including details of the MO that could only be determined through an autopsy, he was tying his hands. Working these homicides with a bunch of hillbillies was ticking him off.

He opened his eyes. So much for Sage's bright idea; she didn't have to work with the crew from *The Deer Hunter*.

His gaze shot toward the front door. Every officer within a

thirty-mile radius was strolling in and out to witness the brutality of the crime. At least a dozen stood around drinking coffee, gossiping about small town bullshit.

Un-freakin' believable.

"Everyone, listen up!" He smacked his hands together. "You're contaminating my crime scene. Follow your footprints out the door and make yourself available for shoe impressions. Billy here—" he dragged the kid over by the arm— "will take your name and badge number on your way out." He jabbed his chin toward Gaines. "You don't need him, right?" Daring him to say no.

"He is all yours, Sheriff."

"Maybe you'll learn something," Niko told Billy. "Stranger things have happened," he mumbled, re-facing the officers. "From now on, no one but essential personnel are allowed inside the perimeter of the tape. That means me, my partner, members of my team, and the Medical Examiner's staff. Unless you were specifically asked to assist, get the fuck outta my sight. And don't go crying to your superior, either. Won't do you any good."

Frankie rushed to Niko's side as officers muttered under their breath, things like "Prick" and "Who the hell does he think he is?" as they exited the two-story barn.

She leaned aside. "Little harsh, don'tcha think?"

"Look at the goddam floor. Prints everywhere. Hasn't anyone ever heard of booties?"

Frankie parted her lips to answer.

"That was rhetorical." He resisted rolling his eyes as he glared at the mess of boot prints. "Now we've gotta take the time to get elimination prints from half the friggin' county. Small town heroes. I need some air."

Fire coursing through his veins, he stormed out the side entrance but stared through the doorway. The motley crew stumbled over their own feet, trying to leave the same way they entered. He could not believe the stupidity that surrounded him. Why did he ever quit smoking? These were uniformed officers—cops!—and not one could follow their own footprints.

Once the barn emptied out, Niko entered—mentally regrouped—and scrutinized the crime scene with fresh eyes. Ben Mathews, a new addition to the sheriff's department, hesitated in the doorway. He waved him inside. "You're with me."

A large blood pool gathered beneath the pulley, and he approached to distinguish the blood pattern. Ben followed like a lost puppy. "Frankie, can you finish shooting the scene and collect evidence while I educate Ben in blood spatter?"

With a click of her heels and a snap of her wrist, she saluted. "No problemo, boss."

He didn't find her funny. Not today. He was in no mood. "Come closer, Ben. I'm not mad at you." He glanced at Ben's feet. Baby blue booties over his work boots. Uniform pressed. Razor-sharp creases in his pants. Perfect.

Ben had worked as a police officer in Plymouth before deciding the sheriff's department was a better fit. When he applied for a transfer, Niko took one look at his military background and commendations and jumped at the chance to add him to his team. That was one year ago, and ever since Niko had trained him hard.

Frankie could never replace him as sheriff one day, especially with her gruff exterior. Her knee jerk reaction of running her mouth, usually meant insulting comments aimed at the balls of superiors. Ben was the polar opposite, always ready to take orders.

The barn resembled a slaughterhouse—blood on the walls, floor, even the H on the window dripped like a severed throat.

Chapter Three

Tuesday, July 18, 2006 4:00 a.m.

I jolted upright in bed, a puddle of sweat left on the sheets. Another nightmare. Would they ever stop? Rubbing my belly, my heart ached for the life I lost. If I had tried harder to defend myself, I might not feel like such a failure. A victim.

Something had to change. I couldn't go on this way.

I threw the covers off my legs and swung them to the floor.

Niko groaned and rolled toward me. "You okay?" he mumbled and patted my hip before falling back to sleep.

He was a good man. Patient and understanding, even though part of him probably still blamed me for the miscarriage. Niko and I tried for years to have children. One March morning I awoke and charged for the bathroom, vomiting over and over until I dry heaved. Later the doctor informed me we were pregnant. When I told Niko, he swept me into his arms and danced around the living room.

Six months later that man broke into our home... There was so much blood.

The cordless phone rang, vibrating the nightstand, and gold earrings danced across the natural finish.

To not wake Niko, I whispered, "Hello?"

"Do you want to live forever?" The computerized voice again.

Every muscle in my body tensed. My throat tightened, and the scar on my jugular pulsed to the beat of my thundering heart. A million things raced through my mind in the course of a few seconds; my fingers gripped the receiver like a vice.

Half asleep, Niko stuck out his hand, mumbled, "Dispatch?"

I hung up. "Wrong number. Go back to sleep. You've still got an hour."

Yawning, his hands reached for the ceiling. "Nah. I'll get up with you."

"No, don't. I mean…" My throat worked, trying to swallow the lie. I hurried around the bed to his side and tucked the covers under his arms. Leaning over, I pressed my lips to his forehead. "Shhh…rest, my love."

He closed his eyes.

With the hem of my nightshirt, I dabbed the sweat from my forehead as my mind replayed Niko's reaction the night our son died. He had let out a pained groan and then a bone-chilling shrill. Praying hands held high, his head volleyed side to side. "Honey, *please*. Tell me this isn't true." When I didn't answer, the color drained from his face, as if I'd ripped his heart from his chest, and he crumpled into a ball on the emergency room floor.

Witnessing his reaction, I couldn't tell him what actually happened. Because I'd reported my visual injuries, he knew about my three broken ribs, dislocated knee, abrasions, contusions, and stab wounds. It was so much worse than that. That man stole so much more. Our dreams, our joy, our plans for the future.

Niko waited his entire life to have a son. For a while, we thought it would never happen. Then we got our miracle. A second chance. In three months, I would have given birth to a boy, something I didn't discover until after I'd lost him. When I heard the sex of the baby, I swore the doctor to secrecy, certain the news would kill my husband.

That night in Boston changed everything. That night ruined us. Ruined me.

* * *

I tiptoed down the stairs. Even with the house serenely quiet, sounds amplified. Soft whistles from Niko's nose billowed in the open loft master suite. In front of a stone hearth, Ruger dreamed in his doggy bed, his enormous English Mastiff paws twitching. Colt, my four-year-old Rottweiler, was snoring, passed out on his back, furry feet in the air—and the knotty pine walls threatened to crack in his wake. Outside, red-breasted robins whistled songs of delight, welcoming the day. Bullfrogs croaked in the pond in front of the sunroom, and tree frogs chirped in the canopy of oak, maple, and ash, shielding our cedar-sided contemporary from view.

My gaze flitted around the room for Niko's briefcase. Ever since the attack, he warned me not to snoop through his case files. I never did. Now, however, I had no choice. My husband was hiding something, evident from his hangdog expression last night as he slid his briefcase under the kitchen table. After seventeen years of marriage, I recognized all of Niko's signs. The way he couldn't make eye contact with me when he felt guilty. How he fidgeted with his fingernails when he was uncomfortable. After a brutal day at work, he tended to slump in his La-Z-Boy with a heavy sigh.

After the phone calls, it didn't take much to deduce there was something he didn't want me to know. Perhaps he received a call from his Boston replacement about a break in my case or a clue to the assailant's identity. Either way, I had less than an hour to find out before the alarm clock buzzed.

On the face of the briefcase lock, I dialed in our anniversary—12-21-89—and slid two brass buttons aside. The hinges popped open. I took one last glance over my shoulder and fished out a file folder from under a stack of papers. Colt padded over and nuzzled his face in my lap. I stroked his head. "If anything happens to me, take care of Daddy. I love you guys with all my heart."

Confirming my request, his sad brown eyes closed and reopened.

I wiped a lone tear away.

Head cocked, Colt held my gaze and then plopped at my feet. Within a millisecond, he was snoring, sprawled with his front and hind legs wide-open—out cold on the creamy ceramic tiles.

My attention returned to the file. As I raised the first crime scene photo, a clenched fist tightened in my gut.

Suspended in the air like an angel, a dead woman wore a milky-white flowing gown with wide cuffs, the bottom hem cut at an angle, the back longer than the front. Her eyes and mouth sewn shut with some sort of black wire. X's erased her features from her ghostly pale face.

An unexpected zing shot through me. Angels live forever. My palms sweated, raising the next photo.

Blood had seeped into the stitching of the gown and crawled toward the pleated sleeves. The bodice stained crimson. Jacquard-woven fabric drank her lifeblood like a vampire tasting his first bite of human flesh.

What injuries the woman endured before the killer dressed her in the gown remained a mystery. I wasn't sure I wanted to know, either, but I had no choice. My stomach did an odd little tumble as I read Niko's case notes.

Breasts removed, X's marred the woman's chest. Iron spikes nailed through her palms braced a board that held her arms out like wings of a raven in flight. Feet bound with zip ties, she appeared as though she was floating in mid-air—trapped between heaven and hell.

A prickly awareness told me why Niko was hiding this. I clawed my hair away from my face, vision tunneling on the corpse.

A creak came from behind, and I swiveled in my chair. Colt practiced his yoga pose, downward dog. A flawless rendition.

A weak smile quivered my lips as I returned to the file.

Uttering a yelp, I slid the ghostly image to the other end of the table and raised the next photo—a close-up of her face. Even with her eyes and mouth X'd out she seemed terrified. Did she know what would transpire? Did the killer offer her explicit details of his plan? Or did the unknown frighten her most?

I prayed she was spared the knowledge of knowing she'd soon float like an angel in the middle of nowhere, her body decomposing, until some poor schmuck discovered her remains. I could not imagine her family's pain, having nothing more than a dissected corpse to bury. The remnants of a plaything a lunatic discarded after he had his fun.

Or maybe, I could.

I squeezed my eyes closed, waited a beat, and refocused. As I examined the photographs, I manifested a detective's demeanor.

Calm. Detached. Clinical.

As gruesome as the crime scene appeared in the pictures, the actual scene must have been horrifying to witness. It's one thing to eye a photograph. Quite another to smell the scent of death, something I could not handle.

Now it was even more evident why Niko hadn't shared this—that this specific brand of psycho roamed nearby. Since that night in Boston, he tiptoed around my feelings, shielded me from the world. I despised being treated like a piece of fragile glass that could crack under pressure, but I also understood my husband wanted to protect me.

Still, I had a right to know my assailant was back. The masked man who attacked me had murdered three women in and around the Boston area before he crept into my home. Who the hell was Niko to play God with my life?

I leaned in, scrutinized the details on the woman's face. My assailant hadn't marred his victims this way. Why would he change his MO? Unless he evolved, in the most basic sense of the word. Or, he wanted his crime scenes to match his words of terror—do you want to live forever?—without alerting me to his arrival. Until it was on his terms. I drew in a sharp breath. Did he want to turn *me* into an angel, too?

Did he take the woman's eyes? What was it about them he found so intriguing? Some say eyes are a window to the soul. This could be his way of possessing not only her body, but all of her.

Engrossed in the case notes, I didn't realize I'd spread the file across the kitchen table in disorderly piles of body shots, evidence photos, and Niko's personal findings.

Until I caught the silhouette of a man in my peripheral vision.

Chapter Four

6:00 a.m.

"Is that my murder book?" Niko held my gaze, chin dipped to his chest, like a disappointed parent. He swept the case notes and crime scene photos into a pile and stuffed them in the folder. "You don't need to worry yourself with this."

"But—"

"I told you I wanted things to be different here, and I meant it." He sighed. "This move was supposed to be our fresh start. Remember?"

I sighed, too, but not for the same reason. "Aren't you mad?"

"What? Why would I be mad?"

"I violated your trust and broke into your briefcase. Doesn't that piss you off just a little?"

He refused to answer.

"Well?" I prodded.

His shoulders sprang to his ears, arms out in a wide shrug as if he had no clue what I was talking about. "What do you want me to say?"

"I want you to yell, scream, tell me I can't be trusted. Show some frickin' raw emotion instead of tiptoeing around my feelings."

He rested a soothing hand on my shoulder. "Babe, I am disappointed that you—"

I rose to my feet, and the chair flew into the wall. "Disappointed! What are you, my father?"

"I don't know what you want me to do, Sage?"

Lip curled in a snarl, I got in his face. "I went through your stuff without a second thought about how you'd feel. Actually—" I hesitated. "I broke the law." Spinning away from him, I pinned my wrists behind my back. "Cuff me. Haul me downtown. Do something. Anything. Just don't stand there and tell me it's fine like you always do."

"What has gotten into you?"

"You. Actually, you haven't, but that's a discussion for another day."

"Now wait—"

Ah ha. Found his weak spot. "That's right, Mr. Bigshot Sheriff. You haven't touched your wife since…I don't even know when. Why's that? Huh? Huh?"

To calm himself, he took a deep breath. "Now you're trying to make me mad."

I swatted my hand. "Ah, forget it. What's the use?"

"Fine. I don't even know what we're fighting about."

"That's the problem. We aren't fighting. We never fight anymore. Where's the passion? Where's the excitement of having your blood boil because I've made you so furious? Where's the man I married?"

"Babe—" he reached for me, and I rotated my shoulders out of his grasp. "Maybe you should lie down. You look tired."

"I don't want to lie down. That's your answer for everything."

As if all was normal, he sat at the table and opened the newspaper.

"Why didn't you tell me—?" Tread carefully. If Niko saw any fear in my eyes, he'd bar me from the investigation. "Never mind."

I ambled to the Keurig. Same routine. Day in. Day out. "Want coffee?" Without waiting for a response, I poured caramel apple coffee into his favorite mug—the front emblazoned with #1 K9 Dad on a gold shield—instead of whipping it against the wall.

Controlling my shaky hands, I set the mug on his placemat and swept his short-cropped dark hair to the side. "I used to enjoy hearing about your cases. Didn't we have fun putting the pieces together, just you and me?"

He stared at me as if I was a crazy person. I smiled warmly.

He smiled back though to me it looked more like gas. "Umm, yes?"

I sat beside him and rested my chin on an open hand. "Remember when we lived in that little apartment in Dorchester? We barely had room to change our minds."

We laughed. This time authentically.

His smile faded. "That's when the South Boston Slayer was roaming the streets. The things he did to those poor—"

"And if it weren't for our little game you might never have caught him. We could play that here, too, if you want. Maybe start with this case?" I rolled my fingers over the closed case file.

Niko took my hand, kissing my palm. "Have I told you lately how much I love you?"

Typical. Avoiding my question. If only he'd let me help catch this guy. With him free, all I could think about was the promise he made me that night. The promise he obviously intended to keep. Helping Niko might also help us rekindle what we'd lost these last few years. I couldn't go on like this. It was literally driving me insane. "Honey, please let me help you. I think it could be cathartic, for me and for you."

He offered my hand a reassuring squeeze. "Not this time. If the press caught wind of the details…you know. Three-ring circus. Reporters would have a field day. News vans swarming everywhere."

I parted my lips to speak.

He flashed a flat hand. "Before you answer, think about a murder this brutal in a small country town. Imagine the flurry of phone calls from frightened residents. So far, we've managed to keep it under wraps, but I don't know how long it'll stay that way. I can't risk it."

Don't react. Play the good wife. "You're right. Of course, you're right. But…since I would never tell anyone, I don't know what you're afraid of. It's only you and me here…and the kids, but I doubt they'll tell anyone. Unless we go to the dog park. Even then, the most they'd tell would be Buster and Codie."

Niko glanced at Colt, and then at Ruger, still snoring in his doggy bed in the living room—black nose tucked under furry chocolate paws. "Very funny. Seriously, after what happened, I told you I'd never bring my work home again, and I meant it." Tears welled in the rims of his eyes as he glimpsed the scar on my neck. "That night wasn't your fault. You know that, right? No one could've predicted what he'd do. I just wish…" His Adam's apple rose and fell, fighting the tears.

"Don't go there. Not today."

"Maybe we should talk about it."

"Drop it. Let it go." I could preach those words. Living by them was a different story.

"I'll let it go…once I catch him."

Maybe we weren't talking about the same thing. Didn't he make the connection between my case and the homicide? I played along. "Catch him?" I jolted back in my chair so convincingly I should have been nominated for an Academy Award. "You're still working the case? I thought you passed it off to another detective when you left. Hell, that's not even your jurisdiction anymore."

Dread needled my gut. "How exactly do you plan on catching him? He stopped killing the day we left town. Besides, we live almost three hours north of there now, so…"

So he didn't have to answer, he sipped his coffee. Again, typical.

For now, I let him off the hook but still needed to find a way into this investigation. I tried one last time. "What if I took an itsy-bitsy peek at the rest of the notes?" Batting my eyelashes, I puckered my lips and flashed my best cutesy face.

A grin arched his lips.

I had him cold. "That a yes?"

He let out a sigh.

I hopped in his lap and pecked his face with little kisses. "Oh, thank you, thank you, thank you."

He spread the files out—stopped, and asked with a straight face, "What about the kids?"

At first, I didn't understand. He had a very dry sense of humor and it took me a minute to figure out if he was kidding. "Colt's sound asleep and Ruger— Please…we're cool."

He held my gaze for a moment.

If I knew my husband, he was wondering why I was so slow on the uptake.

"Okay, but I better not see these details in your book. You know how you get."

"I won't this time. Cross my heart." I drew an X over my chest. Granted, that might not have been the best way to acknowledge his request. "What's up with the stitching over the eyes and mouth?"

"He's a sick fuck, that's what. First, he carves out their eyes—"

"Their?"

"Her." He cleared his throat. "I meant her."

I raised an eyebrow.

"Anyway—" his gaze sidled— "he slices off their—her—tits and takes them as souvenirs."

Profilers used the term trophies and not souvenirs, but since he was allowing me to see the case file, I was not about to correct him.

"I don't know if he's eating the fucking things, or what."

"Eating them?" I resisted rolling my lips. "Doubtful. What else?"

"You mean you didn't see the pattern, the hidden message? Ms. Bestselling Author missed something?"

"Shut up." I biffed his arm. "What pattern? I don't see a pattern."

"It looks like castoff spray." He pointed the area out. "I actually thought it was until I got a closer look."

Dumbfounded, I squinted at the blood spatter. "Are you saying this doesn't match any of her wounds? Then what does it mean?" I raised the photo closer to my reading glasses. "Do you have a better shot? I can barely make it out."

"Not here, no. Truthfully, I have no idea what it means. Shit like this never happens around here. This is small town USA, for fuck's sake, not some metropolis. Maybe he's trying to throw us off by leaving fake forensics." He took a sip of coffee and waved his hand. "Ah, who the hell knows?"

Next, I raised the photo of the woman suspended in the air and examined how the killer managed to make her float. "He must be awfully strong to string up dead weight."

He set down his coffee mug and leaned aside to show me the details of the elaborate setup. "It's a pulley system. You can see it better in this one." He swapped my photo with another.

"Her hands are nailed to a board," he said. "Then there's a rope that winds under the board that connects to zip ties around her feet. Almost as if she's hogtied. Only not as tight. And with her hands secured to a board. Aaack, I guess I'm not describing it very well." He swatted the air a second time. "Anyway, he wants the legs to hang down so it looks like she's flying, or some fucking thing."

I could hear the aggravation in his voice. And I couldn't blame him. Before the phone calls, I would have been right with him. Now, however, I needed him off this case. I couldn't take the chance of the masked man hurting my husband, too. Or worse, killing him for revenge, or some sort of twisted payback. I gave my usual response. "Hey, enough with the F-word. You're not with the guys."

"Sorry. You're right." Disgusted at his own behavior, he hung his head.

Another awkward moment came between us. A wife knows when her husband's heart breaks. I'd seen the body cues many times during these last few years. His gaze falling to the floor when I mentioned a special time in our life. A heavy sigh and downturned mouth each time the news reported an attack. Now, his unwillingness to stop hunting the man who'd hurt me. Perhaps this was his way of dealing with what happened. Of course, I couldn't be sure because the subject was taboo in this house.

"Then what'd he do?"

Thankful the tension was gone, his face brightened like a child peering over a candy store counter.

I was grateful too. Lately, we'd had more and more uncomfortable moments. Our relationship had changed, strained by an ugly truth, I refused to share. Before that night in Boston, we shared everything, good or bad. But this secret would kill him. Hell, it would kill most men.

Catching me off guard, he asked, "You see this?" He showed me a close-up of a window with a bloody H in the center pane.

"What's it mean?"

"I have no idea…yet."

I studied the picture. "Could it be someone's initial?"

"Like an artist signing his work? Could be." Niko stared off into space, and I didn't understand why. Unless I wasn't hearing the full story.

"Hmm." I passed him the photograph. "Get back to telling me about the pulley system."

"After he hooked the zip ties with rope, he weaved the rope into a groove on a hard plastic roller. All it takes is a little leverage. It's not a matter of strength at all."

Still playing along, I voiced the possibility, "Could the killer be a woman?" even though there wasn't a chance in hell.

"Anything's possible. You don't normally see women cutting each other's tits off, though."

This time, I slapped his arm. "Don't be disgusting."

"Breasts. That better?" He gulped the last of his coffee. "Shit. I've gotta run. I'm late." He tapped the file's edge on the table. "I kinda like doin' this again." He traced my face with his fingertips. "You're so precious to me. I've missed this."

A warmth flushed my face, beaming for the first time in what seemed like forever. "So have I. You think it's sick, being that a woman's dead and all?"

"We're a weird couple I guess." He shrugged, and then he kissed me softer and more passionately than he had in years, and that old familiar love we once shared appeared before my eyes. "Kiss the kids for me when they wake up."

I followed him to the door. "I can help you with this case. You know I can."

As he offered me a slight smile, gazing lovingly into my eyes, we felt like us again. I missed this closeness, even if we did bond over crime scene photos.

"I know you can," he said, sadness in his tone. "Babe, after what happened, I want you to be safe."

My turn to hang my head. "I know you do."

"Look. Until recently, nothing like this happened around here. Half the time I'm dealing with suicides and overdoses, the other half I'm serving papers, transporting criminals…nothing like Boston. So I guess I got used to not talkin' about it. That's on me."

Meekly, I nodded.

Niko opened the back door. Holding the bottom of his cinnamon brown tie, he slid the knot up to his chin and then glimpsed his watch. "Now I'm really late."

"Go. I'll see you tonight."

Once he left, I twisted the deadbolt and spun the lock in the door handle. A click sounded, and Ruger's head popped up. He plodded into the kitchen and dropped at my feet. My baby was getting old. We'd had Ruger since puppyhood. Niko smuggled him home on our tenth wedding anniversary. He'd turn seven in a few months. I jotted a note to surprise him with a special cake from The Barkery in Franklin. He loved it last year. A fluffy cake made from bacon grease, wheat flour, and peanut butter, three of his favorites. Seven was the average lifespan for a mastiff. All in all, Ruger wasn't doing badly. Arthritis flared his wrists and hips, like Mommy, and he struggled with stairs.

Ruger opened his mouth, and I set a pain cookie on his tongue—our usual morning routine.

The irony of my dog also taking pain meds to survive was not lost on me.

* * *

Over the years, I learned the best way to find the truth, or cope with tragedy, was to write. When allowed to wander, the creative mind is a powerful tool. Writing might also help me determine why the masked man changed his MO.

After I created a rough outline of my story—a story I based on the recent murder—I reworked scenes, enhanced characters, and added dialogue. The story was jelling nicely, words magically flowing from my fingers, every sentence in perfect harmony with the next. The crime scene photos had woken my muse, who'd been asleep or on vacation for weeks, months, God only knows how long, seemed like forever. My soul was on fire, creating as I hadn't in years. Giddiness tickled my insides, my fingers racing over the keys, ideas shooting through my mind faster than I could type.

The afternoon sun blazed through the kitchen window. My back ached from staying hunched over the keyboard for hours. I took a break and made myself a chicken salad sandwich on a ciabatta roll, my favorite. Leaning against the kitchen counter, I stared out the window at our vegetable garden in the side yard. Mayo dripped down my chin as I let my mind drift, devouring the creamy chicken with the right snap to the lettuce and a hint of celery salt and paprika. Swallowing the last bite, I topped off lunch with homemade sweet tea in a tall glass filled with ice wedges.

As I admired rows of tall corn stalks, I couldn't shake the feeling something dire happened to Chloe. After lunch, I paced the house. Did my short conversation with Joe yesterday have anything to do with the phone call this morning? Or was I making a connection where there was none?

I couldn't get back to work because my mind was not on writing. The masked man's threat repeated in my head—*"I'll see you soon, Sage Quintano"*—and I couldn't concentrate on anything but his words no matter how much I pushed them away.

The phone rang.

Thank goodness she's all right. Without checking the caller ID, I answered, "Chloe, I—"

"Did you like my angel?" the strange voice asked.

My mouth opened and closed, but no words escaped.

"Let me cut to the chase. I have your sister. If you don't do exactly what I say, I'll—"

"Please don't hurt her. I'll do whatever you want." The phrase echoed in my head. *"I'll do whatever you want."*

"That's better."

"Can I talk to her? Is she all right?" Of course, she wasn't all right. Some lunatic was holding her hostage. My thoughts scattered, questions whirling in my head. How did Chloe cross his path? Did he target her because of me? I swallowed. Would Niko find my sister floating in mid-air in some shack like the woman in the photographs?

"Sage, do exactly what he says." Chloe's hoarse voice was barely audible. "Please. I'm so scared. He's got a knife and he says…"

A lightning bolt of adrenaline shot through my core. "I will. I promise. Did he hurt you? Tell me where you are."

The creepy voice cut in. "That's enough."

"What do you want?"

"To start, fifty thousand dollars."

"Fifty grand? I don't have that kind of money." I rubbed my sweaty palms on my jean-clad legs and re-gripped the handset.

Several seconds ticked by, and the silence ate me alive.

"You don't think your sister's life's worth fifty grand? Fine." There was a shuffle, muffled voices, and then Chloe screamed.

"Wait. Please. I can get it…I think. Tell me what you want me to do."

"You know, Sage—" His tone dripped with malevolence. "You're an extremely beautiful woman. Long legs…full, round breasts…tight ass…and those eyes. Shame, really."

"Please don't hurt her."

Saliva built in my mouth as I pictured his sadistic gaze tracing Chloe's body. Because she was my mirror image, Chloe changed her appearance after I was assaulted. She colored her hair flaming red, wispy spikes fringing the sides of her face, cut right below the jawline. Very chic. A vast difference from our usual shoulder-length, sable brown hair.

At the time, I assumed she changed her look in case the masked man returned. To ensure he didn't mistake her for me. A lot of good that did her. Did he follow us to Alexandria, or did Chloe lead him here? It wouldn't be the first time she took a stranger home from a bar. Perhaps pillow talk led to Chloe releasing the details of our whereabouts.

"Sage!"

I flinched. "I'm still here. I'm listening. Tell me exactly what you want me to do."

His tone softened but still crackled with detestation. "I have demands. Cross one of them…Chloe dies. Got it?"

I couldn't believe this was happening. Why wasn't I more careful? Why didn't I keep her close? She wasn't safe in Cambridge, on the outskirts of Boston. This was all my fault. I couldn't let her die because of me.

He shouted my name, and I nearly fell off my chair. "What? Yes. I understand."

"Number one, your husband cannot know what you're doing. He finds out, Chloe dies. You feel me?"

I didn't dare budge, didn't dare think. I concentrated on his demands. "Yes."

"Number two, no one in the sheriff's department can know what you're doing. Do *not* try to pull some sneaky shit like going around your husband to his partner to trace my calls. I *will* find out, and your sister *will* die." Anger poured into his voice. "Don't fuck with me, Sage. I hold all the power. You'd do well to remember that."

"Please don't hurt her. *Please.*"

"Number three, I want the cash delivered to an unnamed location. I'll call you back with the details. If you don't show—Chloe dies."

A sob writhed low in my chest, rose, and tangled around my heart. "Take me instead. Chloe has nothing to do with this. We can meet and do the swap. I'm the one you want." There was nothing I wouldn't do for my sister. Until now, I always believed we had time to mend our relationship. Inseparable all our lives, she was the yin to my yang, my other half, my best friend and confidant, apart from Niko.

A low, boisterous laugh, sharp and snide, echoed over the line. He loved the control he had over me. "Number four, I want you to write my memoir. Gacy and Dahmer have one. Why not me?"

This guy was clearly insane. "Memoir?"

"Published memoir. I want the world to know what I've accomplished. You'll have to use a pseudonym. I'm not stupid enough to confess, so don't even try playing that game."

"That could take a good year or more, and that's only after it's written and revised. You can't keep Chloe that long."

"First of all, Sage, I can do whatever I damn well please. I'll keep her forever if I feel like it."

"*Please.* She's diabetic. She can't handle it. Take me instead."

"Relax. I didn't say it had to be published before I release her. All I want is a letter from your agent stating she'll sell it to one of the big five."

The big five was an industry term for the largest publishing houses. Was he a fellow writer? Someone from the writing community destroyed my life? That was hard to believe. What I admired most about the community was how writers helped other writers, offered support and encouragement. To assume a fellow author could do this made no sense.

During the call, I collected as many useful facts as possible, scribbled key words and phrases that might lead to his profession, location, or anything that could help determine his identity. "For me to get the letter, I'll have to tell her about you," I pointed out. "You sure you're all right with that?"

Silence came over the line.

I blew it. If anything happens to her because of my stupidity, I'll never forgive myself.

"Fine," he said, and I exhaled. "But if she tells anyone—"

"I know." I lowered my voice. "Chloe dies."

"Don't be smart with me, Sage. And another thing, if your agent—Jess is it?—does anything stupid like go to the cops, you won't even recognize your twin's corpse. So you better make damn sure she keeps her trap shut."

His raspy voice transported me to the months before he shattered my life. We had owned a quaint Gambrel on the outskirts of Boston in a family-oriented neighborhood. A perfect place to start a family. After years of miscarriages, we were finally pregnant. Niko and I had a good ten years on the other couples in my OB's waiting room, but we outshined them all. The only plan that hadn't worked out was my writing career. Until one

June morning when Jess Morgan called from the Morgan Literary Agency and told me how much she loved my story. An audible sigh escaped my lips. I thought I'd never hear those words.

My first novel, a mystery entitled "Don't Look Back," did not win any awards. I sold a few thousand books, a respectable amount for a debut, but I hadn't achieved my dream of success. I was, however, a published author, a title I strived for years to attain. Who would have thought the worst night of my life would kick-start my career?

"Sage, do you trust her?"

"Yes. Of course I do."

"You better trust her with your sister's life or the deal's off."

"I will. I mean, I do."

"Call you in a day or two. Make sure you answer by the second ring. If you don't, Chloe dies."

"Day or two? No. I told you she's diabetic. She can't go a couple of days without insulin. She needs a shot every twelve hours."

"You don't think I know that? I did my homework. As long as you cooperate and follow the rules, Chloe will get her insulin."

"Oh, thank God." I needed a new tactic. He held all the cards in this twisted game. "Can we please start earlier? I have so many ideas for your book. This could be unique. A bestseller, even. Come on, let's start now."

"Don't play games with me, Sage." Every time he said my name, I heard a bite of indignation. "We'll start when I say we start."

Another shuffle came over the line as if he was about to disconnect. "Wait. When will you call back? At least give me a day and time."

"Why? So you can try and trap me? You have no clue who you're fuckin' with, do you?"

I knew exactly who he was—a vicious, cold-hearted killer.

The dial tone flat-lined.

As I dropped the cordless phone in its cradle, a dull ache throbbed in the pit of my stomach. What was that animal doing to my sister?

I wasn't strong enough to handle this. I could barely drag myself out of bed in the morning, never mind deal with whether my twin lived or died. One misstep and I'd never see Chloe's perfect smile again, or hear her boisterous laugh, or watch as she turned grown men into blubbering idiots. A move in the wrong direction and Niko would have to escort me to the morgue to identify her body.

Something her captor said earlier flitted through my mind. *"Did you like my angel?"* How would he know about my story? I wrote it this morning after I found Niko's case file. Unless…he hacked my computer. Or…bugged the house. My gaze shot to a floor lamp, behind Niko's Lay-Z-Boy. In the movies, the bad guy always planted the camera in a lamp or on top of the window dressing.

Standing on the couch, I felt along the top edge of the living room windows.

Nothing.

I dragged over a kitchen chair and slid my fingers along the top of the picture glass window.

Nothing.

I scoured up and down the corners of each wall, flipped over picture frames, and ran my fingertips along the edge of a massive painting of a black bear, above the hearth.

No listening devices or cameras. What if he stashed barely visible, tiny equipment? Without a proper bug detector, there was no way to be certain. I plopped on the sofa, let my head fall back, and stared at the ceiling. I couldn't find Chloe on my own.

Dear God, tell me what to do. Please don't let her die.

I jolted upright.

Maybe there was a way to alert Niko without the voice hearing. He couldn't have bugged the entire house. Perhaps he only had time for the kitchen. That's where I crafted my story, the one based on the crime scene photos.

Earlier, I didn't set out to blatantly defy my husband. I was desperate, with an outline due weeks ago and not one word written. Basing my story on the recent murder got me writing again. I knew it would too; it worked once before. A year after the attack I penned a crime novel entitled "Hurt," a story loosely based on the events of that night in my home. To my delight, sales skyrocketed. My name hit the New York Times bestsellers' list, and the title jump-started my career. During many hours of research for the book, I studied the different types of serial killers. The masked man was an omnipotent killer. Someone who believed the local authorities weren't equipped to catch a mastermind like him. Not being caught probably intensified his certitude.

I twirled toward the picture glass window. Maybe he had someone watching me, and they were waiting to see what I did next. Who I called, what move I made in response.

As if death threw his wicked cloak, spasms built in my toes and gradually gyrated my body. My home was no longer impervious to outside dangers. I was exposed, naked. The masked man could do anything he wanted, and there wasn't a damn thing I could do about it.

Unless…

I swiped my notebook and shuffled to the sofa. As I flipped through the pages, I studied the man's words, tried to decipher hidden clues that might help determine who he was or at least point me in the right direction.

I couldn't concentrate. *Chloe must be terrified, alone with a monster.*

Jess. I needed to contact Jess. I darted toward my laptop and then stopped mid-stride. If he hacked my computer, I couldn't use my email. I picked up the cordless handset—hesitated—and rifled through my leather bag for my cell. In one of my books, a killer listened in on cell phone conversations with a baby monitor. Perhaps the landline was safer. Twice I dialed the wrong number, before finally managing to thumb the correct sequence. "I need to speak with Jess right away," I told Claire, Jess's gatekeeper and all around pain in the ass. "Tell her it's urgent."

She snapped her gum in my ear. "What's this about?"

"Put Jess on the phone. Now." Before today, I had never raised my voice to Claire. I couldn't help it. I didn't have time to pussyfoot around, not after what he said he'd do to my sister if I didn't comply.

Claire groaned. "Geesh, what's wrong with you?"

I softened my tone until my voice sounded eerily calm. "Claire, put Jess on the phone, please. Put. Jess. On. The. Phone."

"Sure, tell me what it's regarding first."

Fire raged through my veins. "Put Jess on the damn phone. Put her on the phone, Claire. Now. Now. Now." Wiping the sweat from my brow with the back of my hand, I took a deep breath to collect myself long enough to explain the urgency to Jess. If she ever decided to pick up the damn extension.

"Sage, what's wrong?" It was Jess. "Claire said you were upset. Everything all right?"

I inhaled a deep breath and then slowly released it. "No. Everything's not all right. I need to speak with you. But now I'm thinking the phone isn't a good idea. Can I come by your office? I wouldn't ask if it weren't important."

"Of course. Can you tell me what it's about? Something happen to Niko?"

"Niko's fine. I'll explain when I get there. Don't leave. It'll take me a couple hours."

"I won't." She paused. "Sage, you in some kind of trouble?"

"I'm on my way. Rein in your watchdog. I can't deal with her right now."

"Okay. I'll see you when you get here."

I disconnected without saying goodbye, loaded my laptop and reading glasses in my bag, and flew out the door.

* * *

Two and a half hours later, I was staring at my reflection in the gold-mirrored elevator walls. Eyes puffy, my face was sallow from the shock of speaking to the man who ruined my life, the man who could ruin Chloe's life, too, if I wasn't careful.

It was imperative that I convince Jess to loan me the money. If she didn't—

The elevator dinged at the fifteenth floor, and the doors slid open. A rose border accented beige walls, with large gold letters that read, Morgan Literary Agency. I veered left and opened the first door on the right. Claire was sitting behind a tall resin-coated desk, a half-circle shielding her body from view, only her wild blonde mane and heavily made-up face visible.

She refused to make eye contact with me, and I didn't care. The young secretary stared at her computer screen, snapping her gum, a pen wiggling behind her ear. "Jess told me to tell you to go right in. Apparently, she's expecting you."

Without responding, I hung a right behind the reception desk and speed-walked toward Jess' office, at the end of a small hall. A natural wood door opened by Jess's hand. Claire had announced my arrival. Big shocker there. She always was a rat.

"Come in." Jess ushered me inside and closed the door. Concern etched her olive-skinned face. "Want coffee? Tea? Something a little stronger?" She smiled as if that could break the tension.

I did not return the gesture. "I think you better sit down."

In her mid-forties, Jess reclined in a high-backed executive chair behind an antique desk, her auburn locks swept away from her face with a jeweled barrette. I strode to a bank of windows overlooking Boston's Copley Square. Electric-blue, mirrored skyscrapers neighbored an old brick church. Its cardinal-red steeple promised sanctuary, and an inviting plush lawn lured visitors to bask in the hot July sun. There was a time when this view was my version of paradise. Now, however, the city triggered gloomy memories of crushed dreams and fractured lives.

"I don't know where to begin," I said with my back to Jess. "Did you hear about the woman murdered in Alexandria? What am I saying, of course you did. I mentioned it in the email I sent this morning. Oh…my…God. The email." My gaze darted side-to-side. "Did he hack that too?" I whirled toward Jess. "Did you read it?"

She swiveled toward her computer and punched a few keys. "I don't see an email here from you."

I scuttled around the desk. "What're you talking about? I could've sworn I saw your response. I didn't open it, but I'm almost positive you sent one."

"Sage, I haven't heard from you in weeks. Matter of fact, I'm still waiting for the outline you promised me." She scrolled through sixty, if not seventy, emails. With aspiring writers sending query letters in the hopes of representation, daily emails flooded her inbox. On average, Jess received about two hundred per week. Needless to say, finding a specific message was not an easy task. Why she hadn't implemented a separate address for queries as she talked about many times was beyond me. Typical Jess. Great agent, but she lacked organization, and Claire was useless.

"No. There's nothing here." She clasped her hands on the desk. "Now, about that outline…"

"That's what I sent. The outline for my latest project." I tsked my tongue. "Honestly, Jess, I'm disappointed. I know I haven't had a bestseller in a few years, but I produce at least three books a year. Doesn't that warrant some preferential treatment?"

With an open hand she slapped the desktop. "I did not receive an email from you. And I should have. The publisher wants what he paid for." Adamant, she held my gaze and then wavered. "Wait. Let me see if it got stuck in the spam folder." She clicked the mouse a few times, scrolling, searching for my name. "Nope. Nothing in here, either."

Rubbing the back of my neck, I wandered away from the desk. How did he hack my computer? "He must have intercepted it. That's how he knew." I was talking to myself, but speaking loud enough to confuse Jess.

"Why wouldn't he let it go through? Or at least forward it to you after he read it? Doesn't make sense. Unless he didn't want me writing— Of course." I slapped my hip. "He wants me working on the memoir. He wants all my attention on *his* story, not a fictional account. That's why—"

"Sage." Jess waved her arms like an umpire calling a time-out. "What are you talking about?"

Consumed with my own thoughts, I faced the windows and mumbled, "That's why he said…"

In seconds, she was yanking my arm. "Talk to me. What's

going on?" My body went limp, swaying...back and forth...until she let go. With a furrowed brow, her stare intensified.

I broke eye contact and slid my gaze toward the ceiling.

A pencil dangled from one of the dropped tiles. I listed my head to one side. What would a pencil be doing up there? "Maybe he— No. That can't be right." Mind buzzing with endless scenarios, I zeroed in on the pencil.

Jess mumbled something.

The pencil captivated my attention hanging there like that. A strange little oddity. A number two pencil jutted from the middle of a cushiony white tile.

Jess stomped her foot. "Sage."

I winced.

"Please...I need you to stay with me. Tell me what happened."

All I managed was, "Chloe."

"Chloe? What about her?"

"He has her. And if I don't write his memoir, he'll kill her."

"Who has her?"

How long has that pencil been hanging there?

She shook me by the arms, and my limp body swayed with her. Rote, like I had nothing left inside. No fight. No hope. A mere hollowed-out shell. Empty.

"Sage, who has Chloe? Talk to me."

A jolt shot through me as though I'd touched a live electrical wire. I curled my fingers around Jess' upper arms. "The killer...the guy I told you about in my email...he has Chloe. He'll kill her if I don't *do* something." I neglected to mention he was the same man who attacked me. If I did, she might not believe anything I said.

"For the last time, I do not have an email from you." Relenting, her tense shoulders dropped. "Never mind that. The one who killed the woman on the news has Chloe? Is that what you're telling me? A killer has Chloe?"

I wagged my head up and down. "This morning I sent you an email outlining my new book. In it, I explained I was basing my story on a real case. A case Niko's working." I dropped onto an overstuffed, chocolate leather sofa, and the pillow-topped cushions snugged the sides of my hips. "The killer called me." I told her about Chloe's abduction, the caller's demands, and the restrictions placed on me. "The only one I'm allowed to tell is you."

Her head jerked backward so fast I thought for sure she'd given herself whiplash. "Me? What do I have to do with all this?"

"He wants it published, the memoir. I need you to write a letter promising that you'll sell it to one of the big five. I don't know how he plans to get it afterward. We never got that far." What *did* he have in mind? A secret drop off location? A PO box in someone else's name?

"How can I possibly promise something like that? You know how this business works."

"Huh? Oh, it doesn't have to be true." I pulled my attention away from the pencil, determined to get what I needed. "Write the damn thing, Jess. I can't let Chloe die. Please…don't let her die."

With a heavy sigh, she sat cross-legged on the sofa, facing me. "Of course I'll write the letter. I'll do anything I can to help, you know that."

"Thank you." I fell back against the sofa cushions. A split-second later, I jolted upright. "Is there any way to get a loan against my advance?"

"A loan? How do you expect me…you haven't even given me an outline yet, never mind the manuscript."

"How many times do I have to tell you? I sent it this morning."

"No. You didn't."

"Jess, I'm not lying to you. I sent the damn thing, and he intercepted it. Have you not listened to a word I've said?"

"Have you? I told you I didn't receive any email. Not for nothing, Sage, fifty thousand is a big ask. I can't advance you that kind of money."

I held her hands in mine, anxiety niggling my chest. "I'm sorry. I can't think straight. I promise you, I've outlined the book and have even started writing it. Please." Tears gathered, fierce and forceful. "I have nowhere else to turn."

"What if it's not enough? What if this guy wants more?"

"I can't worry about that. For now, I need to do what he says."

"I'm sorry, but you're gonna have to give me a little time to think about it."

"*Please.* If you don't…Chloe's dead." I cradled my head in my forearms, my shoulders curled over my chest, and rocked. "My sister's gonna die, and I can't stop it."

"Shh, shh, shhh…it's all right. I'll give you the loan."

Behind separated arms, I blinked owlishly at Jess. "You will?"

With a dip of the chin, she confirmed.

"I knew I could count on you. I'll figure out the rest on my own. I don't want you involved. This guy's nuts. I can't put you in any more danger than I already have."

"Oh no. You can't come in here, drop a bomb like that, and then tell me I can't help. Don't shut me out. Not again. Besides, how are you going to handle it? You're not a detective."

"I'm married to one. So it's not like I don't have an idea of how to investigate a crime."

"You know what I'm saying. Let Niko deal with it."

"I told you, I can't." As smoothly as Jess thought she slipped in the insinuation, I caught it. Sadly, she wasn't wrong. I hadn't exactly been a pillar of strength lately. "I can't sit here and do nothing. Don't worry. I'll figure it out."

"Come." Extending her hand, she rose from the sofa. "I've got an idea. Trust me."

Once I took her hand, there was no turning back.

Screw it. I had nothing left to lose…except my life.

Chapter Five

1:30 p.m.

Niko drove down a winding trail to an abandoned barn on a six acre wooded lot, and a blistering sun shot a beam in his eye. With hooded lids, he waited for the tall conifers to shade his vision. Approaching a bend in the dirt road, he let his foot off the gas.

Warm air wafted through the vents. The air conditioner was on the fritz again. Nothing new there. He cranked open the window and the aroma of fresh cut lumber filled the interior. To his left was a skidder, log chipper, and excavator that appeared abandoned. He made a mental note to have Ben check for witnesses.

With a closed fist, Frankie jabbed him in the bicep. "Hey, you awake? I'd rather not die on the way to a homicide."

Even though she couldn't weigh more than a hundred and ten pounds, she hit like a man. Rubbing his arm, he shot her a cutting glare. "This morning I found Sage rifling through the murder book for Shelly Winters."

Frankie thrust her back against the seat. "She what?"

"Relax. It's cool. We've done this for years." He didn't want to share the game they used to play, where they acted out homicides to help determine perpetrators' height, the angle of blows, and unravel complex signatures. "I haven't shared this part of my life with her since we moved here. I liked talkin' to her about it again."

He caught the expression on Frankie's face—lips twisted, an eyebrow cocked. "You think that's strange, huh?"

"Uh, yeah." She turned her gaze to the passenger window.

"Hey, different strokes and all that."

Now he was compelled to explain what happened to Sage the night he took a bullet defending her. A perfect example of why he rarely shared anything about his relationship. It always led to more questions, and it was no one's business, anyway.

After all these years with Sage, they were happier than most. Granted, the last few might have been strained, but he wasn't worried. Hitting a speed bump on the road to life everlasting was bound to happen. With any luck, they'd be back to normal again soon.

"It's just that… How can I put this? In Boston, I always brought my work home with me…that didn't turn out so well. So when— Ah, never mind. We're here, anyway."

"Whew." She drew the back of her hand across her forehead. "For a minute there, I thought we were gonna have a moment."

* * *

In the barn, Niko studied a bloody N scrawled on the front window. Why would he veer away from his usual H? Was this was part of a message? Oh no. Was it Niko's initial?

His mind whirled with possibilities. First, his wife was assaulted by a serial killer, he couldn't catch. Now, a new threat was gunning for him. What if he targeted Sage? The odds of surviving two serial killers must be astronomical. In her forty-six years on this earth she'd been through so much trauma already.

Living without her wasn't an option. Perhaps he should send a car, have them sit on the house. How would he pull it off without Sage knowing? She'd panic. Her mind was fragile enough. If she knew… No. He refused to go down this particular road again. There was only one solution. Find this killer and thwart his plans. Fast.

Ben approached.

With a swipe of the hand, Niko cleared the tears from his eyes. "I'm sorry we got interrupted yesterday. With every cop in the area in and out of the barn, I had to do some damage control before any more evidence got compromised."

"No biggie, boss. You know I'll do anything you need me to."

Niko resisted the urge to beam with pride.

"Is it unusual for a mutt to strike again so quickly?"

"Not if he's a spree killer. But I don't think that's what we're dealing with. I think they connect...somehow. Autopsy shows Karen Thatcher was killed three days after Shelly Winters. But until we get the time of death for her—" he jabbed his head toward the body hanging from the rafters— "we have no way of knowing how long she's been here. My guess...she was killed sometime last night."

He gestured to Ben to follow him to the back of the barn. Beneath a second floor loft, he pointed at blood splattered across the barn-board flooring. "This is low-force velocity, low-velocity spatter. Each drop is at least four millimeters long. That tells us this blood is from the vic's wounds dripping and not from blunt force trauma or stabbing. See the irregular edges? That's because the wood floor is rough. It has no finish. So when the blood falls, it leaves a jagged edge. If these were sanded and polished like most floors today, I'd expect to see smooth edges." He paused. "Any questions so far?"

Ben's forehead rippled, the creases almost as sharp as his pants. "Without the ME's report, how'd you know it's from dripping and not something else?"

"A stabbing, say, would result in medium-velocity spatter. Depending on the force of the blow, it causes the blood to break into smaller-sized splatter. The velocity is determined by how hard the killer strikes the victim and not how fast the blood falls."

With deep nods, Ben scribbled notes in his notepad.

"I'll tell you how I was taught. Look closely at the blood drops. Don't they look like little tadpoles?"

Ben shrugged one shoulder. "I guess." He leaned closer. "Okay. I see it now."

"Great. So, let me ask you—" Niko paused, waiting for Ben to look up. "Knowing the droplets are four millimeters long—"

"How'd you know that?"

"Trust me. I've been doing this awhile." Nothing irked him more than being interrupted. He let it go. The eager deputy was hungry to learn, and that was a good thing. Shame he couldn't say the same for Frankie. "How do *you* think I got that figure?"

"Umm…"

"Think of it this way. These are tadpoles, right? Slice off their tails like you would a fish and then measure. Cut once, measure twice, as in woodworking."

The nodding started again, a wide grin blooming on Ben's full lips. "Now you're speaking my language."

"I thought that might work." Inside, he chuckled. Ben was a smart kid. A bit green, but with direction and encouragement he could make a fine sheriff one day. "Moving on." Three strides forward and he pointed at a second blood pattern. "This is medium-velocity spatter."

To review his notes, Ben flipped back a few pages in his notebook. "Medium is from blunt force trauma or stabbing."

"Correct. In this case, the medium-velocity happened when he slammed her over the head, knocking her out. I'm guessing he used the butt of a gun or something equivalent. We now know the tails show directionality. Meaning, from which way the blood fell. Right?"

A groan escaped from Ben's awkward smile. "Uh-ha."

Niko motioned as if he was stabbing his six-foot-two deputy in the gut. "If I stabbed you like this, then the tails of the tadpoles would face which way?"

"Toward you?"

"That a question?"

Ben checked his notes. "Toward me."

"Very good." He enjoyed teaching. During the early years of his marriage, he'd dreamed of the day he could teach his son how to ride a bike and throw a baseball. Sadly, that day would never come…without another miracle.

"You're the source of the blood so the tails would face you. Now, look at the way the tails are pointing here. Where was the mutt standing when he struck the vic?"

Panic taking hold, Ben's head shook like a metronome on speed. Niko wanted to help, tell him to breathe and calm him down, but he couldn't. If he didn't allow him to process things his own way, he'd never learn.

"I can't tell anymore. There's so much blood. I'm not even sure where the medium-velocity is compared to the rest." Defeated, his shoulders dropped. "Maybe I'm not cut out for this."

"Nonsense. This knowledge doesn't come overnight. It's learned through hard work. I'm giving you a crash course 'cause I need you. Believe me, if I thought you couldn't handle it, I wouldn't waste my time." He patted Ben on the back. "Take your time. Concentrate. I've given you everything you need."

Ben got down in a squat and studied the blood.

He had to step in. "Sometimes it's easier to visualize from a standing position. But hey, if that works for you…"

Right on cue, the deputy rose and leaned over the spatter. Seconds later, a horrified expression crossed his face. He didn't know the answer.

"Look closely," Niko instructed. "A lot of this blood is from the vic being carried. See here and here and here?"

He showed him a blood trail that led from a butcher-block table to the pulley system, suspending the victim in mid-air. "When he abducted her, he must've first knocked her out. Then he transported her here and laid her on the butcher block. This is where he removed her eyes, I'm guessing. We know she came to at one point because he struck her again. Here." He pointed to a blood pool coagulating near the table. "Still with me?"

Again, Ben nodded, as if he was afraid of answering incorrectly.

"Great. So, where was he standing when he struck her the second time?"

The young deputy thought about it for a few seconds and took one-step to the left. "Here."

"Excellent. See? I knew you could do it. All it takes is some practice. Now for something harder." He ran his finger down the side of the butcher block, showing Ben a bleached-out streak. "He's smart, I'll give him that," he remarked, more to himself. "He used bleach, but you can still see where the blood dripped over the edge, onto the floor."

Ben's amber eyes followed the clean spot down to the floor, where a wide smear lightened the old barn-board. "Oh, yeah. Cool."

Cool was right. For the first time, Niko saw retirement in his future. Not that he was ready to hang up his handcuffs, but before Ben transferred in, there wasn't one of his deputies he felt comfortable nominating for sheriff. Except Frankie, and she lacked tact, a skill needed to work with DAs and judges, not to mention victims' families. He tested his theory. "Why would he use bleach on this spot and not on the rest of the blood?"

Ben's face lit up. He knew this one. "Because that's his blood. He cut himself."

"Excellent. That tells us something about him. Bleach destroys DNA, so he probably has a working knowledge of forensics."

"Or he watches cop shows."

"I don't know about you, but if I was gonna kill someone, I wouldn't take the chance the cop shows were wrong. I'd make damn sure I couldn't be ID'd by my own blood. At the very least, I'd Google what it took to destroy DNA. I'll tell you what, let's say he at least has a *limited* knowledge of forensics. That fair?"

"Actually, I think *a working knowledge* was right. If I was gonna kill someone, I'd probably read everything I could about forensics." Visible excitement building, Ben bounced on his toes. "Let's check the libraries. I bet he checked out books on forensics."

"Now you're thinking like an investigator."

Bagging a cigarette butt near the front door, Frankie mumbled something unintelligible. Niko didn't catch what she said, but figured it was a cheeky remark like, "Gold star. Go to the head of the class." Or, "Pass go. Collect two-hundred dollars." Classic Frankie, brooding when she wasn't the center of attention.

Niko locked eyes with her. "You think you can do better?"

She ignored him and bagged a gum wrapper.

"Ignore her," he told Ben. "Tell me what happened next."

Tiny dots streaked across the wood floor and pooled in two areas—a few feet from the pulley and directly beneath.

"After the mutt struck our vic, he carried her to the pulley."

"Before he strung her up, though, he paused," Niko said, "right about here. See the blood pool?"

"This must be where he wrapped the ropes around the zip ties…right?"

"Yes and no. He probably sewed her eyes and mouth while he had her on the butcher-block. Nailed her hands to the board there too. And, I'm betting, zip tied her feet. Then he carried her to where you are. Paused. We know that from the pooling. And that's where he removed her breasts." Niko's gaze darted around the barn. "This is roughly the same area where he got spooked in the farmhouse."

"How'd you know that?"

"What? That he got spooked? Because at the first scene—the shack where we found Shelly Winters—it showed a blood pool in roughly the same area."

"What about the farmhouse?"

"You didn't let me finish. He got interrupted at the farmhouse by the homeless man. That's why Karen Thatcher still had her tits. Excuse me, breasts." Even while the cat's away, the mouse still rules. As usual, Sage was right. The sheriff should speak professionally, and not like one of his men.

"I'm betting he likes to face his victims. It gives him power. The fact that they're unconscious and can't see him is irrelevant." He positioned Ben above the blood pool and demonstrated using Ben as the victim. "He slides the knife under the breast and slices back and forth while applying upward pressure." He backed away. "That's my working theory, anyway."

Ben couldn't make eye contact with Niko. Whether it was because he had a question or because Niko used him as the stand-in for a chick was anyone's guess. The deputy's eyes slid upward toward a splattering of blood above his head, on the edge of a ten-inch support beam that ran between two side walls. "What about this?"

"That's castoff. Look down. See the correlating blood spray? This is where he struck her with a heavy object." Deep in thought, he added, "I still say it's a butt of a gun."

"Then what's this pattern over here from?" Ben walked farther away and pointed to a second castoff pattern separate from the rest of the blood, on the underside of the loft.

"I saw this at the last two scenes, too. I can't make sense of it yet. At first glance, it looks like castoff, but there's no corresponding spatter or injury to indicate…" He stepped closer, directly under the mysterious pattern, and strained to examine each individual drop. "Looks intentional. Like it was purposefully left here." Studying the drops, he raised to his toes. "They're round—perfect circles. Castoff doesn't happen this way. It's impossible. It almost looks like it was done with the tip of a fine paintbrush or ballpoint pen."

"You saying you don't know?"

The doubt in Ben's eyes hit Niko's ego, and he couldn't admit he had no idea how the blood got to where it was or by what means without guessing. The strange pattern was too far away from the victim and didn't match any of her injuries. Something wasn't right. Maybe this was a calling card of some sort. A clue to his identity. "I need to study this further before I can make any determinations. Let's move on."

With Ben on his heels, he ambled to the butcher block. Every so often, his gaze strayed to the suspicious castoff. "Anyway." He cleared his throat.

"We know something spooked him at the farmhouse because he didn't finish his ritual. Serials construct a fantasy in their mind. That's why every kill follows a kind of script, each detail done precisely the same way in order to fulfill a fantasy. The only reason for him not to cut off Karen Thatcher's…uh, breasts…is because he was in a hurry. Which, by the way, probably ticked him off. That's why he didn't get the right spot in the hands. Mr. Murphy was on his way inside at that point."

Ben wrinkled his nose. "Mr. Murphy?"

"The homeless man."

"Whoa. That's one lucky dude."

As he stared at the hanging body, he decided not to point out the irony in Ben's remark.

The dead woman's pale yellow gown billowed in the breeze

from the open barn doors. The rustic old barn had two stories, the second open to the first. A wooden ladder leaned against the lip of the loft floor that held bales of hay stacked to the ceiling. With the exception of the butcher-block and a slop sink, downstairs held farming tools and equipment. Pitchforks, sickles, a bow saw, garden claw, brush cutter, trench shovel—some of them antiques—riding mower, small tractor, an air compressor that appeared as though someone had taken their frustrations out with a sledgehammer, parts scattered beside it.

"Questions?"

"Nope." Ben shut his notebook. "I think I got it."

"Great." He slapped his hands together. The clap echoed through the barn, and Frankie grimaced. "C'mon. I'll show you how to print a corpse." Nearing the victim, he asked the Medical Examiner if he needed help cutting the victim loose.

"That would be great, Sheriff."

"Ben, grab her legs."

Frankie giggled, and Niko shot her an icy glare. She opened her arms in a wide shrug, mouthed, "What?" and then appeared busy collecting evidence.

"Ben. The legs please."

"Why don't I get Billy? He can handle this type of thing a lot better than me."

Gaines mumbled, "You would be surprised."

"Ben," Niko warned, not keen on having this conversation in front of Gaines, "grab the victim's legs."

"But—"

"That's an order."

Without another word, Ben wrapped his muscular arms around the dead woman's thighs.

Niko flipped open a folding knife. "Hold her steady." Careful not to cut the victim's skin he sliced the ropes, and the body fell into Ben's arms.

Sweat trickled down the deputy's forehead as if he'd run a fifty-yard dash. "Can I put her down now, boss? Please."

"Doc, you mind? I don't want the poor kid to pass out."

The Medical Examiner slung the victim's arm around his neck. "I have her." Ben let go, and Gaines lowered the corpse to a white sheet, laid on the floor.

Eyeing the front of his uniform for blood, Ben's hands fluttered like hummingbird wings.

"Death isn't contagious." Niko suppressed a chuckle. "Man up."

"It's cool. I was—"

"Whaddaya think, Doc?" said Niko. "Gotta time of death for me?"

Gaines punctured the liver with a thermometer, read the body's core temperature and then measured the ambient temperature around the body. "Between...twenty-four to thirty-six hours ago. With the heat in here, it is difficult to give you a more precise time until I get her on my table."

In a mini-spiral notebook, Niko scrawled the estimated time of death. "Is it safe to assume she was killed after Karen Thatcher? Or am I missing something else?"

"I believe we have found the victims in order, yes."

"Was she drained like the others?"

He examined the femoral artery. The autopsy reports—delivered after his ME confessed to withholding evidence—showed that the last two victims had a hole in their inner thigh, where an embalming needle was meticulously inserted to drain the blood.

"I believe she was, yes. I see the puncture mark. However, like I said, I will know more once I get her back to the lab."

"I assume you haven't ID'd her yet?"

"Correct. No personal effects were found with the body."

Normally Niko would wait for the ME to finish his initial examination before bombarding him with questions, but because he couldn't trust him anymore to do his job proficiently, he wasn't taking any chances. "Would you mind if we printed her? Then we'll get outta your hair."

Gaines stepped aside, swept his hand toward the corpse. "Be my guest, Sheriff."

Niko withdrew black fingerprint powder, a small camel's hair brush, and two-inch wide scotch tape from his evidence kit. This might not have been the most sophisticated procedure, but it still worked fine for gathering prints from the dead. Besides, the department couldn't afford the latest live-scanner like they could in crime-filled cities such as Manchester, Lawrence, or Boston.

He dipped the brush in the black powder and feathered it across the victim's fingers. Brushed off any excess, and then cut ten two-inch pieces of transparent tape. Working from thumb to pinky, he pressed each digit against the tape by starting in the center and working outward. Because he didn't yet have the victim's name, once he lifted the print he adhered the tape to an acetate card marked with date, time, and crime scene location.

"You wanna do the other hand?" he asked Ben.

"Boy, do I."

"Continue the same way."

With his tongue pressed against his bottom lip, Ben's hands fumbled on the first digit, but he got the hang of it fairly quickly. After completing both hands, he paused. "Now what? I run these through AFIS to get a name?"

"Exactly. Remember to reverse the prints before scanning. Because we use transparent tape, it's a mirrored image."

"You got it, boss."

Frankie sighed loud enough for Niko to notice. He couldn't leave her out, give her all the grunt work. She'd earned her spot.

She slid a business card under a pile of loose debris. With gloved fingers, she swept the evidence onto the card and raised it to her nose. Not exactly a technique Niko would use, but hey, whatever worked.

"Fuck." Eyes wide at Niko, she clamped her mouth closed.

Niko prompted, "What's that?"

"Tobacco. *Cherry* tobacco."

That's why she had that reaction. "Ben, I'm gonna have Frankie do the prints. Why don't you help collect evidence."

"Okay." Hanging his head, he dragged his feet to the front of the barn. Halfway, he stopped and spun toward Niko with the eagerness of teenager asking permission to drive for the first time. "Can I watch?"

"Sure. I'll tell her you'll observe. Don't get in her way, or she'll eat your balls for breakfast."

They laughed.

Frankie's face snapped in their direction. "What's so funny?"

"Relax. Ben's gonna watch you run the prints. Remember to reverse them."

She flung a hand to her hip. "No shit, Sherlock." Frankie was no rookie. She may not have had a ton of experience dealing with homicides, but she learned faster than anyone Niko had ever worked with. Even if she hadn't remembered to reverse the prints, there was no way she'd ever admit it, especially to him.

"You Are the Sunshine of My Life" by Stevie Wonder coiled through the barn. Sage. She'd changed his damn ringtone again. Flashing a flat hand at Frankie, he warned, "Don't say a word."

She lifted her shoulders and shrugged. "Hey, I didn't say anything. I just didn't know you were a Stevie Wonder fan, is all."

"Funny." He grimaced, and shuffled away to speak privately with Sage. Lowering his voice he answered, "What's up, babe?"

Sage was hysterical—crying, rambling on, not making any sense. "You need to come home. Something awful's happened. Come home right now. I can't do this alone. Please, honey. Please."

"Slow down. Tell me what's going on."

"I can't. Not on the phone."

"What're you talkin' about? You're not making any sense."

"I got a call…it's him," she cried out. "He found me."

"Who found you?"

"Come home. Now. I don't know if he's watching me, or listening, or…I don't know anymore."

"Lock the doors. I'm on my way."

"He liked my story, Niko. That's what he said. He liked my story. The new one."

"I'm coming now." He whirled toward Frankie, and mouthed, "I've gotta go" as his wife rambled on and on. "Okay. Shh…don't cry. I'm coming now. Keep the dogs inside."

Frankie bounded over. "What happened? She all right?"

"No." The color drained from his face as he hustled out the barn, and Frankie jogged to keep up. "She said someone was watching her, listening to her. She's bad, Frankie. I've never heard her like this before. Not since—" Thinking back, he rubbed the spot where the bullet entered his shoulder. "She's not making any sense. Something or someone has her all messed up. She's scared to death. I've gotta get home."

Frankie barely got the car door open when Niko put the SUV in drive and pulled away from the barn. "Gimme a friggin' second. I know you're worried about Sage, but let's not kill me in the process."

For a split-second, Niko thought about Ben working alone. He let it go. Sage was his priority. Sage was all that mattered. Catching Frankie's stare, he didn't know how much to share. He didn't plan for her to accompany him home. Not that he didn't trust her. He relied on Frankie daily, entrusted her with his life. But when it came to his wife, he didn't take any chances. He'd made that mistake once. Never again.

Without Sage, he'd end up a shell of a man. They'd been together for so many years, he could barely recall a life before her. If anything ever happened, if somehow this was the same man and he killed her like the others, there was no doubt in his mind that he'd die right alongside her, even if it meant he had to eat his gun.

"Tell me what's going on." Frankie tugged on his shirtsleeve. "I love Sage too, y'know."

"He said he liked her story. Thing is, she only started writing it this morning. I told you we were talking about the case. What I didn't tell you was that she was basing a book on it." A mark of disapproval shone in Frankie's eyes. "Don't say it. I don't need a lecture."

Frankie raised her hands in surrender.

"She was working for hours, crafting her story to resemble the crime scene. And before you say anything, I told her to change the details. But you know Sage. Anyway, from what I could piece together…she was hysterical just now, rambling on and on…the phone rings and this guy says, 'Did your husband show you, my angel?'"

"Aw, shit. You think it's our guy?"

"How else would he know? Unless…"

"Unless what?"

"It's a cop." His frantic gaze found Frankie. "You don't think one of the cops I threw off the scene yesterday would have the balls to call my wife?"

"Nah. Besides, how would they know about her story?"

"Shit." He pounded on the steering wheel. "This is all my fault. I brought this animal to my fuckin' doorstep—again. Dammit. I know better. I swear if anything happens to her…" Tears pooled in his eyes, and he averted his gaze.

Frankie set a hand on his shoulder. "It won't. We won't let it."

A cherry-red Mustang GTO sped by going the opposite direction, its dual exhaust rumbling down the road. As the sports car sailed past his window, his gaze followed through the side mirror.

That guy was lucky Niko was in a hurry to get home. Nothing could stop him from getting to his wife. "But if it does…"

Frankie twisted to watch the Mustang through the back windshield. "It won't." She settled front. "Sage is fine and she's gonna stay that way. You hear me? Nothing's gonna happen to her. Not as long as we're around."

He drove up a mountainside to his and Sage's country contemporary, threw the SUV into park, and bolted down the walkway—the driver door left gaping. Frankie's high-heeled ankle boots alerted Niko to exactly where she was at all times.

Hustling around to the driver side, she kicked the door closed, and Niko cringed, expecting a dent when he returned. Frankie tapped down the flagstone walkway and onto a farmer's porch wrapping around to the kitchen door—the couple's usual entrance—and Niko prayed she wouldn't kick that, too.

When she stepped inside the kitchen, Niko and Sage were in a loving embrace, Niko stroking the back of her hair as she wept on his shoulder, shadows cascading over his face. "It's all right, babe," he consoled. "I'm here now. You're safe." He swayed with his precious wife, then pulled her away from his chest, and gently wiped her tears with his fingertips.

Oh, how he loved this woman.

With an arm draped around her waist, he assisted Sage to a chocolate leather sofa—pigskin leather so soft it almost dissolved in your hand—and sat beside her, lovingly folding her delicate hand in his.

"He…called…back."

As if a ghostly intruder was stabbing him in the heart, he swallowed a lump and didn't react. "Start slow and tell me exactly what he said."

"He asked me…" Her voice faltered. "He asked if I wanted to live forever." She let out a squeal as if she was physically hurt and collapsed on his lap.

"What's that mean?" He had never heard this phrase before.

She wiggled up to his chest, her arms hooked around his waist, and raised her jade-green eyes.

This woman's eyes melted his heart every time.

"I don't know," she said, but her words didn't match her tone. "He knew what I was writing. How'd he know?" She pressed a closed fist to his chest. "How did he know?" She buried her face in his arm, her back heaving, belly cries muffled by his dress shirt.

"Did you email Jess, run the story by her like you usually do?"

She quieted, a teardrop dangling off one of her thick lashes. "Yes, but she said she never received it."

Lifting one cheek off the sofa, he dug in his back pocket and passed her his handkerchief. She honked her nose and passed it back. With two fingers, he held the handkerchief at arm's length and tossed it on the coffee table. Love or no love, there are some things you don't share.

"Show me."

She gave him a look like a doe frozen in the headlights of a fast approaching Mack truck. "What?"

"Show me the email. Where's your laptop?" He scanned the room. Her Chromebook was on the kitchen table. Finger by finger, he unlatched her hands from around his waist and headed for the kitchen. "What's your password?"

She leaped off the sofa. Flat hands flew straight out in front of her. "Wait. I'll do it."

Too late. He was already reading the story. The Chromebook in his hands, his sight glued to the words on the screen, he rotated to avoid her. Sage continuously attempted to get in front of him and snatch the computer away. Obviously something was in here she didn't want him to see.

"Niko, I—"

He held up his index finger, skimming her outline from beginning to end. He closed the Chromebook and scowled at his wife, betrayal consuming every inch of his soul. "You didn't change a thing. Except the victim's name. Every friggin' detail. I trusted you."

Praying hands held close to her chin, she said, "Honey, I was getting the facts down. I was going to change it afterward. I swear."

He didn't know what to say.

"Uh, Niko?" Frankie padded into the room, and Sage jumped like a cat who'd stepped on tin foil, not realizing she was in the house. "What she wrote isn't the point."

Ignoring Frankie, he passed his wife the Chromebook. "Show me the email."

This was none of Frankie's business, but as usual, that didn't stop her. "This isn't her fault."

Silently thanking her, Sage's eyes closed and then reopened.

That was an odd thing to do. What else was she hiding?

"This punk has skills, dude," Frankie added. "He must be a hacker. Maybe it's not our guy."

Sage stared at Niko. He stared at the floor.

"Anyway, maybe we can trace his IP address."

He didn't respond. He couldn't. What he should do was punch a wall. Instead, he closed his eyes, breathed in…out…in… out… Opened his eyes, saw Sage, the Chromebook, and soldiered away, his fingers raking back his hair.

He clasped his hands behind his neck, breathed slow, slow,

slow. Gazed out a picture glass window at gardens speckled among three tiers of grass. Breathed slow, slow, slow. And spun toward Sage. The fear in her eyes wrenched his gut, rendering him speechless.

Frankie repeated, "Maybe we can trace his IP address."

"Fine. Let's get this to the house right away." He snatched the Chromebook and bustled out of the living room.

Sage hooked his arm, stopping him cold. "You can't take my netbook. I have chapters due. How am I supposed to write?"

"Use your desktop. This might be our only chance of catching this guy. Be reasonable."

"No, Niko. I'm not giving up my computer. Think of another way," she insisted, making this ten times more difficult. "Can't your computer guy remotely track him using my IP address, or something?"

Who the hell knew? Computers were never his forte. Unfortunately for him, they weren't Frankie's, either. "How 'bout I send him here?"

"I'm not really up for company."

"Work with me. You're the one who always says I don't compromise. This is me compromising."

"First ask him if he can do it remotely. If he can't…fine. Send him."

A flash of losing his wife raced through his mind, erasing all anger like a mother's hand soothing a crying child. He caressed the side of her face, his voice low, uttering, "Will you be all right here alone? I shouldn't be too long."

She leaned in, brushing her cheek against his. "I love you, pup."

Niko's gaze slid to Frankie, who mouthed "Pup?"

He returned a glower. "Love you too, babe."

As they were leaving the phone rang, and he called out, "I'll get it."

Sage beat him to it, smacking a hand over the kitchen extension. "It's probably Jess. Go. I'll see you when you get home."

"First, answer it so I know you're safe."

She did.

"Well?"

She cupped the mouthpiece. "It's Jess."

The look in her eyes told him she was hiding something. Was she having an affair? He'd kill the man who dared touch his wife. His mind was messed up. Sage would never…would she?

In the doorway, he stared at his loving wife, holding the receiver, waiting for him to leave, and offered her a halfhearted smile. To be honest, he hadn't been there for her in a long time. If he were a bigger man, he might drop to one knee and beg her not to go through with it. But what if he was wrong? The accusation alone could cause a worse rift between them.

This move was supposed to fix everything. Offer them a chance to rekindle the passion they'd lost after that horrible night in Boston. He'd have to try harder, force her to see how much he loved her. If that didn't work, he'd grovel at her feet, hands clasped, and plead for her forgiveness.

First, he had an animal to catch. Apparently someone hell bent on destroying his wife.

Chapter Six

6:00 p.m.

Niko dropped Frankie at the station and drove back to the crime scene. Her mission was simple. Butter up the IT guy. Convince him to hack Sage's computer without a warrant. Frankie was not looking forward to this at all. Granted, no guy had ever refused her, especially when she raised her charm meter to maximum capacity, but if this favor weren't for Sage, she probably would have protested.

Tom Rainhorse was a Native American with a chiseled jawline, bedroom eyes, and velvety black hair tied in a ponytail. Each time she saw him, her heart skipped a beat. Of course, she'd never tell *him* that. She wasn't about to ruin her reputation as a biker babe. That title took years to achieve. Yes, she'd heard the rumors, the whispers behind her back when she wore a kickass outfit. Clearly, she was the only one with any style around here.

"Hey, Tommy." She slid backward onto his desk, next to the computer so she couldn't be ignored. "I need a favor."

Tom rolled his lips. "What is it this time, Frankie?"

"Not for me." She raised an open hand to her chest. "It's for Niko."

"Okay," he prompted.

"Right." Why did he have to be so hot? Too bad it was against regulations to sleep with a coworker. "Umm," she hesitated. Damn. She always found herself tongue-tied around him—so not her usual suave demeanor. "Is it possible to remotely access someone's computer from here?"

"You got the IP address?"

Setting the toe of her boot on the floor, she dug deep into her front pocket and withdrew a scrap piece of paper. “Here. Niko wrote it down.”

He typed the IP address into his computer. “I’ll need consent.”

Hands steepled over crossed knees, she playfully swung her boot. “Consider the consent confirmed. Whoa, talk about a tongue-twister.” She giggled. Stopped quick and fanned her face. “Is it hot in here?”

Tom didn’t respond.

“Anyway…it’s Niko’s wife’s computer.”

His fingers stopped typing. “Does she know we’re accessing her computer?”

“Yes. Of course she does. She’s the one who suggested it.” Pretending to be hurt that he’d think so little of her, she paused for dramatic effect. “Honestly, Tommy, I thought you knew me better than that.”

“Please.” This time he rolled his eyes, his gorgeous, seductive eyes. “I ask because I do know you.” He winked. “All of you.”

Okay, so maybe she’d slept with him once, a couple of years ago. Big deal. She was having a few pops at Shields, the local cop bar in Plymouth, when Tom sauntered in with one of his buddies. The night was sort of a blur. She’d already downed two shots of tequila and was on her third Corona. One minute they were hanging out, laughing. The next, the sun was coming up, and she was doing the walk of shame back to her car.

Ever since that night, Tom hadn’t paid her as much attention. Typical man. Once he got what he wanted, the mystery was over, and so was the thrill of the chase. What possessed her to let him use her that way? Unfortunately, they still had to work together, so kicking him in the balls was out of the question.

Niko should have handled this himself.

“I’m only playing with you, Frankie. I’d do anything for you, you know that.”

Her posture perked up, and she hopped off Tom’s desk feeling better about that night than she had in months. She knew it. Frankie Campanelli still had the magic touch.

On her way out of his office, she waved over her head. "Thanks, Tommy." In the hall she smoothed her hair, plumping the ends with her palms. Head held high, she strode to the elevators. It wasn't until she slammed the button for the main floor with a closed fist and the doors slid shut that she recalled Niko's orders.

She thumbed the fifth floor button again and again.

The elevator descended toward the main lobby.

The doors slid open. She thumbed five another half-dozen times. Cherry-red floor digits climbed higher and higher. The elevator dinged at the fifth floor, and her composure ebbed. She'd made such a great exit. Now she'd look like a fool, and in front of Tom, of all people.

She poked her head in his office doorway. "Niko wants me to see if you've found anything yet."

"Didn't you just leave?"

A flush swept up her face. Frozen in place, she readjusted her grip on the doorframe, her leg kicked-up behind her. "Umm…"

His brow furrowed. "Are you coming in?"

She took one step inside the doorway.

"Closer," he teased, his forefinger rolling toward him. "I won't bite."

She took another step, and her stomach roiled as if daring her to puke all over Tom's Nikes.

"Much," he added, and she let out a loud snort that made them both stop and wonder where in the hell that came from.

Why did she ever tell Niko she'd handle this? "Anyway…" she said, covering for the uncomfortable snort. "What'd you find?"

"It looks like her email *was* hacked. He's skilled, too. I can't pinpoint his location because he bounced the signal from Korea to Japan to somewhere in the Virgin Islands. Then it disappeared. Hang on. It looks like…is her name Sage? Niko's wife."

Don't speak and you can't embarrass yourself. Holding a tight smile, she nodded.

"It looks like Sage's spyware blocked him from everything other than her email. She uses two layers of protection. A password and an authentication code that her phone generates. Tell her to protect her email this way, too. Okay? She'll be much safer that way."

Sounded like gibberish. Admitting that to him was not on the agenda. "Anything else I should know?"

"Nope. The note said to check for a black hat."

She swallowed her pride, and asked, "Black hat?" If this wasn't for Sage, she would have never admitted to not knowing the term. *Damn you, Niko.*

Tom flashed his perfect brilliant-white smile, and her knees weakened. "A hacker. Specifically, an illegal hacker. Not like me. I'm a white hat. Course, you already know that."

"Right." With an awkward smile, she dug in her heel and twirled toward the door. The note. She spun toward Tom. Wait. She didn't need the note back. Again, she twirled toward the door. Oh, man. Her face overheated, and she didn't dare speak. What a loser. Nice move, Frankie. Twirling in his office like a frickin' ballerina. Smooth. Real smooth.

She waved at him—*what possessed her to do that?*—and then left Tom's office. This was so not how she envisioned leaving things with him. Whatever. There was no way in hell she was going back in there.

Down the hall, the gravity of the situation took hold. Someone hacked Sage's email and read personal things about her. Earlier, at the house, she could tell something was eating her up inside. It wasn't only what she'd shared with Niko, either. There was something else, something darker, more menacing. Something Niko didn't know.

Her mind spiraled back in time, to when she was seventeen years old and her boyfriend had forced himself on her. Frankie was still a virgin and had begged him to stop. He got this menacing glimmer in his eye, and it still haunted her to this day. After he had raped her, she wanted to die. One lonely night she even slit her wrists in the bathtub, but chickened out at the last minute and didn't cut deep enough. Earlier today Sage had the same faraway look that haunted Frankie's mirror at seventeen—a hopeless, hollow, vacant stare.

Chapter Seven

Wednesday, July 19, 2006 2:00 a.m.

Unable to sleep, I crumpled a thin quilt in balled fists, the hairs on my neck standing on end. Something deep within connected me and Chloe, and I experienced her fright, her desperation. An hour or so had passed before my eyelids became weighted and I faded into the abyss. A deep sleep, or so I believed.

Something was different. I was lucid. This was no ordinary dream.

My soul escaped my body, and I soared over rooftops. An inky black sky, stars waltzing across the astrological plane. Below me, full leafy treetops, billowy canopies of maple, oak, and ash. My senses heightened, and I was more alive and aware than ever before as if someone removed a pair of foggy glasses from my eyes and the world was in focus. Crisp hues of sunshine yellow, magenta, and tangerine painted flower gardens nestled in the richest green grass I'd ever witnessed. I inhaled a clean, fresh, misty scent—oxygen-infused clouds.

Blackness blanketed the area, but my vision remained sharp, clear. A chocolate Boxer with a black muzzle barked at a stray tabby cat in the backyard of a snow-white mobile home. Out of the dog's reach, the feline perched on a wooden rail fence, licking his paws, tormenting the poor Boxer.

A block away, a teenage boy clambered down a trellis outside his bedroom window. He wore all black, and as he ran from his home, bleach-white soles kicked up and down, like a beacon pointing to his precise location. He hopped in the backseat of a waiting Volkswagen Beetle and sped away. The boy's house came alive. Floodlights blazed on, washing the yard in a golden mist.

Upstairs, the boy's mother slid his bedroom window closed.

How could this happen? Was I dead? If so, it didn't bother me any. Where was I going? Did I have a destination, or was I simply out for a spin around the neighborhood? Someone was navigating my journey. But who? Or, what?

Didn't matter. I surrendered to the feeling. Allowed my body to take me wherever. Never in my life had I been so free, so unencumbered. Up here, danger couldn't touch me, evil didn't exist, and wicked men could never follow. If only I could stay forever…far away from life's pain. Where souls ruled the earth, and troubles washed away like sand castles at high tide.

I arrived at a log cabin in the woods. My astral self descended and hovered even with the roofline.

The quaint cabin had strong, ten-inch, exterior log walls, sealed with a thick clear coat and a brick-red metal roof with matching trim and shutters with pine tree cutouts. A fieldstone chimney stood sentry against the left side of the cabin, like a soldier protecting his post from the Taliban. Creamy beige stones had mortar slapped in between. A tall, thick ash tree—ramrod straight and high—was on the right side. A war between nature's elements, fighting over who secured the property. Skeletal branches lightly brushed the rooftop as it swayed in the warm summer breeze.

From a basement window, a sliver of light shot a spotlight. The beam flamed across the dark forest floor and exposed a lone chipmunk scampering into a burrowed hole to take cover from an approaching Fisher Cat. A woman's screams pierced my ears, her bloodcurdling cries resonating from the basement.

Chloe. My soul left my body to find Chloe.

Through the years I'd read numerous articles and books about astral projection, but never experienced it. Sylvia Browne—a world-renowned psychic and medium and the author of over forty non-fiction books—was a huge influence in my life. Chloe's too.

A silver cord tugged at my skin—a cord that connected my astral self, or soul, to my physical body. Sylvia's teachings explained that if the cord severed, I would die. I didn't care. If I could grab hold of the roof, I might be able to climb inside. Hands clasped together, arms high above my head, I dove toward the cabin.

The cord sprang me backward, my tether not allowing me to venture too far away from my physical self.

Chloe floated through the metal roof and hovered a few feet above. Looking haggard, tiredness clung to her face. "Sage, is that you?"

"Oh my God. Are you okay?"

"What's happening? Where are we?" Unable to believe, she touched her lips, cheek, and stroked her hair. "Is this a dream? Am I dead?"

In a soothing but confident tone, I assured her, "No. Our souls escaped our bodies. Astral projection. Remember Sylvia Browne's books? We read all about it before—" I stopped, unwilling to remind her of our argument.

"You mean we both astral projected? Together? How's that possible?"

Our love of the paranormal, spirits, and other unexplained phenomenon was one of the many things we had in common.

"I thought you needed training to do this?"

"I'm not sure how it happened. But remember when we heard Sylvia speak in Colorado? She said it could spontaneously occur during times of great trauma. Maybe because we're twins it happened at the same time. Or it could be because of our circumstances. I don't know. Does it matter? Let's not waste this gift. Tell me who took you. A name, something to go on."

"But I don't know anything. I never saw his face." Her gaze fell to the cabin. "Do you hear someone screaming?"

"Umm…" I swallowed, bracing myself for her reaction. "I think it's you, Chlo."

"What?" Her eyebrows arched. "Why?"

"What's the last thing you remember?"

"The man." She stared at her empty palms. "The man was tearing off my blouse…slicing the buttons with a butcher knife."

She probably wondered why she didn't fight back. During the last three years, I spent many sleepless nights with the same nagging question.

Incredulous, Chloe slapped her hand over her mouth, her sight locked on the cabin, her head shaking. "I can't go back." She eyed the silver cord protruding from her belly button. "If I cut this I'll die…right?" Without waiting for a response, she laced her hands around the base and yanked the cord away from her body. A few feathery strands unwound, glinting as they fell into the blackness and then magically disappeared. "Dammit. Get this thing off me. I can't go back. I won't." She tugged and tugged. Each time more strands unraveled.

"Stop it, Chloe. Listen to me. Jess and I have a plan. Hang in there a little longer." My astral body was flickering. "Time's running out. Tell me what he looks like. Did he give you his name?"

"All he said was, 'Do you want to live forever?'"

I winced.

The screams stopped, and the forest became hauntingly quiet. Chloe's cord disappeared, and yet, there she was in front of me.

Perhaps this was a dream. Even so, I still needed to find her. "Did you overhear him on the phone? Maybe you heard him use a name, an alias, anything. Think. I don't have much time. Did you see any mail lying around the cabin?"

"I can't go back, Sage." She was shaking her head again. Unwilling to listen. Unwilling to believe. Unwilling to help in any way. Like she'd given up all hope of rescue.

"I'm getting weaker." I yearned to slap her, knock her around, and force her to listen to me. If past experience proved anything, yelling and screaming would not do any good. In an unruffled voice, I said, "Stay with me. Concentrate. Did you hear or see anything?"

"Dark hair. Black, maybe, but I think it's a piece." She gasped. "He did call someone. A woman…I think. It was last night after I spoke with you." Her eyes went huge in shock. "Oh God, Sage. I think G—"

An overpowering force sucked me backward as if someone was slurping me through a straw. No matter how much I fought, I could not make it stop. Only seconds later, I sprung upright in bed. Beside me, Niko was snoring so loudly I swear the curtains rippled. Colt lay belly-up across the foot of the bed. Paws twitching, he was chasing someone or something in his dream.

With closed a fist, I pounded the mattress. "No, no, no. Lord, why allow me to see her and then pull me back? This all could be over. I might have saved her. I don't understand." I fell back against the pillows, and Niko rolled toward me.

"You okay?" he mumbled and patted my arm before falling back asleep.

Okay? That was the biggest understatement since Clinton swore he did not have sex with that woman.

* * *

The morning sun reached through the window with spear-like fingers as though God himself was gently nudging me awake. I opened one eye and felt around the bed for Niko. His side was empty, except for a note on his pillow.

Good morning, my love. You looked so peaceful this morning. I didn't want to wake you. Rest. I'll give you a buzz later. For now, know that I love you, and I'll never let anything happen to you. I'm posting a car outside the house for your protection. He'll be here around 6:30. DO NOT turn him away. He has strict orders not to leave you alone and to follow you when you leave the house. Please, babe, work with me. I can't live without you. Love you, pup.

I threw the thin quilt off my legs and leaped from the bed to a window overlooking the front yard.

As Niko ordered, a squad car idled out front.

What would the neighbors think? Small town gossip ran rampant around here. Why, Niko? This could ruin everything. I called Jess. "We've got a problem. Niko put a car on me."

"Stay put. I've got an idea."

The call ended.

Prying the vinyl blinds apart, I stared at the cruiser. Great, *now* my husband gets proactive. I let go, and the blinds snapped into place.

On my way out of the loft, I crumpled up the note and tossed it in a small wooden trash barrel. *If I can't get to Jess, I can't save Chloe.*

The phone rang downstairs.

I jogged to the kitchen extension and answered, "Jess?"

"Not Jess." It was him, the one who had Chloe, the man who attacked me. "Good thing you answered by the second ring. I almost hung up. You know what woulda happened then, don'tcha?"

Chapter Eight

8:15 a.m.

After the call, I made a beeline for the shower, my second one of the day. Sliding down the wet walls, John Doe's words held me hostage, forcing me to relive that night in Boston, my heart breaking for the woman I was. Chloe was enduring the same horror I experienced, and there wasn't anything I could do.

I towel dried my hair, plodded downstairs, and slumped onto the sofa. Colt jumped on the cushion next to me, resting his chin on my hip. I stroked his head. He always knew when Mommy was upset.

Before we adopted him, he was training to be a service dog. The facility was an hour away, in Concord. Niko's buddy trained all the K9 cops, as well as dogs used for the blind, disabled, and handicapped. He was even teaching dogs to detect diabetes and cancer in humans. Incredible stuff. Colt couldn't sit still long enough to satisfy the strict guidelines needed to graduate to a service dog. His playful quality and high energy were what attracted us to him, but those same qualities also made him a bad candidate for the program. A service dog dropout.

I scratched behind his ear. "Fate already recorded your destiny as a member of our family. Huh, buddy?"

My cellphone signaled a text.

Holding Colt with one hand, unwilling to knock him on the floor, I snatched my cell off the coffee table. It was Jess, parked around the corner from my house. "Boys, it's now or never."

Colt nuzzled his head into my lap—his usual ploy to get me to stay home—and Ruger lumbered over and opened his mouth for his pain cookie.

"Oh, Rugey. I almost forgot." I shuffled into the kitchen, opened the Rimadyl bottle and plopped a pain cookie on his tongue. Ruger chewed, his jowls sagging and spitty, and then stumbled back to his doggy bed. "I'm sorry, puppy love. I promise I won't be long."

Ruger groaned, and I understood exactly what he meant. "Yeah right, sure you won't."

"Come, my sweet babies. You need to do your potty before I go."

Colt bolted out the door. Ruger trekked behind, head down, not making eye contact with me—laying it on thick.

A thickness formed in my throat. I had to leave without taking them for a walk. As I prepared excuses for the kids, I wiggled into black jeans, slipped on a dove-gray T-shirt, and pulled an ebony hoodie over my head. Hopping up and down, sliding my feet into leather flats, I let the dogs in one by one. Gave each a peck on the forehead and rattled off my lines, groveling for forgiveness. Needless to say, it went over about as well as a steel anchor on a sinking life raft.

At the back door, I ran my fingers through my damp hair and disguised myself with dark sunglasses. Creeping toward the back fence bordering the Murphy's house, a raised ranch behind my property, the blistering heat was a lot hotter than the news advised. My black hoodie absorbed the July sun like a camel storing water for a hundred-mile trek through the desert.

Halfway over the fence, I remembered I hadn't forwarded the phone. I jumped to the ground and sprinted back home. As I approached the door, the phone rang, and I fumbled to get the key in the lock and get inside before the end of the second muffled trill.

At the beginning of the third ring, I answered, my breath ragged.

"I should hang up." The computerized voice. "I told you two rings."

"Please don't. I was…in the bathroom. I got here as fast as I could. Please, it won't happen again."

"You ready?"

"What, now?"

He didn't answer.

Warding off a headache, I stroked my forehead with my fingertips. "I mean…yes. Absolutely. I'm ready."

"Sage, don't ask me stupid questions. I can't deal with stupid questions. They anger me. You don't want to anger me, do you?" He loved the control he had over me.

"What do I call you?"

"Call me…John, John Doe."

Smart. "Okay, John. For me to outline a memoir I need a little background information. Like, where you grew up, what your family life was like, that sort of thing."

Silence.

Was he considering how much he should share, or constructing lies?

"I grew up in Marblehead."

Marblehead? That was where I was raised. He must be lying, using my birthplace as his own. I tested my theory. "Did you go to Marblehead High?"

"Why, you think we had classes together? Marblehead might be small, but as you know, it has many sections—The Neck, Old Town, Swampscott line, all with different schools. Even if we did attend the same school at the same time that doesn't mean we know each other." Anger poured into his voice. "Enough. You're fishing."

Yes, social classes seemed to segregate, from the filthy rich to the middle class, but there was only one high school in town. This proved he was lying. The only way he could be telling the truth was if he'd lived on The Neck and went to private school. If that were true, his family would have millions. Mansions and elaborate houses overlooked the Atlantic Ocean, many with tennis courts, some with golf courses. A lighthouse at the tip of The Neck, elite country clubs peppered throughout.

Old Town, however, was where antique dealers and custom shops lined cobblestone roads. Where a cup of coffee and a donut cost nine bucks, even back then. My parents raised us near the Swampscott line, a middle class neighborhood. Most families had money. They were far from poor.

My family inherited the house from my grandparents, who built the place long before Marblehead was the in spot for the upper crust. Even so, if John Doe lived in town, as he claimed, our paths would have crossed sooner or later. He never lived in Marblehead. Of that I was certain. "What'd your parents do for a living?"

"Why? You gonna blame my parents for how I turned out?"

"I'm only asking a question."

"My father was a chauffeur for a rich family on The Neck. Mom was the maid. Dad was a mean drunk. Hated his work. Hated the rich. Always took it out on me and my brother when he got home. Mom was a timid woman who let him beat the fuck out of us to save herself. That what you wanna hear?"

Parts of his story had elements of the truth in it. It rolled off his tongue too easily for it all to be fiction. "I'm sorry. That's an awful thing for a boy to have to go through."

"I know what you're doing, Sage, and it's not gonna work."

Shoot. I thought showing compassion, trying to relate to his human side, would make it harder for him to hurt Chloe. Years ago, I read an article about being abducted. The first rule was to say your name, so your kidnapper would view you as a person and not an object. The second, to show empathy for your abductor's background if he shared his background. Do anything you can to make yourself appear as his equal and not merely a plaything or piece of meat for him to torture.

"I don't know what you're talking about, John. I'm genuinely interested in the circumstances surrounding your choice of—" I was veering off course. Forget the mind tricks. Talk to him, lend an ear. "I think I know what you want to discuss." This wouldn't be easy, but I had no choice. For me to gather intel, I had to get him talking. "Who was your first victim and how did you choose her?"

"Now we're getting somewhere." This line of inquiry elated him. "Let's see. I was sixteen…had this girlfriend, Mary Ellen Cheney. She had the best smile. Perfect teeth. Pretty brunette hair. Didn't mean to kill her. It was an accident. But I did enjoy playing with her corpse afterward." He chuckled ghoulishly. "Doesn't make me a bad guy."

My stomach backflipped as I imagined what a budding serial killer must have done to his first dead body. Dissection. Mutilation. Necrophilia. Maybe there wasn't any human being left in him, and that's why I was failing to connect with him. I hated to ask, "How did she die, John?"

"I'll let you figure that out. It made the papers. Not my name. Her parents were devout Baptists. No one knew we were an item except me and her. Dead women tell no tales." He was enjoying this much too much.

Imagining how Mary Ellen's parents felt hearing about her death made my heart twist into knots. "Who was number two? Actually, how many victims were there, exactly?"

"Five. I think. No, six. I lost count. Anyway, the second was this whore I picked up in downtown Lynn. Early nineties, I think."

"How old were you then?"

"Nice try. Doesn't matter. She was a total pig, asked if she could suck my cock for twenty bucks. Who was I to deny her? Afterward, she wanted another twenty for swallowing. That wasn't the deal. Fucking whores. Never happy. I sliced her throat with a switchblade. Back then, I always kept a blade in my sock. Blood sprayed everywhere." Having a ball reliving his glory days, the memory tickled his ego. "It was raining blood inside my car. Glorious blood. My windshield was covered in it. All over the interior of my Z28. Loved that car, too. Fucking bitch bled like a stuck pig."

Saliva built in my throat and coated my tongue—my gag reflex ready to explode. Not wanting to hear the details, I squeezed my eyes closed. "Number three?"

He paused. "I don't hear you typing. You getting this down?"

Shoot. I'd been so consumed by his answers I totally forgot. I rushed into the living room, the cordless phone pressed to my ear, and jotted notes—but not the ones he wanted. "I was writing it on a legal pad. I often take notes longhand."

"What if your husband finds your notes?" Livid, his voice

spiked. "I told you, I don't want him involved. Burn the pages and type this shit out. Burn the pages underneath, too. They have ways of finding out what's on the top page by dusting the imprint. Sneaky fucks. You hear me, Sage? Do it. Do it now. I'll wait."

I tore a blank page from the legal pad, and then another and another and crumpled the pages into a ball and tossed them into the wood stove. For the sound effect, I lit them on fire. "There. Happy?"

"From now on, think, Sage. Use your fuckin' brain."

"I'm sorry. I've never done this before." Heart tripping, my throat knotted. "Please don't take my mistake out on Chloe. Please, John. It won't happen again."

"No. It won't." He quieted as if planning something wicked. "Where was I?"

"Three." I gulped. "You were about to tell me about your third victim."

"Number three." He thought about it for a few seconds. "Right. That was the broad in Chinatown. I remember now. She was working at a massage parlor, famous for their happy endings. I guess she was pretty. Typical chink—flat face, slanted eyes, tiny body—but she had these huge fake tits with white nipples. It was fucking disgusting. I took one look at those albino nipples and instantly lost my hard-on. She made the mistake of laughing. No one laughs at G— I mean…John, and gets away with it."

I scrawled a capital G in my notebook and circled it. I also wrote Marblehead, Lynn hooker, and Chinatown massage parlor homicide for future reference. With any luck, I might find a way to unmask his identity. Chloe mentioned a man whose name began with G. Maybe it wasn't a dream. My soul left my body to find my twin. Weirder things have happened.

John startled me. "She laughed right in my face, the fucking whore. But she wasn't laughing once I pulled out Betty."

"Betty?" I cringed. "Who's Betty?"

"Betty's my knife. Old dependable Betty, the one woman who never failed me."

This guy was clearly insane.

"Me and Betty have been together for years."

I could not hear any more about his undying love for his knife and did my best to steer the conversation back on track. Unfortunately, that meant making him talk about what he'd done to the masseuse. "Sorry to interrupt, John, but I don't want you to lose your train of thought. You were about to tell me what happened to the Asian woman."

"Right. The chink. So, she was laughing at me—I mean hard, too, belly laughing—while staring at my limp dick. That's enough to make any guy snap. Who the fuck did she think she was? She was the one who made it go soft with those fucking albino nipples." His voice crackled—wicked, demonic. "So I sliced that whore up good. Sliced those fucking nipples off too, and tossed them out the second story window."

Through the voice box, or whatever he was disguising his voice with, he roared so hard I could barely understand him. "Down below, on the sidewalk, this dude got pinged in the head and looked up. He almost saw me, too. Can you imagine, walking down the sidewalk and a white nipple biffs you off the side of the head? It was too funny." His tone chilled. "I took her eyes. My first set, actually." A pause. "Chloe has nice eyes."

Invisible fingers strangled my voice. I managed only, "Please, John. No."

"Relax."

"Please don't. You said if I cooperated—"

"I said calm the fuck down. Your sister still has her eyes…for the moment. Now, where was I? Right. I didn't take the chink's eyes because I liked them. I took them because she was staring at my cock. Those slanted fucking chink eyes. Even after she was dead, she was still laughing at me."

I swallowed a chunk of vomit that lurched up the back of my throat. Unable to hear another word, my voice cracked as I said, "Victim four?"

"I think that's enough for now."

Thank you, Jesus.

"I want to make you crave my stories. What fun would it be

if I gave it to you all at once? You'll have to earn it."

A thunderbolt of pain struck me in the gut. Did he say something similar while raping his victims? Niko hadn't mentioned if the woman in the photograph was sexually assaulted, but I presumed she was.

My mind cluttered with images from that horrific night in Boston. I couldn't move. I couldn't speak. Every memory I had pushed away flooded my brain like a tidal wave—crippling me—and I fell backward and landed on the kitchen chair, a hand clutching my heart. An icy chill screamed through my bones, and I was right back in my old living room. Shivering. Alone with a stranger. No control over my destiny, or if I'd even have one once he satisfied his thirst.

"You should have enough to get started," he said. "I want you working on this non-stop. You feel me?"

I fanned my face, my skin flushing. "I understand. Now, may I please speak with my sister?"

"No. Whaddaya think this is?"

"Proof of life. That's the deal. As long as I know she's all right, I'll keep listening. If I find out she's hurt, or worse, that's when I tell you to screw." As soon as the words rolled off my tongue I wanted them back. "I didn't mean that. I need to know Chloe's okay."

Another excruciating pause of silence came between us, and I prayed he wouldn't take my outburst out on my sister. After several agonizing moments, there was a rustling sound, a click, and then, "Sage?"

"Oh my God…Chloe. Did he hurt you?"

Audibly she wept, deep gasps hitching in her throat. "I love you, Sage," she said as though she had abandoned all hope.

"Please don't give up. I'm coming for you. Remember the cabin? Please, Chlo. I need you."

"That's enough." John broke us apart. "You got my letter?"

"Yes. How do I get it to you?" An idea skipped through my mind. "Do you want me to email it?"

"You email it and try and capture my IP address? Nice try.

Keep this shit up and I'll lose my patience. Go to Kelley Park on Lake Street. Look for the bench with the X. Leave the letter on the bench, inside a folded newspaper. Do not hang around. If I see you there, your sister dies. Today. One o'clock. Don't be late."

I thumbed the end button, and a cold shudder ran through me.

My cellphone chimed a text.

"Shoot. I forgot about Jess." I typed in a response, forwarded the home phone to my cell in case John called back, and flew out the kitchen door. After climbing the fence, I trampled over broken tree limbs, dense underbrush, and through piles of old autumn leaves. A muck of dank mush slurped my right shoe like quicksand. "Dammit." I yanked my shoe out of the sludge, banged the excess debris on the side of a pine tree, and slipped my bare foot inside. Squishing and squashing, I cut through the Murphy's side yard and landed on a paved road. A few doors down I spotted Jess' gold Lexus.

I opened the passenger door and explained my delay.

Jess slung her right arm over the passenger seat, her left palming the wheel. "What'd he say? Did you try to get his name?"

"John. John Doe."

"Clever."

"Oh, he's very clever. In lavish detail, he told me about his first three murders. This guy's sick in the head. We need to work fast."

Jess started the Lexus. "What else did he say?"

"Honestly, thinking about it turns my stomach. He scheduled a drop site, though. Kelley Park. One o'clock."

"He's gonna meet you?"

"No, thank God. I'm supposed to leave it on a bench. But there's no way I'm not hanging around to see who picks it up."

"Sage, that's too dangerous to do by yourself. Maybe I should go with you."

"No. He said to come alone. I can't take the chance of him spotting you."

"I don't like this."

"Neither do I."

Jess rifled behind my seat and brought forward a black duffel bag. "Here's the money you asked for." She dropped the bag at my feet. "You don't have to pay me back all at once. Maybe we can work something out where a portion comes out of each advance. Sound fair?"

"You're the best. Thank you." I unzipped the bag. Money bands wrapped crisp one hundred dollar bills, stacked neatly in rows. "Wow," was all I managed. "Do you mind if we hit a library first? I want to look up some of the things he told me."

She agreed.

I stared out the passenger window and imagined threats being whispered in Chloe's ear. "I wish I hadn't been such a royal ass over something as trivial as dating a married man."

"You didn't know. You can't blame yourself."

"But if I minded my own business, she would have stayed in Cambridge instead of coming up here. That must be when he took her. It's all my fault. If I wasn't so bullheaded…if I apologized…I swear if anything happens to her…"

Ten minutes down the road, Jess crossed into Bristol and hung a right onto Pleasant Street. A parking spot in front of the Minot Sleeper Library opened up, and she swung in front of a hunter green Rav4. The driver leaned on the horn, swearing out the window.

"Mass plates. Figures," said Jess. "Friggin' vacationers."

"You're a Mass driver."

"No kidding, but at least I'm not a Masshole like that lady." She twisted the key, killing the engine. "I don't know if you're gonna be able to find what you're looking for in here. It's awfully small."

"Quaint. Around here the word is quaint." I opened the car door and slung the duffel bag over my shoulder. Small town or no, I was not about to leave that much cash in an empty car. "Anyway, it's worth a shot." I kept my eye on the woman in the Rav4, who didn't budge as I hustled to the entranceway.

On a heavy oak door, ancient wrought iron hinges creaked open. Made from brick with church-like windows, the library was a historical building built in 1885, and one of my favorite places in the Lakes Region. With Wi-Fi and a borrowing service, the old library kept current, too. A large cement plaque displayed the name over the entrance. *Minot Sleeper Library* etched in black.

When "Hurt" hit the bestsellers list, I asked the librarian, Judy Cohen, to do a reading here. City after city I signed books across New England and New York. By the time I returned to Alexandria, I was so tired I cancelled. I always meant to reschedule, but time got away from me.

The last thing I needed this morning was a snooty librarian with an axe to grind. "Maybe *you* should ask where they keep the microfiche. Judy wasn't happy about the reading. Remember?"

"That's right. Okay. Go over there—" she gestured to the right— "and hide in the stacks. I'll come find you afterward."

I blended with rows of books. Judy glanced in my direction, and I pressed my back against the spines of several crime novels. Opposite me, one of the titles sent a cold crackle down my spine and down the backs of my legs, as if gnats were gnawing at my skin. "The Autobiography of John Doe - Confessions of a Serial Killer."

Chapter Nine

9:30 a.m.

Frankie typed the latest victim's name into her computer. Nancy Macomber. No criminal record. Not even a speeding ticket in the last ten years. She must have been a friggin' saint. Combing through the victims' backgrounds, credit card statements, and phone calls, she didn't find one connection between the three women. They frequented different grocery stores, prayed in separate churches. Neither Shelly Winters nor Karen Thatcher had credit card charges for the same coffee shops or restaurants within the months preceding their death. Nancy Macomber never ate out. At least, she never paid for it.

Frankie couldn't find a single location where the three women's paths crossed.

Rubbing the back of her neck, she called over to a deputy a few desks away, but kept her voice low so Niko couldn't hear. "Psst...Bradley. You find anything yet? I'm hitting one roadblock after another."

"So am I." Preston Bradley was a member of the squad, who, like Billy, got the job through a family relation. Only Preston was nothing like Billy. His uncle, the former sheriff, gave him his start, but it was Preston who'd earned the respect of his peers through a strong work ethic and investigative skills. He even used his mother's maiden name so people wouldn't make the connection.

Frankie liked that about him. When she first heard the sheriff's kid was transferring in, she immediately thought, great, another spoiled asshole who's bored with his perfect life and wants to play cops and robbers. It took months for her to give him the time of day. Eventually, though, he proved himself. Not an easy feat. Out of the six cops in the squad, Frankie only spoke to three—Niko, Bradley, and Lars Childs, everyone's favorite clown. Don't even get her started on Reed. He was as useless as tits on a bull.

"Niko's gonna be PO'd if I don't find something soon." Bradley had a way with words. Originally from Cambridge, Massachusetts, he had yet to drop his thick Boston accent. "I'm screwed, Frankie. Niko said if I came up empty, I'd be riding a desk."

She had to laugh. Granted, Niko had the power to put a deputy on desk duty, but with only six in the department, he'd never do it. Apparently Bradley hadn't figured this out, and she sure as hell wasn't about to tell him. After all, Niko was her partner. Partners stuck together, even if it meant having some fun at a co-worker's expense. "Did you interview the loggers?"

"Yup. The supervisor—" Bradley checked his notes— "Dan Morris, shattered his knee cap in a logging accident that day. But while his apprentice—" again, he checked his notes— "a kid named Donny Sprite, was rushing him out of the woods, he saw a couple pass in a dark SUV. Didn't get a good enough look for a sketch. Said it might be a Ford Explorer, but he wasn't positive."

"A couple? Interesting. He say anything else?"

"That a lot of teenagers use that trail. They party at the barn. One of the kid's father owns it." Frankie flipped back a few pages in her notebook. "A Mister Douglas Garrison. He alibied out. What about the ME's report? Did it come in yet?"

"Billy said they'd fax it when Doc finished his autopsy. He's also supposed to be sending lab results."

As the words left his lips, an ancient fax machine spit paper out its mouth.

"I got it." Frankie rushed the fax machine to see what, if anything, the killer left behind. She skimmed the five-page report, nodding deeply, acknowledging the findings.

"Okay, here's something." She perched herself on the edge of Bradley's desk, legs crossed, her black leather ankle boot playfully swinging. "No semen in the rape kit. No fingerprints, latent or otherwise, but we do have a partial palm print on the handle of Karen Thatcher's passenger door. We also might have DNA from cigarette butts recovered from the barn and the cabin. Marlboros."

She glanced up from the report at Bradley. "Course that could take weeks. Typical bullshit. No one ever accused the wheels of justice of moving too fast. Am I right?"

"If we've got DNA, we've got 'im." His voice rose three octaves as if someone had punched him in the gonads.

Poor kid had a lot to learn. Because there may or may not be DNA didn't mean a match could be made. Contrary to many police dramas on TV, law enforcement did not have a database filled with every citizen's DNA. The Supreme Court hadn't yet upheld a law to allow law enforcement to take DNA swabs from people arrested for serious crimes.

The general rule was that law enforcement could only obtain DNA evidence from a suspect once a judge signed off on a warrant. Meaning, she'd have to show probable cause that a suspect's DNA would lead to evidence of a crime. Talk about a pain in the ass. Probable cause. What a joke. More than one so-called solid citizen slipped through the cracks using that excuse.

Ben strolled into the middle of the conversation. "We got 'im? That's awesome. How?"

"Don't get your panties in a bunch. We don't got shit." Hot blood seethed through her veins at the mere sight of the deputy. Niko should be training *her*, not him. She wasn't stupid. Obviously, he was grooming him for Sheriff.

Frankie was his partner, his friend, his confidant. Why'd he choose Ben over her? Okay, she admitted, so maybe she shouldn't have pulled the mayor's toupee off at last year's Christmas party. Big deal. She was only joking around. Besides, it looked like a dead rat on his head. He wasn't fooling anyone. And maybe she shouldn't have told the police captain to take a picture of her ass, but he was googling at her as she was walking away. That wasn't very professional, either. Whatever.

"Why are you here?" she derided Ben. "Your nose need a break from Niko's ass?"

"Why do you hate me so much? I never did anything to you."

"I don't hate anyone." She hopped off Bradley's desk and settled behind her computer, her back to Ben.

"Niko said I could watch you run the prints, so I know how to reverse 'em."

"I'll call you when I'm ready. Hey." She spun in her chair. "Weren't you supposed to go to the library or some shit?"

"I did. Three of them, actually. No one checked out books on forensics except college students." His voice softened. "I guess it's a dead end."

She'd heard the same tone in her own voice when she was first learning the ropes. The absolute certainty that a course of action would render results and then the uncompromising defeat when it didn't. "Pull up a chair," she relented. "I was going over the autopsy report and rape kit."

Smiling like a kid with his first ice cream cone, Ben rolled a charcoal-cushioned office chair next to her desk. "Thanks, Frankie. I'm psyched we get to work together. You were the one I wanted to shadow. I never expected Niko to volunteer."

Even though something inside her yearned to tell Ben, "aww, that's sweet," she yammered, "yeah, yeah. Don't get all mushy on me." Since Niko had dibs on Ben, she'd school Bradley as her protégé. She leaned around Ben to Bradley and said, "Hey, if the mutt isn't in the system, we don't have shit. I mean, sure, we can match DNA once we find a suspect, but until then…" She'd made her point.

"What else?" Frankie drew her finger up, down, and across each page pretending she was speed reading. Bradley was so gullible he believed almost anything she told him, and she never missed an opportunity to have fun with that particular personality flaw.

Right on cue, Bradley's mouth formed a perfect O. "Wow. How'd you learn to read so fast? You're amazing."

"Thanks, kid." She winked. "You'll get there someday." One second too late, she spotted Niko behind her, arms crossed on his chest, sight locked on the three deputies. "Niko." She sprang to her feet, and her chair sailed across the room and smashed into a spare desk. "How long have you been standing there?"

"Long enough." A smile lurked beneath his scowl, giving him away. He was putting on a show for the newer members of the team. "You guys having a good time at the taxpayers' expense?"

With one arm across her waist, the other swept out to the side, Frankie bowed. "I'm sorry, sir. Forgive me."

As usual, Bradley was the last to catch on. "We were—" His voice pitched and cracked as though he could faint at any moment.

"Niko," Ben chimed in, "Frankie was showing me the autopsy report."

Huh, the kid was actually covering for her. This little display earned him a few brownie points.

"Got anything for me?" Niko glowered at Bradley, albeit not very convincingly. He was no more of a hard-ass than she was a… umm…pushover.

Bradley's eyes bulged, and then slid to Frankie. What the hell. Might as well save his sorry ass. "Partial palm print, cigarette butts, possible DNA, and a boot tread. Columbia work boot, size ten."

"That's something, at least. Did you cross-reference for past crimes with the same MO?"

"Yeah, and I got a hit." She retrieved her swivel chair and rolled it to her desk. She typed the killer's MO into Spillman—a database that shares information between sheriff and police departments. "Three years ago local police found a body in Kingston. New Hampshire, not Mass. Didn't you and Sage used to vacation at Kingston Lake?"

"Yeah, but so did a million other people." Niko slid back on to an empty desk, next to Frankie. "Walk me through the case."

"The body of a thirty-five-year-old woman, later ID'd as Sophia Lambert, was discovered in the old schoolhouse, a historical landmark turned residential home. Per order of Bank of America, the foreclosed property sat empty for nine months. On July 19th, 2003, a prospective buyer and real estate agent for the bank found Ms. Lambert hanging from a hole in the ceiling. Apparently, the home had the old horsehair plaster and low ceilings. The mutt cut a hole with a jigsaw and set up a pulley system."

Gathering facts, she read ahead. "Same cigarette burns on the soles of the feet. Stitching on eyes and mouth. Breasts and eyes removed, never found. The body drained of blood and a bloody H on the window facing the main drag."

Something she said registered with Niko. "Did you say July 2003?" He hopped off the desk to read the case file over her shoulder. "You positive it's 2003?"

She glanced back at him, wrinkling her nose. What's with the panicked reaction to the date? "Yeah. Why?"

A bead of sweat dripped down his forehead and dangled from the tip of his nose. With the back of his hand, he wiped it away.

"You okay, Niko?"

Sheepish white, the blood drained from his face from the mere mention of the date, and he didn't respond. Stumbling backward, he stuck out his hand—a death grip on the side of the nearest desk.

"Boss?" she prompted.

Voice shaky, his chin was quivering. "Leads?"

"Nope. They were looking at the boyfriend, a Mister Chuck Smalls, but he alibied out. All other leads ran cold."

"Perfect." Sarcasm laced his tone. "For shits and giggles, call the lead detective and see if he'll share the leads that dried up. They had to have more than one suspect."

"I'm on it." She searched Spillman for the detective's contact information. Every so often, her gaze traveled to check on Niko

He took out a pressed handkerchief and dabbed sweat off his forehead, took a minute to collect himself, and said, "Ben, you're with me. We need to notify Karen Thatcher's parents that their child's dead."

"Good luck, Ben," Frankie remarked, masking delight. "You're in for a real treat. Death notifications suck."

"Wouldn't you rather take Frankie? I can call the detective in southern NH."

"You need to learn. This is part of the job. The worst part, but a necessary task."

Eyebrows arched, Ben silently begged Frankie to save him. Covering the mouthpiece of the phone, she said, "Time to break your cherry, kid."

* * *

The moment Frankie mentioned the date, the noise in the squad room had distorted as if Niko was underwater. He thought about that night, thought about Sage. He couldn't tell his wife the man who assaulted her was here in Alexandria. The room spun out of control, and he felt around to brace his imminent collapse. Scooting his butt onto the corner of the desk, he waited for the feeling to pass.

During the summer of 2003, Niko was hunting the most prolific serial killer Boston had ever seen. The murders rocked the city. After dark, brunette women were petrified to leave their homes. The jogging paths all emptied by 5 p.m., and the residential neighborhoods appointed a crew to smother trees and lampposts with tiny white lights like Christmas in July.

People feared for their lives. The task force was stumped. The killing spree lasted three never-ending months before the mutt assaulted Sage at home. Niko had only shared three of the murders with his wife. There were actually six before September 12, 2003. But the Romeo Killer's MO was nothing like the recent homicides. No eyes taken, no stitching on the face. No evidence to make him believe the same killer traveled north.

Except the date.

* * *

10:30 a.m.

Knocking at the door of the Thatchers, Niko cautioned Ben. "When notifying parents of murder victims, you never want to blurt it out. We need to extract as much information as we can before telling them. Once they hear the news, they can't think straight. For now, follow my lead. Unless they specifically ask you a question, don't speak. Let me handle it."

Ben released an exaggerated breath. "Oh, man. I thought I was gonna pass out."

Niko allowed a faint grin and then thinned his lips when an

elderly woman answered the door. "Are Mr. and Mrs. Thatcher home?"

The woman touched an open hand to her chest. "I'm Mrs. Thatcher. Or do you mean my daughter-in-law?"

"Are you Karen's mother?" The words slipped out before he could stop them. Damn Lambert case had him all messed up.

"She's my granddaughter." The elderly woman palmed the side of her face. "Is she all right? Did something happen?"

"Ma'am, if it's all the same with you, I need to speak with Karen's parents, please." No matter how much planning beforehand, death notifications rarely went smoothly. This was no exception.

"Come in." She ushered them inside. "Wait here, please."

Like a lot of area residents, the Thatchers lived in a rustic home. Unlike the others, this massive log home sat directly on Newfound Lake with an awe-inspiring view out the kitchen sliders. Billowy treetops hugged a sandy shoreline, an occasional house nestled in between. A backdrop of rich green mountains, the air so thin it seemed to nurture misty clouds as if embraced by a mother's loving arms. Speedboats with jet skiers, pontoon boats with folks casting fishing lines off the side, vacationers frolicked in crystal-blue water.

The smell of wood permeated the hot July air from a soft pine interior. A black cat nuzzled his face on Niko's shoe and squirmed in and out of his legs. He loved animals, but a black cat during a death notification was a bit much, even for him. "Nice kitty." He bent to one knee and gave the cat a gentle nudge, pushing him away. "Go lay down."

Ben leaned aside, hushed from the corner of his mouth, "He's not a dog. Cats don't take orders."

The black cat made one last round in and out of his legs and then plopped on Niko's left foot, purring like a mini buzz saw.

"What's wrong with him? Why won't he leave me alone?"

"There's nothing wrong with him. He's only being friendly." Ben squatted, scratching the cat's belly, still on top of the sheriff's shoe.

"Get him off my foot, Deputy. If you think he's so cute, slide him over to you."

"Mean ol' uncle Niko," Ben told the cat. "You want lovin'. Huh? Yeah. You're a good boy. Aren't you?"

Niko held a tight smile for when the family arrived. He shook his foot. "Get him off me."

"Don't listen to him. He's a meanie."

"Deputy Mathews, I am ordering you to get that—" He gave his leg one firm shake and stepped over the cat, hand extended to the couple. "Hello, Mr. and Mrs. Thatcher. I'm Sheriff Quintano from Grafton County. May I have a few minutes of your time, please?"

"Sure. Right this way." Bob Thatcher, a husky man with linebacker shoulders, escorted Niko and Ben into the living room. Without saying a word, Barbara Thatcher followed obediently behind her husband. The couple sat on a stiff sofa that squeaked when the cushions depressed, and Karen's grandmother perched her tiny frame on the armrest beside her son.

Didn't take much to deduce the family dynamics in this house. Bob was king, his mother second-in-command, and Barbara had no opinion of her own. Niko opened his notepad, pen at the ready. "When was the last time you saw Karen?"

Karen's grandmother let out a squeal. "Why? What's happened? Oh, dear Lord, Bob, something's wrong. I can feel it." She pressed a clenched fist to her heart.

Would she go into cardiac arrest once he broke the news?

Ben snapped into action, knelt in front of the elderly woman and set her frail hand in his. "We need to ask you a few questions." With two fingers he caressed huge brown age spots on the backside of her hand. "You have beautiful hands, Mrs. Thatcher, so youthful and soft."

"Oh, my." Her cheeks blushed rose. "Aren't you a charmer, you sweet boy."

Incredible. Niko's instinct to bring the kid was spot-on. He was personable, good with victims' families, not afraid to schmooze an old lady. Impressive indeed. "So, the last time you spoke with Karen was…?"

"Friday night," offered Barbara. "She usually has dinner with us on Sundays, but she said she had plans."

"Did she say with who?"

"No." Eyeing the grandmother, she weaved her fingers with Bob's, staking her claim. "Now that I think about it, she *was* acting quite secretive."

"How so?"

"Normally she's open and honest with me, but when I asked about her plans, she changed the subject. I knew not to push. She is an adult, after all."

"Was she dating anyone?"

The mother's upper lip curled in a snarl, eyes shifting to her husband. "Not that I'm aware of, no."

Niko's detective antennae dinged. The mother was covering for Karen. She'd met the man on the sly and the husband had no idea. "What about friends? Did she have a close friend that she confided in?"

"Becky Adams," Karen's grandmother provided. "They've known each other since grade school. Karen hired her as her personal assistant once her publishing firm got up and running.

"Publishing firm?" That, he never expected. Why didn't Frankie tell him about this? "Karen's a book publisher?"

"Yes. Newfound Thriller. It's a small press, you know. She's done pretty well for herself. I'm so proud of my granddaughter."

A speedboat full of college students sailed by the window, hooping and hollering, and Niko could not pull his sight away from the girl water skiing off the back. She was doing well, too, until a catamaran cut her off. One ski shot straight up in the air and she flew backward, into the water.

The boat circled around. One of the boys scooped the ski and dropped it by the girl, now treading water. The girl fidgeted under the water, slipping her foot into the ski boot. With an exaggerated nod toward the boat she signaled she was ready. Straight arms held out in front, her fingers gripped around a rope handle, the boat glided her out of the water.

It would have been a flawless start if her bikini top wasn't around her waist. With a Miss America smile, she waved at beachgoers on the shoreline.

Eyes widening, Niko gulped and loosened his tie. Catching his reaction, Karen's father was about to swivel toward the window when Niko brought him back with, "Mr. Thatcher," in an elevated, anxious tone. "How 'bout you? Do you know of anyone bothering Karen?"

"Karen doesn't have any enemies. Everyone loves her." He tucked his wife's arm under his; their hands still weaved together. "Please, Sheriff, tell us what's going on with our little girl."

The scene on the beach kept drawing his attention, beckoning him to watch. The college girl did three laps past the house—male beachgoers on their feet cheering her on—before she realized it wasn't her ability and grace that excited her fans. She dove into the water, and the shoreline booed in protest.

A trickle of sweat needled Niko's hairline, the room growing hotter by the second.

"Sheriff?" prodded Bob.

"Yes? Oh, right." He ran his finger under his shirt collar while he reviewed his notes. "Had Karen been getting any strange phone calls lately? Or did she say she felt like someone was watching her?"

"You mean stalking?" Barbara raised an open palm to her cheek. "No, no, no. Not my baby. Not Karen."

Bob leaned forward, urged, "What's happened? Is she all right?"

"I'm sorry to inform you that Karen's remains were discovered in an abandoned barn, Monday afternoon."

The grandmother wailed and collapsed onto Bob's lap, clutching her heart. Barbara rocked, tears streaming down her cheeks, and Bob shielded his face with his hands.

"How'd she die?" asked Karen's father. "Please don't tell me she's the body I heard about on the news, with her eyes removed."

The news? How'd they get ahold of the details? Vultures.

The worse part of the job indeed. There was no easy way to

tell a grieving couple, their daughter was severely mutilated before death. Setting a grief counselor's business card on the coffee table, he answered, "Her death's been ruled a homicide."

Chapter Ten

10:30 a.m.

In front of the library's microfiche machine, I read the Boston Herald, 1990 editions and searched for articles about a Chinatown murder. For hours, I breezed through one article after another.

Jess was at the machine next to mine. "I can't find anything. How 'bout you?"

"Not yet. There're plenty of murders in Chinatown, but not one at a massage parlor. Maybe John Doe lied about where he killed her." I rolled to the next article. "Wait. Here's something." My gaze fluttered back and forth across the screen, digesting the article. "This must be it." I read further and smacked the table with an open hand. "Shoot. The police don't mention a suspect. All this work and we're nowhere. This was a stupid idea." I proceeded to stand when Jess yanked my arm, forcing me into the chair.

"Don't give up so easily. You always do that. Patience, my dear friend, patience."

"Easy for you to say. You don't have some psycho holding your sister hostage."

"That's not fair." Her voice raised ten decimals, angry and hurt blurring her tone. "You know I love Chloe. Would I be here if I didn't?"

Judy Cohen, the librarian, let out a "Shhhh…" a stick-straight finger to her lips, her marble-like navy eyes in tiny slits over half-moon glasses.

Jess lowered her voice, but kept it firm. "You think I don't have a million other things I could be doing right now?"

"Then go. You're the one who wanted to drive up and help me.

All I asked for was a letter and a loan. I never told you to come here."

"You ungrateful—" She swallowed, waited a beat. "I cannot believe how you're talking to me." Without taking her eyes off me, she rose—two women locked in a battle of wills.

"Leave." I waved her away, dismissed her like a petulant toddler, but watched her reflection in the microfiche screen.

She exhaled through her nostrils the way a bull prepared to charge a matador's cape. A split-second later her shoulders relaxed and she retook her seat. Using her feet, she inched her rolling chair closer to me. "I know you're upset." Her tone was conciliatory. "I'm upset too, whether you believe it or not. Taking your frustrations out on me is only going to make matters worse. Please, Sage, we've been friends a long time. Let me help you. Don't shut me out like you did before."

"I've told you a gazillion frickin' times I wasn't shutting you out back then." My gaze shifted to Judy, glowering at me to lower my voice. "I needed time to process what happened." I frowned, my eyes tilted downward. "You can't understand unless you've been through it. No one can."

As if sick of hearing the same tired excuse, Jess sighed. "It's been three years. When are you gonna get past this?"

"How *dare you*."

The librarian shushed us.

I leaned aside, loudly whispered, "How dare you? Who do you think you are, telling me when to get over being raped?"

No one was more furious than me about reliving the assault over and over. If Jess hadn't guessed "Hurt" was about my life, I would never have told her. I should never have told her. She and Chloe were the only ones I confided in, and they both expected me to move on. But I couldn't erase the images, the odors, the viciousness of rape. I doubted any victim could. It was always with me, growing inside me like a fungus. Jess throwing it in my face only intensified my angst.

I swiveled toward the microfilm machine. "Go. I don't want your help, and I don't need it."

"How will you get home?"

"Don't you worry about me. I'll be fine."

She rested her hand on mine. "Sage, be reasonable."

I jerked my hand away. "Honestly, I can't even look at you right now."

"You do this every time life gets the least bit complicated. You retreat to your own little world. Someday you'll realize the world is not out to get you. Yes, something terrible happened to you. Get over it. Women are raped every eight seconds in this country. Do something to help yourself. Join a support group. Talk to other survivors. Anything that might help you deal. I can't take this anymore. I've had enough." She stormed away from me, and out the library exit.

Disgusted at myself, I dropped my forehead on folded arms. In the past, I opened up to a counselor. All it got me was a stack of bills my insurance refused to cover.

The tears came full-force, and I cried for what a mess my life had become. For what that man stole from me. I cried for Chloe. For what I now believed she would experience if she hadn't already.

I cried for Niko. The poor, sweet man didn't deserve a wife like me. I was no longer the woman he married, and he certainly didn't sign up to care for an emotional invalid. Maybe everyone would be happier if I disappeared. Tears puddled on the desk, my chest heaving up and down as my emotions spilled onto the natural pine.

Judy marched over with her hands on her hips. "I'm going to have to ask you to leave, ma'am. You are upsetting the other patrons."

I raised my drenched eyes.

"Sage Quintano?" She sat in the empty chair. "Heaven's sake, I didn't realize that was you."

Sure, she didn't. She looked straight at me. I searched my leather fanny pack for a Kleenex.

Before I found one, Judy snapped a tissue from under her cuff. "Here. It's clean. I always keep one handy for my stories." When she smiled, she was missing teeth on the top row, toward the back. A plate held two teeth on either side of her incisors, evident by metal wires, and then bare spaces in place of molars. "Don't you still owe us a reading?"

Blowing my nose in the tissue, I wagged my head up and down. "Sorry about that. My tour lasted forever. I'll make it up to you. I promise."

She swatted the air. "No need to worry about that now, dear. Just a friendly reminder, you know."

If it was only a friendly reminder, she wouldn't have brought it up now when I was obviously upset. Passive aggressive bullshit. Classic Judy. "Thank you, Judy." I gritted my teeth. "Sorry, if I disturbed your patrons. I'll leave."

Again, she swatted the air. "Nonsense, dear. You stay as long as you want. Perhaps you'd like to do a reading now."

I yearned to say, "I'd rather eat glass." Instead, I went with, "No, thank you. I'm working on something. Besides, I don't have any books to sign. Wouldn't you rather have a proper event, advertise first and what-not?"

"You mean like I did last time?" She pursed her lips, her chin dipping to her chest, staring at me over those glasses she used as a weapon.

"Is there anything else?" I jabbed a chin at the microfiche. "I should get back to work."

"Sure, sure. You go right ahead, dear. I am sorry to have bothered you. Please keep it down. The other patrons, you know."

"Absolutely, Judy." I crossed my heart and then caught myself. I had to stop doing that. "Not another word. I promise."

Judy never asked why I was crying, which I found odd. She probably didn't care, only that it disturbed the other visitors. She returned to a narrow oak table, a few feet away, found the page she had dog-eared, gave me one last spiteful glare over her glasses, and melted into her story.

I scrawled a note to remind myself to reschedule the signing.

Before I left the library, I slung the duffel bag over my shoulder and made my way to a row of computers, chose the last one at the end, and typed in the MO depicted in the crime scene photos. Within seconds, pages and pages of articles appeared on the screen. A masthead caught my eye. Woman Butchered near Kingston Lake, dated July 2003. I clicked the title.

The news story filled the screen, and my blood chilled to ice.

A thirty-three-year-old female, Sophia Lambert, found dead in the old schoolhouse in Kingston, early this morning. Her eyes removed. Breasts carved from her chest. X's sealing the wounds. A source close to the investigation said Lambert was viciously raped…

Raped repeated in my mind like a shout echoing through a canyon. Raped…raped…raped…raped… I jumped to my feet, clutching my heart. The room whirled—round and round, faster and faster—and I wobbled, clawing the table edge with my nails.

I stumbled forward.

I needed fresh air, needed to be outside, needed to feel freedom. Alive. As if some semblance of normalcy still existed. *Breathe, Sage.* I gulped what scarce air I could find. Smeared sweat dripping down my forehead with my sleeve.

Eyes bulging, I gaped left, right.

Library patrons stared, muffled voices in the background. A loud, steady hum…vibrated through my core. Judy stood to say something.

I couldn't stop. The door was in sight.

Vision blurred with tears, I waved splayed hands out in front of me.

The door was breathing. The wood swelled, contracted—taunting me, daring me to near.

I staggered forward.

The door seemed less and less real the closer I got. A mirage. A delusion in my head. One misstep and it could vanish. Then I'd be stuck. Trapped. Held hostage like that night in Boston. A wretched stench of decay overpowered my senses, my body rotting inside out.

I zagged into the stacks. Books crashed onto the hardwood and sent me reeling. I dropped to my knees, rocked my head in my arms.

I'll never escape, never make it out. Tears deluged my eyes, and I lost sight of the door. I surveyed left, right. Focused on the stained glass. The door was in between two windows. If I aimed for the windows, I'd find the exit. With flat palms, I pushed off the floor, steadied myself, and crawled to my feet.

It felt like miles to the door—my feet heavy, legs tired and weak. Why didn't Niko tell me? Why would he hide something like this? The Lambert murder had happened two months before the killer broke into our home. My husband knew what he was capable of, and said nothing. Did he want me to die? Lose the baby? Why didn't he warn me? I would have taken precautions. I would have had deadbolts installed on every door, bars on the windows, sealed the sliders. All he said was he was chasing another sicko. That was nothing new. But if I had known…rape, mutilation, taking body parts as trophies. Now that animal had my sister.

I hurtled toward the door.

A few more strides. A few more feet until…

With two hands, I shoved open the door and devoured the air, as if emerging from an underwater cave.

Damn my husband for always treating me as though my mind could snap at any moment. Nothing irked me more than being treated like a child who wasn't mature enough to handle the truth. The cautious way he chose his words when he needed to tell me something minor. Major things, life or death matters, he never discussed. Not anymore.

Why didn't he tell me?

I glimpsed my watch. 12:31 p.m. Oh no—Chloe.

I hurtled down Pleasant Street—zero to twenty—as if a gun fired to signal the start of a race. When Pleasant Street turned into Lake Street, the park was still a mile or so down the road. I'd never make it in time.

I sprinted faster, my arms pumping harder and harder.

The toe of my flats hit a fissure in the sidewalk and I sailed through the air, skidding across sun-bleached pavement—a flat stone skipping the ocean. Road rash stung my hands and ripped holes in the knees of my new jeans. Blood snaked down my shins and through the torn denim. "I can't do this," I wailed, curling into the fetal position. "I'm sorry, Chloe. I'm not strong enough."

As I lay on the sidewalk car horns beeped. People stared out car windows. They probably thought I was drunk, or homeless, or plain nuts. This small town was getting smaller by the second.

I sat upright, pulled my hood over my head to hide my face, and rummaged through my fanny pack for dark sunglasses and cell. It was eighty-five degrees outside, and I was wearing a hooded sweatshirt with a duffel bag on my shoulder.

I must look like the friggin' Unabomber. Super, more gossip for the townsfolk.

I dialed a trusted friend, my spiritual adviser. "Mr. Chen, I need you. Something's happened."

"Talk to me, child," he said in his usual serene tone. Originally from China, Mr. Chen was the most spiritual person I'd ever known. At only five-foot-four he was a force, a powerhouse, a master of the arts. His deep faith allowed his mind to travel beyond the realms of this world, into the unthinkable, the magical. "You tell me anything," he said in broken English.

"Something terrible's happened, and I don't think I can handle it. I told you about Chloe, my twin."

"Many times. Another married man?"

With a quick glance in all directions, I cupped the mouthpiece, lowering my voice to a whisper. "No. Worse. She's been kidnapped."

"Until you see the rabbit, don't release the falcon." Quite often Mr. Chen would offer his wisdom by way of Chinese proverbs. He'd held my counsel for so many years I knew almost all of them by heart.

"Yes, I'm sure. Her abductor called me. He's using her so I'll cooperate."

"What he want?"

"You mean besides fifty-thousand-dollars? He wants me to write his memoir, or so he says. He's made me listen to his past murders and now has me delivering a promissory letter of publication along with the money to a drop-off point. Personally, I think he wants to keep me busy so I don't look for Chloe."

A drawn out silence.

"A monk can run away, but not the temple."

"I'll have to face it sooner or later because he has Chloe. Is that what you're telling me?"

"Yes. Remember, the gun always shoots the bird with his neck stuck out."

"I know. I'll be careful and keep my eyes open. Thank you, Mr. Chen. I can do this…right?"

"Put people under pressure and they will hang themselves. Put pressure on dog and it will jump over wall. Be the dog, Sage. Be the dog."

"Be the dog." I mulled it over. "Be the dog." I was Chloe's only chance of survival. "I am the dog, Mr. Chen." His encouraging words of wisdom energized me, filled me with the confidence I needed to continue. "I am the dog," I echoed. "I…am…the…dog."

He grunted his approval.

I tossed my cell in my fanny pack and hightailed it toward the park with a renewed power, sheer unadulterated fear driving my very existence. Within minutes, I managed to propel myself down Lake Street, rounded the corner through the park entrance, and then slowed. Speed walking, arms scissoring by my side, I had three choices of groups to blend with—dog owners utilizing the public park as a doggy park, mothers and nannies watching their children play on the jungle gym, or fathers pushing their little girls on tire swings. Anyone would do if it brought me anonymity.

Normally when I appeared in public people gawked. A bestselling author around here garnered as much attention as a movie star. I unzipped my hoodie and shed it like a snake leaves its skin. Glasses too. I didn't care anymore.

Let them stare. I could use this to my advantage. Someone might notice who sat on the bench after me, or if I was lucky, a fan would take my picture as Chloe's abductor stepped into the frame. I combed the area for an X but didn't see one anywhere. Did I walk into a trap? Did he lure me here to trade my life for Chloe's, or to have a matching set?

My eyes stung—probably bloodshot, definitely puffy—as I scoured the park.

Mower lines crisscrossed a checkerboard pattern over a manicured lawn, the aroma of freshly cut grass left lingering. Different breeds of dogs ran freely, their owners embarrassed when they scuffled over a ball. Children's laughter pierced the blazing heat. Elderly citizens read newspapers and took strolls on the walking path, around the outer edge. The park was a joyous place to come and relax.

Not today. John Doe's presence made it ugly. The laughter and high-pitched screams overshadowed by murder, spoiled by a menacing air of contempt.

I circled each bench, hunting for the symbol. After examining six, I spotted a chalk-white X on a bench's cement frame. The bench sat at the far end of the park, edged by a dense wooded area encircling a small patch of grass.

For all I knew he could be hiding behind a tree, waiting to strike.

I sat on the bench and drew the letter from my back pocket.

Damn, I forgot the newspaper.

A few feet away, an elderly man was reading the morning news. Typical grandfather type, who would bounce a little girl on his knee and serenade her with songs from his era, when, as he would say, music still sounded like music, not like the crap out there today. Perfect mark.

With a glance in all directions, I scooted to his bench. "Excuse me, sir?"

"Yes."

I offered my standard warm smile. "Would you mind sharing the newspaper? I forgot to pick one up on the way. Any section. I'm not picky."

The old man split the paper in two, sliding out the sports section for himself. "Here you go, little lady. I want to get the scores on a couple games I put money on."

A gambler? Never expected that.

Not people watching was a new experience for me. All good

writers people watched now and then. I could watch strangers come and go for hours as I made up tiny details about their lives. I never knew if I was right of course, but often they became characters in my books. The park was one of my favorite places to go for inspiration.

Not today. This was the last place on earth I wanted to be.

As I stink-eyed the old man, I questioned what secrets he held. A wedding band wrapped his ring finger and cut deep into the flesh from years of wear. Did he divorce and couldn't let go, or did he murder his wife in gambler's rage? He was alone at the park in the middle of the day with no child or dog, and he didn't appear sociable, other than answering my question. Did he possess enough evil to abduct, torture, and maim another human being?

Unease clawing at my chest, I mumbled, "John Doe?"

He cupped his ear. "Pardon? You'll have to speak up, honey."

"I said, thanks for the paper." With a tight smile, I muttered, "You don't fool me for a second, old man. Deaf, my ass."

He leaned closer. "Huh? I didn't catch the last part."

"I said, have a good day."

"Oh. You too."

I rose from the bench, goose bumps popping all over my skin and scuttled to my designated seat. As Mr. Chen encouraged, I had to get my head in John Doe's deadly game. Instead, I saw evil in people's eyes, detestation in their souls, and auras black with hatred.

I slipped the letter into the folds of the newspaper and set it on the bench beside me, scooted the duffel bag under the seat and then meandered to the west side of the park, about ten yards away. Assuming Chloe's kidnapper was watching, I strode out the entrance and zigzagged through parked cars to a side street, running alongside the walking path.

The bench was too far away. I cut through the woods behind the park.

The sun's rays couldn't illuminate the dank forest floor through a thick canopy of leaves. Intermittent spots of blue sky peeked between full treetops. Critters scurried through dry, crunchy leaves. Hawks soared overhead, waiting to swoop down and capture smaller prey in their talons. Pine needles littered dense foliage and emanated a Christmassy scent. Sticks crunched underfoot as I trampled over fallen trees, through picker bushes, under limbs cracked in half by spring's torrential downpours, until finally I found an opening, behind the bench. I crouched low, shielding my body with a wide-bottom oak tree—eagle eyes on the X.

Within five minutes, a person wearing a baseball hat and dark sunglasses passed the bench. His face snapped toward the newspaper, but only for a moment. He wore baggy gray sweatpants and an oversized navy T-shirt, a close-up of a wolf silk-screened on the front. He had muscular, tanned arms with heavy black hair. He was taller than I, stronger than I, and definitely more menacing. Gripping the bark of the old oak, I stalked the stranger, who sat beside the old man. He lingered for what seemed like forever.

I thought he'd never leave.

With a snap of his neck, the stranger eyed the newspaper again.

I leaned forward in anticipation.

The man quickened his pace toward the marked bench. He stopped in front of the X to tie his sneaker though I hadn't noticed if it had come undone. With one fluid motion, he swiped the newspaper and duffel bag and kept moving.

Now was my chance. I hugged the park, trampling through the woods, following him as far as I could without stepping in plain sight. He got in a black SUV with tinted windows, parked on a side street—the same road I came down earlier.

By the time I made it to the road, the SUV was speeding away.

I had no way to follow. If I hadn't picked a fight with Jess, I might have discovered where he was hiding Chloe. This all could be over with Chloe home safe. The nightmare done, with only the wounds left to heal. But I did pick that fight.

No matter how much I wished I could turn back time and relive the moment when I pushed Jess away, it would never happen. To make matters worse, I was too far back to get a good look at him. I never saw his face, only jet-black hair protruding from under the cap, which Chloe believed was a hairpiece, anyway. I was no closer to finding my sister than I was before.

With my head hung low, my soul crushed, I changed directions and began the six or seven mile walk home.

A horn blared from a black SUV as it swerved, missing me by inches. The truck had tinted windows, the same make and model as the kidnapper drove.

I took off after it.

The SUV stopped at the end of the road. The left blinker flashed on…off…on…off…

I charged at full-speed toward the rear bumper. The faint outline of a hand waved furiously against the back windshield.

"Chloe, I'm coming," I called out—sprinting, my arms pumping to increase momentum.

The hand banged against the glass.

I fought against the wind, ignored the blistering sun scorching my back.

The SUV was almost within reach.

I stuck out my arm and almost made contact.

The SUV took the corner.

I careened diagonally across Lake Street. Cars lined up at a red light. I finally had the advantage. My fast strides shortened the gap between us, and I banged on the glass. "Chloe, I made it." Tears of joy wet my lashes as I twisted the handle on the back window. "I told you I'd—"

The window flipped open. Two six-year-old boys played patty-cake, slapping each other hands, singing, "Miss Mary Mack, Mack, Mack. All dress in black, black, black. With silver buttons, buttons, buttons. All down her back, back, back."

My heart sank.

The driver got out and slammed the door. A petite woman marched toward me. "What the hell do you think you're doing? What are you, some kind of pervert?" She forced the window closed and told the boys, "Lock it."

I had bent over with my hands on my knees, attempting to

catch my breath. Agonizing pain screamed through my legs. I wobbled, grabbed hold of the bumper to keep from falling.

The woman scowled. "What is wrong with you? You drunk or something? Do I need to call the police?"

"I'm sorry," I said, breath catching in my throat. "My sister… she's been kidnapped. I thought I saw her in the back of your vehicle. I never meant to scare your boys. I love children. I would never…" Choking back tears, I ground my jaw.

The woman studied me a moment. "Aren't you Sage Quintano?" With a gleam in her eye, a smile bloomed on her freckled face. "Gosh. It is you. I love your books." Her weaved hands raised to her chin.

As much as I appreciated a fan enjoying my novels, I found it strange that she disregarded my mention of a kidnapping. Some people were so self-involved, they barely acknowledged anyone else. A trickle of sweat rolled down my nose as I straightened. "I'm so glad you like my books. Thank you."

"Hey, would you mind…" She held up a straight finger. Not the middle one thankfully, though I couldn't blame her if she had. "Don't run off now. Be back in a jiffy."

Believe me, I wasn't going anywhere. My arthritis flared, and I could barely walk never mind run away.

She shuffled to the back seat, pulled out "Hurt" and returned to the bumper. "Would you mind?" She nudged the book toward me.

I offered my standard warm smile and held out my hands. "Got a pen?"

"A writer without a pen." She tittered like a schoolgirl.

This woman was wearing my last nerve raw. I fished a pen out of my fanny pack and signed the back of the first page. "There you go. Again, I'm sorry if I caused you any undue stress."

"Don't be silly. You're *creative.*" She flashed air quotes. "I understand. Kidnapping." She cupped her mouth, and her titter evolved into throaty chortle. "You are very funny. You probably wanted to get my reaction for your next book. Am I right?"

Through a thin-lipped smile, I said, "You caught me."

The traffic light turned green minutes ago, and the drivers

behind us laid on their horns. Deafening, steady honks vibrated through my bones. My head throbbed in protest, and I waved at the silver Camry, feet from us, and mouthed, "I'm going." I told my new best friend, "I've got to run. It was nice meeting you." As I hobbled away, she said the magic words I longed to hear.

"Can I drop you somewhere?"

After all the running, the walking, the waiting, the crouching, my legs cramped, my joints screaming at me to sit. At that moment, I could almost kiss her. Almost. "You know, that would be nice. Thank you."

"Won-der-ful. Hop in." She was lightly clapping her hands, and I swear she skipped all the way to her door. Behind the wheel, the top half of her body rotated to face me. "I'm Sandy, by the way."

"Nice to meet you, Sandy." Longing for solitude, I hugged the passenger window. Sandy rambled on incessantly. It was better than walking five, six, seven miles home, but not by much.

"So, where ya headed?" Her excitement was bubbling over, bordering on disgusting.

"Alexandria," I droned. "You can drop me at the corner of Cass Mill and 104 if you don't mind please." I controlled the urge to add, "Because you sure as hell aren't coming to my home."

Sandy rattled off something. I wasn't paying attention. If she told me I won the lottery, I would have uh-ha'd her to death. From my peripheral vision, I spotted another SUV, identical to Sandy's, heading in the opposite direction, a few car lengths ahead of us. Facing the windshield, my gaze narrowed on the vehicle. Specifically, the driver's baseball cap.

My biggest fan noticed what drew my attention and she floored the gas, her head volleying between the SUV and me. I think she said, "Do you know that person, Mrs. Quintano?" But I couldn't say with any certainty because I was focused on the driver.

"Mrs. Quintano?"
"What?"
"Do you know him? Gay."
"Gay?" What the hell was she talking about?
"Gay. Driving that SUV."

Chapter Eleven

3:00 p.m.

Niko and Frankie drove two-hours to Plaistow—one town over from Kingston—to interview the lead detective on the Sophia Lambert case, and Niko's nerves had him drumming the steering wheel. Five months after a realtor discovered Lambert's body, Detective Mason retired. Had he worked the homicide hard, or did he go through the motions, biding his time until retirement? Unless this case was the reason he'd left the job. It wasn't unusual for a serial case to end a good cop's career. He'd seen it many times over the years.

Niko knocked at the front door of a modest home on the outskirts of town.

"You gonna tell me why this case is so important?" pressed Frankie. "Don't tell me you're only checkin' it out because you don't do anything on a whim."

"I wanna see if he had any alternate suspects or avenues we haven't considered yet."

"Nice try. You're forgetting one thing. I know you, Niko. You're not an impulsive man, and you sure as hell don't chase your tail. If you don't wanna tell me, that's cool. Say so."

"Fine. I don't wanna tell you." He knocked again.

She crossed her arms on her chest—her usual mad-as-hell position—and he could barely make out a wisp of smoke streaming from her nostrils.

The door swung open. A middle-aged man greeted them, a Budweiser in his chubby hand.

"I'm Sheriff Quintano from Grafton County. I have a few

questions about one of your old cases."

The ex-detective took a swig from his beer and flashed a toothless grin. "Which one?" He held the door at an angle, ready to slam it shut if he didn't like the answer.

"The Lambert case."

Mason's smile dropped. "No. No way. Sorry, you wasted a trip." He shoved the door closed, but Niko stuck his foot in the way.

"We drove two hours. Can't you at least give us five minutes?"

"Move your damn foot." Like a rabid dog ready to lunge at his throat he sneered at Niko. "I'm retired. Go bother someone who's still on the job."

With a flat hand, Niko stopped the door from crushing his foot any more than it had. "Mr. Mason, please. It's important. Five minutes, that's all I ask."

Mason's gaze ran up and down Frankie's body in a visual rape. A shit-eatin' smirk emerged, and Niko resisted the urge to wipe the filthy look off his face. "*She* bought you five minutes. Not a second more." He tapped his empty wrist as though he would time them. How, without a watch, was anyone's guess. "We'll talk out back."

He showed the Sheriff and his deputy through a living room that hadn't been cleaned in weeks, if not months. Dirty glasses left ring marks on end tables, framing a ratty rattan sofa and on several spots on a rickety wooden coffee table. Newspapers stacked high on one side of a faux marble Formica table, with soiled plastic placemats and a flimsy napkin holder. Empty chip bags, plates cemented with bits of last week's food, a cigarette stamped out in a streak of dried ketchup, half-drunk liquid, mold floating on the top—the place was a sty. Once they left, Niko would have to order tetanus shots for each of them.

Did the Lambert case cause psychological damage, scar him in ways that led this ex-detective to live the rest of his years in filth? It wouldn't surprise Niko. Seemed like the telltale signs of depression. Either that or he was a pig impersonating a police officer. Pun intended. Suppressing a chuckle, he slipped through the sliders onto a deck. "What can you tell me about the Lambert case that isn't in your report?"

"Like what?" Mason gestured for them to sit at an umbrella table. "I never caught the bastard who killed that poor girl, if that's whatcha mean. But I'm guessing you know that."

"Yes. I read the case notes in Spillman."

"Right." Mason lowered his head, moving it back and forth in a slow shake.

To see how forthcoming he'd be, Niko tested him. "Was there anything on the windows?"

"Yeah. H dripping in blood. Like that bastard dipped into her open wounds and used her blood as finger paints." Visibly he shivered as though he was reliving the crime scene.

Frankie leaned forward. "Any alternative suspects besides the boyfriend?"

Mason chugged his beer and let out a loud burp that stunk of stale booze and cigarettes. "The boyfriend alibied out."

"Let's cut the bullshit," she said, reading Niko's mind. "You know what we want. Tell us and we'll get outta your hair. Don't and we'll stay all muthafuckin' day. Your call, asshole."

The retired detective crunched his beer can against his forehead, and smashed the empty Bud on the glass-top table. "Whattaya wanna hear, huh? That I wanted to eat my gun after I saw the crime scene? That I couldn't bear to live with what that mutt did to her? That the nightmares got worse and worse until they finally crippled me, and then my wife left? Shit, man."

His hands shot up above his head, slapped the table as they fell. "What do you want from me? The Lambert case ruined my career. Hell, it ruined my whole damn life. I was a good cop with a solid arrest record. I screwed up. Okay? That what you wanna hear? I screwed up and now that animal's free."

Tilting to one side, he rooted around in his sweatpants' pocket for a pack of smokes. Lit a cigarette, and loudly exhaled toward the umbrella. The smoke billowed under the umbrella, dissipating into the blistering afternoon heat. His eyes shifted toward the heavens as if searching for divine intervention, and he softly echoed, "I screwed up."

Frankie seemed almost as shocked as Niko. Her mouth fell open, speechless for the first time in years.

"No one's here to lay blame at your feet." Niko's throat fisted shut, and he swallowed hard as he swung his gaze toward Frankie, summoning the courage to continue. "The Lambert homicide happened in July 2003. My wife was attacked the following September, in our home. And now, whoever killed Lambert is back. Only this time he's hunting where I live."

With a steadying breath, he said, "I need to make sure it's not the same man who assaulted my wife." He shifted his gaze to Frankie, whose mouth went totally slack—eyes bulged like Colt's when he drooled over a juicy steak.

"That's why I'm actually here," he relented, leaning back in his chair, grinding his jaw, suppressing the impending tears. This was the first time he had shared what happened to Sage. The first time he said it aloud in years. Bitterness coated his tongue. How dare that bastard touch his wife.

Thank God, she wasn't raped.

Mason took a drag off his cigarette, and thick smoke swirled out his mouth as he responded. "I'm sorry to hear that. I am. I couldn't imagine someone raping my wife."

"Rape?" The word stopped Niko's heart, and he pitched forward. "I never said anything about rape. She was attacked. Assaulted. Dislocated knee, broken ribs, stab wounds. Not rape. Thankfully, not rape."

"Really?" Confusion rolled over Mason's face, brows furrowed, deep ripples in his forehead. "You read my case notes, right?"

"Yeah. Why?"

"Sophia Lambert was viciously raped before death. Vaginal and anal tearing. Bruises on her inner thighs…it was awful. The things he did to her…" He rubbed his closed eyelids with the fingertips of one hand as if trying to clear the image.

"I didn't read that in the file." The air on the back deck turned to mud as Niko searched the ground for his briefcase. "You sure it was the Lambert case?" He peeked under his chair, under the table. Damn. He must have left the case file on his desk.

"Am I sure? I'm positive. Believe me, I'll never forget hearin' the details from the ME. He raped her for hours as he beat her. Matter of fact, *her knee* was dislocated, too. She had broken ribs, stab wounds..."

With enraged hands, Niko shoved the table and rose so fast it made Mason and Frankie both jump. "I've gotta go. Thank you for your time." Without making eye contact with either of them, he bustled toward the deck stairs—sobs erupting in his throat.

Mason hurried after him and hooked Niko's arm. "Hey, man. Listen. I guess it's possible he didn't rape your wife. Doubtful, but possible. In any case, I'm sure she woulda told ya."

Tears built and built, brimming his eyes. The ex-detective was humoring him when now, more than ever, he needed to know the truth.

"Hell, maybe I've had a few too many, and I'm mixing up the cases."

In clenched fists Niko crumpled Mason's shirt collar and threw him against the vinyl siding. "Think. Think real hard, and tell me whether Lambert was raped the way you said she was. I don't have time to play fuckin' games with you. This is my wife we're talking about." He slammed him harder into the siding. "My *wife*. Was she raped, yes or no?"

Mason's shoulders sprang to his ears, voice rising with hesitancy. "I don't know what he did to your wife."

"Not my wife, you idiot. Lambert. Did you mix up the files or did you tell me straight?"

"Okay, okay." He raised his palms in surrender. "I told you straight, man. What he did to Lambert is burned into my memory. Sorry, man. If I worked a little harder...didn't drink myself half in the bag every night...maybe your wife wouldn't've suffered. It's all my fault. If I were you, I'd kick my sorry ass. Go ahead. I deserve it. It may as well've been me who hurt your wife."

Lip curled in disgust, Niko released his grip. Mason was a pitiful excuse for a man. A disgrace to the badge.

Frankie was pacing back and forth behind Niko, hands balled into fists, restraining herself from decking the ex-detective. Niko cocked his arm and punched a fist-sized dent in the siding, next to Mason's face, then clambered down the stairs.

As he banged the corner of the house, Frankie said, "You're lucky, dude. I would've aimed for your balls." She hustled after Niko. Rounding the corner to the front yard, she called out, "Wait up."

Niko cradled his right hand in his left. "You wanna drive?"

"Does Raggedy Ann have cotton tits?" She clapped for the keys. He tossed them. She caught them with one hand and darted around the front of the SUV, her heels clicking on the pavement. "This is so cool. You never let me drive. Where to, the house or home?"

He couldn't straighten his fingers. "We need to stop by the hospital first."

"You all right?"

"I think I broke my hand."

She ignored his comment, probably too focused on the case and what had happened to Sage. Niko couldn't blame her. The last twenty-four hours…a roller coaster ride, with two homicides back-to-back. Dropping a bomb about Sage only added to the madness.

"Wouldn't the rape kit be on file with the ME?"

Niko didn't answer. Nor did he speak the entire ride home. His mind spun. How could Sage survive a rape and keep it secret all these years? Granted, she'd been distant since…no, she'd never hide something like this. They shared everything, good or bad. One of Sage's early demands was that they always took the time to talk with one another. "Communication is key to a good marriage," she said. That's why they'd stayed together for so many years. Maybe he made it to the house in time that night, and if he had delayed even two minutes, things might have turned out differently. No way was she raped. Impossible.

* * *

6:00 p.m.

Parked in the driveway, his hand wrapped in an Ace bandage, Niko told Frankie to take the SUV home and swing by in the morning.

"I'm going back to the house," she said. "If you need anything..."

"Thanks, Frank. I need to soak this hand. I'll see you in the morning. Call me if anything interesting happens." He got out and slammed the passenger door harder than he intended. Leaning through the open window, he joked, "I guess I don't know my own strength." He smiled to hide the deep ache in his heart and the throbbing pain in his knuckles.

The SUV idled in the driveway as Niko strode down the walkway. At the door, he waved over his head to signal she could leave. When he strode through the kitchen, Sage was asleep on the sofa. So innocent, so gorgeous laying there, a chartreuse toss blanket draped over her toned legs. Without so much as a whisper, he pulled the blanket over her shoulders and softly kissed her cheek.

Her eyelids fluttered open. "I didn't know you'd be home so early." She scooted over so he could sit beside her. With her legs draped over his lap, he traced her knee with his fingertips.

Oh, how he loved this woman.

"Babe, we need to talk." That came out wrong. The last thing he wanted was to pressure her into a confession. What if he was completely off about this? He should tell her to forget he said anything, curl next to her, and go to sleep. Feel her in his arms, make love to her the way he used to before— Oh shit, maybe she *was* raped. Rape victims often couldn't handle sex afterward.

Dear God, don't let this be true.

"What happened to your hand?"

"I hit a wall. Cracked a couple knuckles. Hairline fractures. No big deal. At least it's not broken."

She took his hand and gave his bandage tiny kisses. "My poor baby. Did the wall start it?" She grinned, knowing exactly what transpired.

"The wall told me something I didn't know," he countered. "Something I should've known a long time ago. Something that really pissed me off."

She feigned innocence. "What?"

Was she playing stupid, or did she not know what he was referencing? Did he have this wrong? For the first time in hours, a twinge of hope seeped into his soul. He should have dropped it then, but he didn't. He couldn't. He had to know for sure. Facing her, his arms draped over her legs, he said, "Babe, I know you don't like to talk about it, but I need to ask you something about the night of the attack."

She fell backward, against the toss pillow, laid over the armrest, and stared at the ceiling—closed off. He was familiar with the position. Whenever he broached the subject, this was her usual MO.

"Whatever it is, it's not important."

Normally this was when he'd drop it. Not tonight. "It is important, Sage. It's everything." She continued to stare at the ceiling—her way of avoidance. She'd practiced this technique and had it down. "How did he dislocate your knee?"

She bolted upright. "Excuse me?"

"The man who—"

"I know who you mean." Her lips pursed. "Tell me, why are you bringing this up now, all of a sudden? What's so special about tonight? Is there something *you* want to *tell me*, Niko?"

Yes! He yearned to tell her about Sophia Lambert. What she went through, how she suffered. He yearned to tell her how lucky she was that the perp hadn't raped her, too, and that Niko's worse fears were becoming a reality because the man who attacked her was back. Instead, he prodded, "How did he dislocate your knee?"

With a heavy sigh, she dropped her feet to the floor and folded the blanket. Laid it over the back of the sofa and smoothed the cashmere with her hands. He loved the way her hands moved, so graceful, so ladylike. As if nothing was wrong, as if they hadn't snapped at each other, as if it was another ordinary night, she asked, "Want coffee?"

"Sage, don't do this. Sit. Talk to me." He patted the cushion next to him. She didn't move. "I asked you a simple question, and I deserve an answer."

She gave him a wide shrug. "I don't know what you want me to say."

A fire burned in his belly, and he jumped to his feet. "I want you to tell me the truth…for once."

She neared, and her eyes zeroed in on him like an owl spotting a mouse scurrying below the perch. "What did you just say to me?"

"I didn't mean that. It slipped out. But I do expect an answer. Then I'll drop it. Promise."

"I'll answer your question when you answer mine." With a fist on her hip, she spoke adamantly as if she already knew about Sophia Lambert.

How could she possibly know? He took a wild guess that he was right. "There was a similar murder two months before your attack. The MO matches the recent homicides. Might be the same guy. Your turn."

"How could you not tell me he was back?" Her eyes darkened as if she wanted to stab him in his sleep. "Don't you think I have a right to know when my life's in danger? Shit, Niko. This is like last time."

"Babe, I only found out tonight. I swear I was gonna tell you. I—" He studied her expression. "Wait a minute. You already knew. It's written all over your face. This news doesn't surprise you. You're only pissed that I didn't tell you sooner."

"I…umm…"

He stepped closer, nose to nose, staring her straight in the eye. "How did he dislocate your knee? And don't lie to me."

Her gaze sidled.

"Answer me, dammit."

She shot him a look that told him to pay attention. "Okay… if you must know…he raped me," she cried. "Are you happy now? Is that what you want to hear? He. Raped. Me." She crumbled to the floor, buried her face in cupped hands, sobbing, trembling as if it happened yesterday.

An invisible strike to the gut buckled Niko in half.

She raised her face. A haunted memory in her eyes. "When he ripped my knee to the side…to…to…he tore the cartilage. The pop was so loud." Her eyes rolled closed, and she was right back in that Boston living room.

"That sound. I'll never forget that sound." With her arms wrapped around her midsection, she rocked—swaying back and forth. "And the pain. That excruciating pain. I can still feel it. His hands touching me. I can still smell his breath on my neck. And when he entered me…I felt our baby…our baby. . ."

Please. Stop. He couldn't hear anymore. He no longer wanted to know.

Dear Lord, make her stop.

"And then he was inside me ripping me to shreds, slaughtering our unborn son."

"Son? The baby was a boy?"

"I tasted the blood on my tongue when he hit me with the butt of his gun. I wanted to die. I wanted him to kill me. I wish he had killed me. I begged him to, but he said he'd make me live forever." Her eyes flashed open. "Now I don't have to wait. He's back to finish the job."

"Live forever? As in, what the caller said?"

For a split-second, her gaze met his. A vacant stare as if she had nothing left inside. Like she was an imposter in an empty shell of his wife. He did this to her tonight.

Why hadn't he seen it before? His wife was in pain. He should have run to her, consoled her. He should have told her that together they could heal, that together anything was possible. He yearned to tuck her head on his shoulder and tell her everything would be all right, give her the absolution she so desperately needed, but he didn't. He said nothing.

All that repeated in his mind was that he would kill the man who'd done this. How dare that animal touch *his wife.*

Sage reached for him, but he recoiled. He couldn't. Not now. Not yet. She lied. She kept secrets after they'd promised never to do that. What else was she lying about? What else hadn't she told him?

"Pup, please—I need you." Her whole body pleaded for him to hold her.

He curled his arms around the top of his head, hiding the devastation on his face. "I can't, Sage. I need time." He escaped into the kitchen.

She followed. "Where are you going? What are you going to do?"

Detestation shot through his core and he spun toward her, a rage burning inside him. "I'm gonna kill him. Hunt him like he hunted you. No one fucks with my wife. No one."

"Niko, please." Begging him to stay, her splayed fingers hovered inches in front of his chest. "I need you. Please don't leave me alone. *Please.*" Her voice quavered. "*Please, pup.*"

"I can't, Sage. I love you, but I can't. You've been lying to me for three years. Don't you think *I* had a right to know?"

Pinpricks of guilt needled at his bones as he unhooked her keychain from the rack, next to the door, tears swelling in his throat. "I'm taking your car. Frankie has mine." He swung open the door, fighting to keep his voice steady. "I won't be home till late. Don't wait up."

She bounded over. "But you are coming home, right?"

Soldiering up the walkway, he didn't turn around. Tossed, "I don't know" over his head. "I need time to think. I can't say how long that'll be."

"Pup, please don't do this. I was ashamed. I was afraid of how you'd take it. And rightfully so, it seems."

He stopped, whirled toward her. "So this is my fault now?"

"*You* brought that animal to our doorstep."

There was so much hatred in her eyes. Was this how she actually felt? Did she always feel this way? "So you do blame me. You blamed me, so you punished me by not saying anything."

"No." Arms outstretched, hands searching for her husband, she shook her head in slow motion. "I never blamed you. I don't know why I said that. I don't want you to go. Please. We need to talk this through."

"Apparently you've already decided that I'm the bad guy." He stomped farther up the walkway.

"No. Aren't you hearing me?" In her nightshirt, she took off after him, barefooted. "There's shame in being raped. Unbearable shame. You have no idea how dirty it makes you feel. Haven't you noticed I shower three or four times a day? I can't get his stench off me. I can smell him on my skin."

A cold blade pierced his heart, thunderous pain twisting his insides. When he thought he couldn't take another second of agony, her words cut deeper, until an excruciating ache shattered his soul. Part of him desperately yearned to hold her in his arms, tell her he understood. But he didn't understand.

If she had only told him, he would have been there for her. At least he always assumed he was the kind of man who would. What would he have done back then? Would he have been able to make love to his wife? Now that he knew the truth, could he ever erase the images from his mind?

"Rape is a dirty four-letter word," she said. "That's all there is to it, honey. It's dirty. It's ugly. And no one wants to talk about it."

With a vice grip on her wrists, he shouted in her face, "Why didn't you fight? Why didn't you kick him in the balls? You didn't even defend yourself. You just let him—" Eyes wide, he clamped his mouth shut. Why did he say that? Why was he acting this way?

As if he'd slapped her across the face, she gasped, eyebrows knitted together. "You think I let that monster rape me? Fuck you." She flipped him off and sprinted down the walkway, into the house, slamming the door behind her.

With a slacked jaw, blood froze in his veins. More because of what he'd said than of her reaction. Why did he want to hurt her? He couldn't think straight. He only needed her to get away from him for a little while so he could process this. Let him leave the house. She always pushed and pushed. Never let him have two goddamn seconds to absorb anything.

Tears doused his red-hot cheeks, and he bolted up the walkway and jumped in the driver seat of Sage's Ford Edge. "Fuck!" He pounded on the steering wheel. "Dammit!" He cradled his bandaged hand. "Why did he have to rape *my wife*? Why *my wife*?"

Chapter Twelve

11:59 p.m.

Swaddled in a blanket, I lay on the sofa and blankly stared at the TV. After my argument with Niko, the last thing I could concentrate on was a crime drama. After three years, I didn't understand how Niko found out about the rape, or why it surfaced tonight.

Colt's head popped up behind me, and his gaze volleyed back and forth across the room, black wet nose twitching in the air. Ruger followed suit; only he knew exactly what he was smelling. His massive paws clomped over to the living room window, and he sniffed the air as though an intruder loomed nearby. His sienna-brown eyes widened toward his brother. As if he had prompted him, Colt threw back his head and howled. Ruger chimed in, his voice cracking with age.

Colt sprang to his feet, standing over me on the sofa, belting a low, steady bay. Intermittently he barked in Ruger's direction. Deafening voices. High and low pitches, chirping barks back and forth—communicating about whatever was outside.

"What is it?" I tossed off the blanket, shuffled to the window, and peered outside at pitch-blackness with only a glimmer of a waning moon. In this part of the state, no streetlights illuminated the roads. We were lucky to find a sidewalk now and then.

Above our heads, the loft floor creaked. All three of us twirled toward the staircase. Colt dove off the sofa. Lightning fast, he shot up the stairs. Incessant barking alerted me to danger.

With a foot on the bottom tread, I cupped my hands around my mouth, hushed, "Colt."

Silence.

"Colt."

Silence.

A low guttural rumble thundered deep in Colt's throat.

Someone's in the house. My skin tingled as if the masked man was digging me a fresh grave. What if the intruder had a gun? A knife? "Colt."

Ruger trampled over and set his paw on the bottom tread.

With two fingers, I hooked his collar. "No, Rugey," I whispered. "Stay with Mommy."

He sat in a perfect sit at my feet—head held high, squared hips, a cold stare toward the loft, investigating the air like a K9 cop hot on a suspect's trail. Colt appeared on the top landing. Gazed down at us like Jesus on the Mount.

A shadow emerged behind him.

To mask a squeal, I slapped both hands over my mouth.

Colt cocked his head.

I patted my thighs. "Come to Mommy."

After a glance over his shoulder, he trotted down the stairs and took his place next to his brother. Two statuesque heroes. Their bodies in perfect harmony, complimenting each other's strengths and weaknesses. Both willing to sacrifice their lives to save mine.

I couldn't allow that. "Who's there?" I hollered. "I'm calling the police, so you better leave now."

The shadow sashayed across the room, and my bladder weakened.

"Leave now and don't come back." I bent to Colt's level, whispered, "Bring Mommy the phone."

Seconds later, he returned, the handset between his teeth, wagging his stubby tail.

"Good boy." I petted his head, and then dialed Niko's cell. It rang four times before the call transferred to voicemail. "Dammit, Niko, now is not the time to punish me." I thumbed nine-one… and a tap at the living room window riveted my attention.

The dogs raced over. I dropped the phone and caught up, flattened myself against the wall and lifted the side of the curtain.

A shadow swayed in the moon's golden smolder.

My heart thrashed in my chest. *Thump, thump, thump* echoed inside my head, drumming at my ears. Craning my neck to the window, I forced myself to look.

On the side of the house, a broken tree limb hung from a rock maple tree. Each time the wind caught its fanned branches it tapped on the glass.

I snatched Niko's baseball bat from the coat closet and climbed the loft stairs. One foot, then the other, I crept to the top landing.

A red balloon swept across the master suite—its ghost-like shadow waltzing—thin rubber stretched to transparency.

Something was inside.

To coax the balloon closer I stood on my bed, swinging the bat. After several attempts, I managed to grab hold of the knotted end and lowered the balloon to my chest, squinting at the contents.

A note.

I hopped off the bed and swiped a ballpoint pen from my bureau. With one hard poke, I popped the balloon. It sounded so much louder than I expected.

In a flash, Colt was in the loft, his furry head swiveling left and right.

Ruger's blocky head crested the top stair.

"It's okay, puppy loves. Mommy's fine." I unfolded the note. A tremble erupted in my core and spread into full body spasms. I read it again.

Do you want to live forever?

My knees buckled, folding me to the floor. Colt and Ruger lunged to my side, whimpering, licking my cheeks as they had that night in Boston.

I cradled their frightened faces in my arms. "I don't know what I'd do without you."

With a heavy groan, Ruger nudged his muzzle into the side of my neck, and Colt flopped across my stomach, sobbing as if I was dead.

"Babies," I soothed. "I'm all right. Hey—" I tousled their

fur— "look at Mommy. See? I'm fine."

They quieted.

I wiggled out from under them, pressed my lips against Colt's and Ruger's snout, and then brushed stray hairs off my nightshirt. The last thing I wanted was to remind my boys of the horrors in Boston. I crumpled the note and tossed it in the barrel. "I have work to do, kids. This has gone on long enough."

I closed and locked the sliders and pressed my foot on the security bar. Then ambled downstairs and over to my computer, on the coffee table. Before Niko left for work this morning, I downloaded copies of the crime scene photos. *Lord only knows if I'll get another chance to study them while he's home. Especially now.*

The first photo filled the screen—a close-up of the strange blood spatter. Fake forensics the killer purposefully left behind to divert the authorities. At least that's what Niko believed. I, however, disagreed. Everything this killer did had a purpose, a ritualistic meaning.

I scrutinized the photograph. The blood drops were in some sort of pattern, but I couldn't identify what the killer was telling me. As much as I strived to believe, I was no detective.

I shut the Chromebook.

How would someone enter the loft? I climbed the stairs and flipped on the outside floodlight. Flashlight in hand, I slipped through the sliders and onto the balcony. Hung over the railing and waved the light over the surrounding ground. In the dirt below, footprints indented soft soil up to the lattice, beneath the balcony. Tiny squares cracked in half from someone climbing to the loft, using the lattice as a ladder.

This was how he got inside.

In the summer months, I kept the sliders ajar, falling asleep to soft serenades of crickets and tree frogs, fireflies twinkling in the dark—the cool night air melting the heat away.

Did I forget to lock the sliders this morning?

To escape the madness overshadowing my life, I turned to my love of astronomy.

The balcony overlooked miles and miles of forest with a

backdrop of Cardigan Mountain. At night, especially with a full moon, it was a majestic place. Tonight, I'd make due with a slivered moon's feeble attempts to brighten the area. I reclined my head, turned my gaze to the millions of stars sparkling in a velvety black sky.

My tension ebbed as I ruminated about life on other planets. I believed wholeheartedly in aliens, that they walked among us and studied our way of life. Contrary to some, I also believed they were gentle beings. They did not have oversized heads and hooded eyes like in the movies. Their form was much like ours.

I focused on the stars themselves.

During the many years I had studied astronomy, I memorized the constellations. I unveiled my Celestron NexStar 6SE computerized telescope and aimed into the night sky. The summer constellations were some of my favorites. Cygnus, the Swan, was the first to catch my eye. Some people called it the Northern Cross. The swan's outstretched wings formed the bar of the cross, while the head of the swan, a double star called Albireo, sat at the bottom.

One of the easiest constellations to find was Lyra, the Harp. The legend of Lyra told the story of Orpheus. The god Apollo gave him a harp. Orpheus' music was sweeter than that of any other mortal man, soothing savage beasts, bringing joy to the heart of the weary. Some said rivers changed course to stay near its beauty.

Orpheus married a beautiful maiden named Eurydice. After the wedding ceremony, as she walked with her bridesmaids, a snake bit her and she died. Grief stricken, Orpheus journeyed to the underworld to win her back. His music not only gained him entry to Hades, but it also caused Pluto, the god of the underworld, to soften his heart and grant Orpheus' wish. With one condition—Eurydice must follow Orpheus, and not look back until both gained the upper world. Orpheus followed his instructions until he reached the surface. Before Eurydice entered the light, Orpheus turned, and Eurydice vanished from sight with one word left for her love: Farewell.

The story brought tears to my eyes each time I witnessed the beauty of Lyra.

I punched the keypad and zoomed in.

"Is that?" Readjusting the focus, I examined an unexpected constellation.

"Oh. My. God." I fell against the balcony railing, and my mind spiraled back in time, reliving the ordeal when I'd first spotted the masked man—a gun trained on my head.

"Please, I'll do anything you want."

"Anything?" Through a hole in the ski mask, a crooked grin formed on the stranger's lips. "Strip."

Cornered with no escape, a tremor shot through me. I had no way to outrun the monster who planned this while Niko was hunting him. With no choice, I unbuttoned my pajama top and let it fall behind my back. Dropped to the floor, and hugged my bent knees.

The intruder was in front of me and all I could do was shiver and beg for my life. Niko was right. I never once defended myself.

Before I knew what was happening, the man lunged on top of me and tore off my panties. His jagged nails left deep scratches down the sides of my thighs. "Do you want to live forever?" he asked, stale booze and cigarette breath souring my stomach. Pants around his ankles, he rammed himself inside me…over and over. "Do you want to live forever?" He had grime on his skin as though he hadn't showered for a month. "Do you want to live forever?"

"No," I shouted. "Kill me. Please. Kill me now." My husband couldn't handle having a raped wife, and without him, surely I would die anyway.

His slimy tongue licked the side of my face and slid to my breasts, and he bit my nipples so hard I thought for sure they detached. With crazed black eyes, he bucked up and down, and then flipped me over.

I screamed in agony.

His excitement was palpable as he threw me on my back and wrenched my legs apart. A loud pop coiled through the living room.

"Kill me. *Please*...kill me."

When it was over, he ordered me into the bathtub. Didn't matter to him that I could barely stand. If anything, he got off on my suffering.

During the rape, he wore a condom. I felt it break. For weeks I worried he had given me an STD. Had I gone to the hospital and admitted to the rape I would have had a rape kit done. I might have been able to put him behind bars, get justice for what he did, but that would have required me to tell my story to Niko, to the police, to the DA, and to the jury.

Truth was, I was ashamed. Somehow, I must have asked for it. Perhaps I'd made eye contact with him in the grocery store or the park, and he misinterpreted a pleasant smile as an advance.

If I could do things over again, I would have told my husband and anyone else who'd listen, and locked that animal away for the rest of his natural life. But I didn't, and now, he'd make me pay for my lapse in judgement.

"Do you want to live forever?" That phrase would haunt Chloe, too.

A mighty force of adrenaline slashed open my veins as I stared at the constellation.

Two parallel lines capped two of the brightest stars in the night sky. The legend that endured was of Castor and Pollux, two brothers—one good, one evil—sired by different fathers. According to legend, the queen of Sparta gave birth to four children—two boys and two girls. One boy and one girl fathered by her husband, the other two by Zeus, king of the gods. She raised the four children together. The two boys—one mortal, the other immortal—were inseparable. They went on many adventures, joined Jason, and the other Argonauts in the search for the Golden Fleece.

During a fight with landowners, the mortal Castor was viciously killed. Pollux became inconsolable and begged Zeus to allow him to die so he could join Castor. Moved by Pollux's love for his brother, Zeus agreed to keep them together for eternity. They spent half their time in the underworld, the other half in heaven.

The name of this constellation—Gemini, the Twins.

Same pattern as the mysterious blood spatter. The message obvious.

He wants the twins.

Chapter Thirteen

Thursday, July 20, 2006 6:30 a.m.

Niko awoke on the couch in his office from the throbbing ache in his shoulder. No need to tell him it was raining outside. Ironic the old injury flared today. Another reminder of that night. Like he needed another reminder.

Last night wasn't the first night he spent at work during a major case. It was, however, the first night he slept here in Alexandria. When he was a Boston homicide detective, he often worked round the clock, chasing multiple murderers. After the move, he vowed to concentrate on his marriage and not allow the job to come between them.

Add that to his list of failures.

He wasn't blind. Anyone could see that his wife was having a hard time coping. Hell, Sage even cringed during violent TV shows. What he never expected was that she was a rape victim.

How does a woman hide a secret like that from her husband? Why didn't she tell him the baby was a boy? Didn't she think *he* had a right to know? He whipped the thin blanket to the floor—it barely covered his legs anyway—and stomped to his desk. Threw open the bottom drawer and snatched his travel bag containing a shaving kit, washcloth, soap, toothbrush, and comb.

Before leaving the office, he chanced a peek out the door to make sure no one was in the squad room. Across the hall in the men's room, he washed in a sink that could barely hold a full-grown cat, old pipes rattling—a racket that instantly gave him a headache. At Boston PD, the detectives had locker rooms, bunks, and showers. You'd think the Grafton County Sheriff's Department would at least have better facilities than the Boy Scouts.

Wrong.

Before the troops rushed in, he changed his shirt. As much as he despised wearing the sheriff's uniform, it was all he had handy. While wrangling his arms into a shoulder holster, a knock sounded at his office door. "Come in."

Dunkin' Donuts coffee in hand, Frankie stayed in the doorway. Niko preferred Starbucks, but good luck finding one in the boonies.

He pulled a Styrofoam cup from the cardboard tray. "Thanks. You comin' in?"

Her eyes shifted to the blanket on the floor. "What's goin' on?"

Great. A lecture. Exactly what he didn't need now. "Whaddaya mean?"

"That how you wanna play it?"

Balled fists on her hips in a power pose, he waited for her foot to tap as he opened his arms in a wide shrug. "I seriously don't know what you mean."

"Whatever. There's been a report of a missing woman. You comin'?"

"No. You take it." He sat behind his desk and shuffled papers. Not that he could concentrate on work, but if he appeared busy she might leave him alone.

Frankie didn't budge an inch. Again, her fists flew to her hips and, this time, her foot tapped expectantly.

"You're dismissed, Deputy."

"I'm dismissed? You being serious right now?"

"What?" He slapped his forearms on the desk and leaned forward, careful not to hit his knuckles. "You said a woman was reported missing. You gonna make her family wait all day?"

She narrowed her eyes, and Niko would swear he heard her growl. "Fine," she said, a bite to her tone. "Fine!" She slammed the door. A foggy glass pane with the sheriff's name and title etched in gold vibrated for several seconds.

He cringed, waiting for it to shatter. It didn't. "Huh. Imagine that." Reclining in his leather chair, he crossed his ankles on his desk and weaved his fingers behind his head. Shooting pains stopped him cold. Dammit. He couldn't even relax in his own office without—

Sage opened the door. In a deadpan voice she said, "We need to talk."

He dropped his feet to the floor, and his back straightened in a flash. Again, he shuffled papers. "Not now. I've gotta lot of work to do."

As usual, she didn't listen, perching her slender hips on the edge of an upholstered chair in front of his desk. "But I need to tell you something." She rifled through her leather bag and withdrew some sort of sketch. Looked like scribbling, no doubt a product of her overactive imagination.

The soft aroma of Shalimar tickled his nose. He always loved the way she smelled, so ladylike, so sensual. With the back of his hand, he rubbed his nose, regaining his all-business attitude. "I'm busy. We'll talk when I get home."

"When's that happening?"

His gaze met her radiant green eyes. Such beautiful, vibrant eyes with thick dark lashes.

"Are you even coming home tonight?"

The grim twist to her mouth broke the spell she had over him. "I don't know, Sage. I have three murdered women—four if you count the cold case—and another reported missing an hour ago. I'm sorry I can't drop everything and rush home."

She stood in front of his desk with an unnatural stillness. "Fine. You want to act like a child. Fine. I'm taking my truck. I shouldn't be left without wheels because you want to brood." She also slammed the door.

How long until the women in his life knocked the darn thing off its hinges?

Tugging at his collar, he uttered, "I'm sorry," a few seconds too late. What compelled him to act like a jerk? Why didn't he tell her she was his whole world, his everything?

He fished a bottle of Tums from his bottom drawer. Chomping the chalky fruit tabs, he stared out a bank of windows. In this part of the state, almost every view had a backdrop of mountain ranges. He and Sage loved that about the area.

As he gazed at the slopes, his mind on Sage and how he'd hurt her, a fiery sun illuminated a plateau nestled in the summit of the tallest pinnacle. Slicing through the fog its gleaning smolder reminded him of a celestial, heaven-like place. Where troubles disappeared and violent crime never occurred.

If only they could live there. Maybe then he could erase all the monstrous acts people committed against one another—and the horrific act done to his wife. If he and Sage resided on the heavenly summit, they could heal together, live the rest of their lives in peace and harmony.

Sadly, that dream would never come true. Could he ever come to terms with what happened to his wife? A man broke into his home and violated Sage in ways he could not begin to fathom, and Niko added to her disquiet with his macho bullshit.

Why hadn't he handled this better? If only he could turn back time and relive last night. If someone could grant him one wish—to look past the lies and forgive, hold her in his arms and tell her how much he loved her, together they could begin to heal.

His behavior this morning wasn't much better. How could he fix things? He'd made a fine mess of an already explosive situation. How could he ease his wife's pain? The pain he caused.

She didn't deserve this. Sage was the kind of woman who should have a loving, compassionate husband, one who would stand by her through the direst of situations. Last night as well as this morning, he fell short of being that man. Real short.

* * *

8:30 a.m.

Because Frankie didn't feel like listening to her coworkers, she took the call solo. Ben and Bradley would ask questions about why Niko didn't handle this himself. She couldn't tell them the truth. That Niko slept in his office last night. After she dropped him off at home, he and Sage probably had a blowout fight. Typical man. A man brutally assaulted his wife, and it's her own fault.

Maybe he didn't blame her, but he didn't stick around and

comfort her, either. People wondered why she stayed single. Okay, so maybe a small part of her still missed her ex. Before Niko accepted the position of Sheriff, she almost walked the isle with Chance Rocco, a veterinarian who saved her dog.

Three years ago, Gunther, a Saint Bernard she adored, broke free from his outside run and chased a squirrel into the street. A blue F250 swerved, but not in time. The truck struck Gunther in the hindquarters and he rolled onto the windshield, contorted in ways she still couldn't forget, and crashed onto the asphalt. The smell of burning rubber permeated the area as she raced to his side, resting her cheek against his, sobbing incoherently, her heart fractured into tiny bits.

How she managed to get him to the animal hospital remained a blur. By some miracle, Chance saved his life. Gunther had a broken hind leg that required periodic checkups. Whether it was the Florence Nightingale effect, or Chance's handsomeness, which first sparked her interest, was anyone's guess. She had dated him for a year before he proposed. As usual, she ruined the relationship, said she cheated when she hadn't—an aftereffect of rape, her seventeen-year old self wreaking havoc…again.

In front of the Longo residence, she dialed Chance's number. She didn't speak as his Barry White voice filled her with memories of a happier time, warming her insides. Cliché or no, he was the one who got away, the one she'd always care about, her white horse in the black of night.

Certain he wasn't still single she clicked off her cell. Women had their claws in men like Dr. Rocco milliseconds after hello.

Frankie kicked the car door closed. Her heels tapped across the tar and then sunk in soggy grass. The sun burned through dark clouds, stopping the rain. On the front stoop, she tousled her hair to get rid of the dampness and then raised a fist to knock as Joe Longo opened the door, wearing a pink polo shirt, a navy blazer, and tan chinos.

Preppie, much? She resisted rolling her eyes.

"Thank goodness you're here." He waved her inside, waited for her to step on an entryway mat, and jabbed his head toward the kitchen. "Please wipe your feet. We can talk in here when you're done."

In the kitchen, Frankie rested her hand on a round oak table and peeked over her shoulder to see if she left prints across a snow-white carpet. Joe slumped in a chair. The claw-foot table legs and ornate chairs seemed a little much for a kitchen until she scanned the rest of the space. The Longos weren't hurting for cash. She had never seen so much stainless in one room. White-and-gray marble accented stainless steel countertops. A stainless refrigerator built into the wall had a matching dishwasher, trash compactor, and an appliance she didn't recognize. Recessed lighting dotted cathedral-high ceilings and a high-gloss oak floor was ideal for dancing in your socks.

Why would a woman want to leave all this? Unless…she married a bastard or didn't leave on her own accord.

Across the table from Joe, she said, "Tell me, Mr. Longo—"

"Please, call me Gordo."

She had no friggin' clue where he got that nickname, but didn't care enough to ask. "Okay, Gordo, when did you last see your wife?"

"Yesterday. Gloria and I had breakfast together before I left for the office. When I came home, she was gone. She hadn't made supper and her car was still in the garage." He stuck a pipe between his teeth and flicked a gold butane lighter.

"Do you mind waiting? I'm allergic to smoke." She wasn't. She hated the smell of pipe tobacco. It reminded her of her alcoholic father who used to pass out drunk with a pipe in his mouth. To this day, the smell of cherry soured her stomach. "So, did you try calling your wife?"

"Yes. I called her cell all night, but it went straight to voicemail." Joe flipped open the lid of his lighter and then slammed it closed—over and over.

"Uh-ha," she said, glib. "How do you know she's not with a friend?" Staring at the lighter, she gritted her teeth, the noise sending shivers up and down her spine like fingernails on an elementary school chalkboard.

Hm. A nervous habit. Gordo might not be as innocent as he claimed.

"Please find my wife. She's not with a friend. She doesn't have any friends." No matter what he said, there was something other than worry in his eyes. "We haven't lived here long. Something happened to her. I can feel it."

Not sadness, not fear. Was she wrong? She'd been wrong once or twice, or so Niko claimed. Speaking of, he'd have her badge if she arrested a grieving husband without evidence. Small town politics dictated that she must remain professional and first go through the list of possibilities, because you never know who a witness' relative might be or what connections they might have. Accuse the wrong person and get walloped with a million-dollar lawsuit. Blah, blah, blah. "Your wife doesn't have *any friends*? None?"

"No. I mean, not exactly. She has one friend, Karen, who comes over now and again, but mainly she spends time with her brother. He's slow," he whispered the way some old timers might say homosexual.

"Karen? What's Karen's last name?"

"I don't know. Why?"

In her notebook, she scrawled "Karen Thatcher?"

"My wife is not a social person, sheriff. She's more of a—"

"Deputy Sheriff."

A fissure cracked his Botox'd forehead, and he shoved the table away and rose. "You're not the sheriff? Where the hell is he, then? This is an emergency. For Chrissakes, someone took my wife."

Frankie slapped the table. "Calm down, Mr. Longo." She softened her tone. "Listen, Gordo." What a stupid ass nickname. "Sheriff Quintano's working on a different matter. I'm his number two, and I can assure you we will do everything we can to find your wife."

Joe slumped into the chair. "I'm sorry. He must be busy with the murders I heard about on the news. Dear Lord, you don't think—" He snapped up his lighter and wildly flipped it open, closed, open, closed.

Click, click, click, click, click, click. She should take his precious lighter and shove it up his ass. "We have no reason to believe your wife's absence has anything to do with the recent homicides." That sounded so professional. Niko would be proud. So maybe she told a white lie. Big deal. There must be thousands of people named Karen. Testing her theory, she said, "You say you heard about the murders on the news. Did you recognize any of the victims' names?"

"What? Why? Is that important? For cryin' out loud, my wife is missing."

Frankie scratched a line through Karen Thatcher's name. "Never mind," she droned. "Where does your wife work?"

"Franklin General Hospital. I already called them. She didn't show up for work today and they haven't heard from her."

Jotting down Gloria's absence from work, she prompted, "Your wife's cell number?"

Joe Longo cleared his throat, and Frankie made a note of his hesitancy. "Why?" he asked. "You don't believe I called?"

Should I? "We need to pull her calls. Maybe she called someone to pick her up. Like her brother, for instance."

"I told you there's no one to call."

She rolled her head, cracking her neck. If ever there was a man who needed his ass kicked… Through a tight-lipped smile, she ordered, "Her cell number please, Mr. Longo."

He wiggled his fingers for the notebook. She flipped to a fresh page, passed him the mini-spiral and leveled a ballpoint pen. As if his wealthy hands deserved better, Joe pursed his lips and slid an expensive gold pen from his shirt pocket.

"While you're at it write down Karen's number too." *Jerkoff.*

"Now what happens?"

Frankie tucked her notebook in the back pocket of her favorite jeans. "I'm gonna take a look around, see if there's any forced entry. One more thing. Did she take her bag?"

"Her purse? Haven't seen it."

Purse. Excuse me. Bags must be for poor people. What would he say about a clutch? "That's a good sign."

With a loud exhale, Joe set his hands on the table and rose halfway.

"I need you to stay here, Gordo. Don't worry. I'll let you know if I find anything." *You smug bastard.*

To eliminate forced entry she checked for tool marks on the front and back doors. Then she scrambled upstairs to the master bedroom and searched for anything that resembled blood.

The place was spotless. No sign of an assault. Or worse, a murder.

Off the master suite, she moseyed into the bathroom and opened the medicine cabinet. Gloria Longo was taking several different medications—Klonopin, Lexapro, Trazodone, Benperidol, Xanax—obviously depressed about something. Couldn't blame her. If Frankie were married to that horse's ass downstairs, she'd slit her own throat…or pull a Bobbitt.

Maybe Gloria committed suicide.

As she closed the medicine cabinet, she caught her reflection in the full-length mirror on the opposite wall. The outfit she wore today was killer—long-sleeved sheer raven top with cutout shoulders and a deep neckline, a black lace, strapless halter underneath, black stretchy jeans that hugged her slim hips, deep burgundy hues woven into the fabric. In the right light, the jeans changed color like a chameleon. So cool. She topped off the look with her signature black leather ankle boots, with a five-inch heel and a zipper up the back.

Perfect. She blew her reflection a kiss.

Frankie scurried down the stairs and into the kitchen. From her standpoint, this was good news. The entire ride over—all right, more like five minutes—she worried the mutt abducted Mrs. Longo, and in a couple days, they'd find her body hanging like the others. Of course, Joe might not find relief with her findings. His wife was still missing and possibly dead.

Nonetheless, she was almost positive Gloria took off with a friend or lover. Worse case, she committed suicide. Still, she found nothing to indicate her disappearance had anything to do with the recent homicides. She was probably thrilled to be away from her controlling husband or lying in bed with another man in a fancy hotel somewhere.

As Frankie rounded the corner, she smelled the bleach.

Chapter Fourteen

9:45 a.m.

Tossing my bag on the kitchen table, the cords in my neck tightened. If Niko wouldn't listen, then I had to solve this on my own. Screw him. I only wanted to share what I learned last night, what I discovered in the stars. He didn't have to throw me out of his office. Now I didn't feel the least bit sorry for not telling him about Chloe's abduction.

I checked the phone to make sure it still had a dial tone. Nearly twenty-four hours had passed since I left the ransom money and still no call. I sighed. *Where's my head?* I'd forgotten to release the forwarding. Here on the mountain, cell phone signals went in-and-out at random. I thumbed star seventy-three so I wouldn't miss John Doe's call.

After checking and rechecking the phone service, I crossed into the living room and reclined on the sofa. Colt darted over, jumped onto the cushion next to me, and nuzzled his head into my lap. He was so smart. Instinctively he knew Mommy was having a rough day. Ruger flopped on top of my feet—his way of ensuring I didn't leave without him knowing. The kids weren't used to me being gone this much. I spent most of my time writing.

Apologizing, I scratched my puppy loves behind the ear. Ruger groaned his acceptance and Colt gave me one long lick up the side of my face.

I leaned back and unfolded the sketch of Gemini. Eyeing the pattern, emotions spiraled in my chest, unanswered questions buzzing in my head. I set the sketch on the coffee table and shuffled into the kitchen for a cup of chamomile tea.

As I waited for the kettle to whistle, I admired a photograph of Niko and me on our honeymoon. We flew to Aruba, a beautiful, balmy Caribbean island that had a constant gusty wind. Great for wind surfing, not for picture taking. In this photo, my hair was flapping to one side, as if waving to a friend off camera.

I recalled the day.

We were relaxing on our balcony with umbrella drinks, wide smiles on sunburnt faces. I was wearing a Hawaiian tank top and bikini bottoms. Bare chested, Niko matched with his Hawaiian swim trunks. Even then, I was shy. Traipsing around in a thong or string bikini wasn't my style. Unlike Chloe, I simply did not feel the need to flash my best attributes. On summer beaches, my twin was up for anything and everything. She entered wet T-shirt contests and wore skimpy, practically non-existent, bikinis. Proud of her body, her behavior often got *me* into trouble.

In college, I worked in a restaurant with an elite patronage. One hot summer day in August, my boss took a potential investor to a beachside resort for drinks. Chloe strutted by wearing next to nothing, waited to draw a crowd, and poured a bucket of icy cold water over her breasts. The next day he fired me. I explained that I had a twin, but my boss didn't believe me. The investor had made a comment that if that was how his employees acted during off hours he wanted no part of the restaurant.

Classic Chloe. Craved attention and usually ended up the center of it. Truthfully, I envied her confidence. If only I could find some now. Alone with a monster, she must be terrified. God only knows what he's doing to her.

I prayed John Doe didn't rape her. She'd never be the same.

The memory of Boston washed over me like a tidal wave.

In a corner, I had shuddered in a ball on the floor.

"Get up," he demanded.

With trembling arms crossed over my bare breasts, I rose to my feet. "Please don't do this. Please."

He gestured with the gun. "Bottoms too."

My gaze lowered to my pajama pants—a cow print with bleeding hearts—and then roamed up his massive body. Wide shoulders, muscular chest, arms the size of Schwarzenegger's.

He shouted, "Now. I don't got all day, bitch."

I begged, tried reasoning with him. When nothing worked, I hung my head, and the soft material of my pajamas gathered around my ankles.

"Underwear too."

"No. Please. You don't want to do this. If you leave now, I won't tell anyone. Please, mister. Please don't make me do this."

His gaze traced my body.

Where was Niko? Why wasn't he stopping this?

Naked, I quavered in my living room, arms by my side as he studied every inch of my body, spinning me side-to-side as if I was nothing more than a piece of meat. A cold, menacing stare in soulless eyes, his pink tongue salivated along his dark-skinned lips.

The seconds on the grandfather clock ticked…ticked…ticked.

I should force myself to vomit down the front of my chest to create a God-awful mess. Would that disgust him enough to leave me alone? Could I stab him in the V of his neck—in the soft skin pulsing with his wretched, blackened heart?

As I stared down the barrel of the gun, his gloved finger twitched on the trigger. Would I have time to ram his nose with the butt of my hand before he got a shot off? That's what my instructor would advise. Self-defense class, what a joke. Why didn't they prepare me for something like this?

My gaze flitted left, right. Where were the kids? Did he kill them, knock them out?

A crash against the sliders whirled me around.

Ruger and Colt threw their bodies against the glass, scratched, clawed, tried every way possible to get inside.

"They make it in, they're dead, so you better pray that glass holds."

"Please don't hurt them. I won't fight you. I'll do whatever you want."

"Damn straight you will. Now get on your knees…bitch."

* * *

1:30 p.m.

I approached Mr. Chen, who was sitting cross-legged on the high point of a bridge in his friendship garden. Around him, a babbling brook rolled over four waterfalls and into a lagoon with an elevated ring of twelve animals—rat, ox, tiger, rabbit, dragon, snake, horse, goat, monkey, rooster, dog, pig—representing the Chinese zodiac. Around an outer circle were the five elements—wood, fire, earth, metal, water—where we meditated and communed with nature.

Not wanting to intrude, I hesitated. "Excuse me, Mr. Chen?"

Fingers clasped in an O on each knee, he kept his eyes closed. "Sit. Breathe."

I kicked off my sandals and sat beside him in the same position. In a soft voice, I told him, "Niko knows."

He stared straight ahead. "And?"

"He knows my secret. He knows that I was…well, you know."

"He knows what, Sage?"

Mr. Chen knew damn well what I was talking about. We'd discussed it so many times the details were hardly foreign. "You know what. Now Niko's sleeping at the office, and I have no way to help Chloe. I don't know what to do. John Doe is going to kill her. I can feel it."

"When we get to the mountain, there will be a way through."

I could barely think straight, never mind decode his proverbs. "Mr. Chen, I need your help. This once can you give me a straight answer?" Never had I spoken to him this way. I respected his culture, even admired it. Today, however, I needed more. I needed counsel. Something tangible to hang my hopes on.

"Tell me everything. Your dreams, your fears, and your discoveries. I cannot force these things from you. You must give them to me freely. Let go of bad energy. Breathe…" He inhaled through his nostrils, slowly exhaled through his mouth. "Breathe with me."

We must have breathed for ten minutes before the muscles in my body eased.

"Now," he continued, "start from beginning. Keep breathing.

In…out…in…out…"

After a few more deep breaths, I told him how Chloe was kidnapped. How her abductor called me, asked for a ransom, and told me to write and publish his memoir. How I later had an out-of-body experience that I believed was a dream. How I flew to a cabin in the woods, and how I discovered Gemini in the blood spatter.

Mr. Chen stopped his deep breathing. "In dream you traveled to Chloe?"

"Yes, but I think it was only wishful thinking. I doubt it was real."

He rose. "Stay."

A few minutes later, he returned. "Come."

I slipped my bare feet into my sandals and followed him to a part of the garden I had never seen before. All of the elements surrounded a small hut. Inside, the zodiac animals hung on bamboo walls. A leather chaise lounge and a padded chair sat alone in the space.

"Sit." He pointed to the chaise. "I unlock mind. Let dream show you location of cabin."

With a twinge of hope to my tone, I asked, "How?"

"Kick off shoes. Listen to me. As you fall backward, allow body to relax. As you listen to voice, eyelids get heavy, very heavy. You let eyes close, and your body melt in chair. Listen to voice. Focus on voice. You dreamed of cabin, surrounded by nature. Feel nature. Trees sing. Rock of chimney—hard, sturdy, trustworthy. Night sky becomes day and you see bird. Bird tell you where is cabin. What bird say, Sage?"

"He doesn't say anything." Legs restless, I shifted in the chaise. "He's only whistling, Mr. Chen. Why is he whistling at me?"

"Breathe…"

"I am breathing. He's not telling me anything."

"Breathe…"

To calm my thrashing heartbeat, I breathed in through my nose, out through my mouth.

"Again. Breathe…"

I did as he asked.

"What kind of bird?"

In my mind's eye, I stared at the bird to distinguish its markings.

"You hold answer, Sage. What bird?"

"I think it's a…a…"

"Not think. Know."

"A…a…a whippoorwill."

"Good. Fly to next bird. Feel wind in face as you soar. Your body light like air. You move fast. Smooth. Breathe in pines. Taste sweet sap on tongue. What next bird?"

"I don't know." My voice pitched and cracked, fear stuttering my words. "I d-don't k-know where I am. It's d-dark a-and I-I…"

"No," he insisted. "Not dark. Day. Light. You see fine. Clear. Breathe…" He paused. "What bird?"

Rolling my head side-to-side across the chaise, I couldn't envision what he was telling me. "It is dark. I can't see. Please, Mr. Chen. I want to come back."

"No. You see trees. You hear wind. You are wind. Light. Soaring. Day. What bird, Sage?"

I blocked all distractions and concentrated only on his voice, breathed in…out…in…out… Within a few minutes, my body released its frustration, and the area around me brightened. In front of me was a bird fluttering its wings, tweeting a sweet melody. "Partridge. It's a partridge." Giddiness tickled my insides.

"Good. Your body moves. Light like air. Flying. Soaring. Day. Where are you?"

"I don't know where I am. Darkness is coming. It's getting closer…closer. I can't see. I can't see! Help me, Mr. Chen. Help me!"

"Breathe…child. Breathe…"

"I am breathing."

"Listen to voice. Calm. Safe. Day. Light. Breathe… What bird?"

A scarlet bird emerged from the darkness. "Cardinal."

"Good. Follow cardinal. Where he go?"

"I'm flying over rooftops. Wait. I think I'm in my neighborhood. Yes. I see my house."

"Good."

"It's so beautiful up here. You were right, Mr. Chen. I am light like air."

"Journey complete."

"What? No. It can't be over yet. I still don't know where Chloe is. He can't go. He hasn't told me anything. Come back," I called to the cardinal. "*Please,* where's my sister?"

"Journey over," Mr. Chen insisted. "Let bird fly away. Breathe…"

I took a deep breath, held it, and gingerly let it go.

"Good. Listen to voice. You feel body. Body heavy. Grounded. Eyes light. Open eyes. You safe. Back with me."

When I opened my eyes, I remembered everything I experienced, but could not understand why I had seen these things or what they meant. Mr. Chen was no help, either. He told me I held all the answers. If that were true, I might never see Chloe again.

Chapter Fifteen

6:00 p.m.

After I left Mr. Chen's, I drove for hours. Nowhere in particular; I couldn't go home to an empty house, back to where my disquiet skyrocketed. John Doe could be lurking outside, watching my every move. At least in my vehicle, I had some control.

The hypnosis confused me more than it helped. No matter how much I tried, I could not determine what birds had to do with finding Chloe.

Heavy traffic redirected my attention to less important matters—vacationers. Newfound Lake tourists congested this area in the summer months. According to the locals, every week the lake refreshed itself with twenty-two underground natural springs. The crystal-blue water and over twenty miles of sandy shorelines made it a vacationer's paradise. Which meant, from May to October the traffic became impenetrable. License plates from New York, Massachusetts, Canada, Vermont, and several other states, littered the cars ahead of me. Horns beeped. People hollered obscenities at other drivers.

Once Columbus Day rolled around, the real beauty of the area flourished. Multicolored tree-lined streets, acres and acres of farmland, rich green pastures, and rolling foothills rejoiced surviving the summer months. Locals emerged from their homes, free to roam their town undisturbed, and cozy dirt roads became lonely once more.

Up ahead, three construction men patched the road after replacing water lines. A police officer directed traffic to take a detour down a road I'd never been on before. A country back road angled at a steep incline and looped around to a half-paved/half-dirt road.

Another detour.

This time, a man with a reflective orange vest directed me down a hill. I took two rights and a left. With no idea where I was anymore, I presumed I was still in Bristol, but there was no way to know for sure. I followed the cars ahead of me. Was I was being redirected to the main drag near Pleasant and route 104 so I could find my way home? This exhausting day needed to end.

I daydreamed…tucked inside with my boys, the four of us snuggling on the sofa as a loving family. If Niko didn't come home by nightfall, or at all, I had no protection from the invisible eyes—watching, studying my moves, waiting to pounce.

As I hung a right, I happened to glance at the street sign. *Whippoorwill Drive.*

I straightened in my seat. This was it. The key to finding Chloe.

The traffic advanced. In front of me, cars veered left one-by-one. I stayed straight. Nothing could make me leave Whippoorwill Drive.

The sun drained from the afternoon sky and the area around me darkened. A slivered moon rose and offered a paltry attempt at brightening the area. Trees soughed on a hauntingly quiet back road and pebbles crunched under my tires' thick treads. A low rumble sounded far off in the distance and grew louder as it approached.

A man on a Harley sped toward me, his bushy mustache flattened across his cheeks. As he sailed by my window, he gave me a nod and revved his engine—deafeningly loud pipes saying hello. Twin engines roared, gunning it up the dirt road. A puff of smoke and gravel trailed behind him, and the ends of his bandana skullcap and gray ponytail flapped in the wake of his escape.

Then I was alone.

The dirt cloud fell in slow motion as I raced through, twisting and turning my way down the hill. When I finally stopped, the road ended. I could go either left on Myerton Street or right on Angel Hill Lane.

No Partridge. How could there be no Partridge?

I banged a U-turn and followed the road up a hill—chugging along, swiveling my head left and right so I wouldn't miss a street sign. Partridge. Where was—? I slammed on my brakes, tires skidding in the dirt as I hung a sharp right onto Partridge Way.

The Ford Edge putted along a private road not maintained by the town. Gravel kicked around me, coating the SUV in grit. I flipped on the windshield wipers to clean a spot, jouncing in my seat as if I was riding a fake bronco in a country music bar. Turning on my headlights helped somewhat, but I still couldn't view the street signs until I was practically on top of them.

The area had a sinister feel.

My hands grew clammy against the leather steering wheel, and my thoughts cluttered with images from The Chainsaw Massacre, a low-budget horror flick I saw years ago. The B-rated movie starred a chainsaw-wielding maniac who slaughtered stupid teenagers who refused to get out of their own way, or screwed each other at the oddest times, oblivious to the killer's presence.

Up ahead on the left, my headlights caught a road sign. *Cardinal Terrace*. I spun the wheel. Delayed. In my dream, I was heading home when I found the cabin. Was the cabin on Cardinal or Partridge? Had I passed it, not recognizing it in the dark?

I pulled over. With gravel flying as if I'd driven into the eye of a tornado, I could barely see anyway. Might as well walk the rest of the way.

In the backseat, I rooted around in the pocket behind the driver seat.

I had to have a flashlight somewhere. Niko packed my vehicle with items I might need in an emergency—jumper cables, first-aid kit, magazines, maps of New Hampshire, Maine, Massachusetts, and Vermont. Everything…except a weapon to defend myself.

Blackness blanketed the area as if someone cloaked this neighborhood from the rest of the town. Flashlight leveled in front of me, I ambled down Partridge Way. Stones crunched under my feet. A hawk soared high above my head, his mewling cry ricocheting off treetops. Steaks sizzled on a nearby grill, and my mouth watered. I hadn't eaten since breakfast.

In a tight fist, I clutched my and Chloe's Gemini symbols that I had blended into one charm, zipping them back and forth across the chain. Teeth chattering in seventy-degree heat, my neck turtled in my shoulders. Roaming through a killer's neighborhood without a weapon was not the smartest move I'd ever made.

A squirrel scurried across the road, and I flinched. Eyes wide, my harrowing gaze shot to a German Shepherd, barking, guarding his property against unwelcome guests. I encircled him with light. The ferocious canine lunged on a chain link fence. Huge paws stuck through tiny squares, spit dripped from sharp canines as the dog gnawed on the wire, beady eyes glaring at me.

Heat assaulted my face and neck, yet my hands were cold and clammy. I practiced my deep breathing.

To my right, a single house light blazed a half-circle into the road. I aimed my flashlight across the street. To my left, a narrow ledge-pack driveway traveled far off the road through a wooded lot. A small cabin, nestled among tall trees and thick brush, had about two acres of uncleared land with a high wide-sectioned fence that edged the property line. The exterior was peeling, weather-beaten. A worn front porch dipped in the middle, its curved ends arched in an awkward grin. Old four-pane windows hung slightly off-kilter as if someone knocked them around in a brawl.

A dull ache throbbed in the back of my throat. This was the place. I prowled to the front door. A stone chimney ran up the side of the home—ramrod straight and tall, exactly like in my dream. Light shot from a basement window, not as bright as I'd envisioned but with the same menacing intensity.

I ducked low, scuttled over to the half-window and cupped my hands around the glass. Grimy prints smeared the glass as though someone was trying to claw their way free. Because I couldn't see past decades of crusted dirt and soil, I abandoned the idea of entering this way and hustled to the front porch.

Jiggling the knob caused the door to creak open.

I skulked across an empty living room, and my imagination kicked into overdrive. Everything came alive. Tattered black lace curtains hung on either side of the front windows, like service widows awaiting their husbands' casket to return from war. An old rope rug lounged across a wooden floor and a stone fireplace sat empty, wishing it still warmed the home. In the kitchen, a mustard-yellow stove and refrigerator had their doors wide open in a silent scream. The porcelain sink dripped single drops from its antique faucet, sounding a repetitive *clink, clink, clink.*

Off the kitchen, I aimed my flashlight down a narrow staircase with a cement floor at the bottom. As I set my foot on the first stair, it creaked and moved as if it was moaning in pain. Halfway down, my foot broke through one of the treads, and I crumbled to the stair above. A diffuse pain spread across my foot, ghostly skeletal fingers preventing my escape.

Chloe could be around the corner. I had to keep going. I limped down the stairs. "Chloe, it's me. Where are you?"

The temperature dropped ten degrees in the deserted basement. Dank. Moldy. Dark.

My flashlight illuminated a massive blood pool against the far wall, skirted by a stone foundation. Next to the blood was a wooden stool that held a tape recorder.

A metallic odor churned my stomach—the scent of death. If an average man possessed eight pints of blood and a woman Chloe's size had about five then…I was too late.

With a trembling finger, I pressed "play" on the recorder.

"Sage?" Chloe's shaky voice. "Please do what he says. He has a knife and…"

A loud, steady buzz echoed inside my head. I stumbled backward, my arms outstretched behind me, blindly searching for a place to land. Nothing made sense anymore. The phone calls, the ransom, the letter…it was all for nothing. Chloe was dead and probably had been the entire time. I collapsed on the bottom stair, keening over my loss. "Why, God? Why let this happen?"

He didn't fail my sister. I alone shouldered that blame. If I hadn't snapped at Chloe for dating a married man, I might have been able to protect her, at least warn her to be careful. Why couldn't I let her live her own life? I always pushed and pushed. Why didn't I listen? What a fool. Ms. Bigshot Author who knows everything. I got my sister killed.

My sight flicked around the basement and tunneled on the blood. Gripping the railing, I hoisted myself to my feet and inched toward the thick crimson plash in the corner. As I bent over the blood, my reflection stared back at me. An icy chill trickled down my spine.

A nipple floated to the surface. Wobbled…back and forth… ducked its head under the blood and bobbed face-up.

I shrilled, "No!"

Chapter Sixteen

9:00 p.m.

A nosey neighbor on Partridge Way reported an intruder had broken into the house next door, and of course Niko told Frankie to take the call. Ever since Ben transferred in she always got stuck with the grunt work. Bullshit at its finest.

"Stay in the car," she told Bradley, "while I speak with Mr. Ames."

"But shouldn't I go with you?"

"Look. I let you tag along. Don't push your luck."

Bradley sulked in the passenger seat as Frankie kicked the driver door closed. This mentor crap was much harder than it looked. She approached Mr. Ames, who was waiting on the sidewalk with his German Shepherd, the dog practically foaming at the mouth.

He'd better not drool on the outfit, or this interview will go downhill fast. "Mr. Ames, I'm Deputy Campanelli." She withdrew her notebook and pen from the inside pocket of the Sheriff's Department jacket Niko forced her to wear while spouting some crap about looking presentable. Whatever. "Please describe what you saw."

"I heard Buttons barking and—"

"Buttons?" Oops. She meant to keep that to herself.

"My dog."

No shit, genius. She was referring to his ridiculous name. No wonder the dog looked like he wanted to chew someone's face off. She'd probably be pissed too, if she had to walk around with a name like Buttons. "Go on."

"So Buttons was really carrying on. I went to check on him and spotted a flashlight, someone skulking around over there." He pointed to a long driveway across the street. "I think it was a woman, but I can't be sure."

"A woman? Interesting. Did you confront this alleged woman?"

"No. I brought Buttons in the house and called you guys." The dog snarled, growling at Frankie.

I hear ya, pal. Sorry, but I can't shoot your owner for you. "Are you sure this woman doesn't live there?"

"Positive. I knew the couple who owned it. They used to rent it out, but it's been empty for a while now."

"Okay then. I'll go check it out. Thank you for your time, Mr. Ames." She shook his hand like Niko would. *Unprofessional, my ass. That was a flawless interview.*

"Will you let me know?"

She cocked an eyebrow. "Let you know?"

"About the woman. Who she is and why she's there. I didn't notice a vehicle. I think she came on foot."

"We can't comment on an open investigation. If I need anything further, I'll contact you." If only Niko wouldn't chew her out over telling the guy to mind his own friggin' business. Maybe she should leave before she loses her cool. No need to give the boss something else to gripe about.

"But if it wasn't for Buttons, you wouldn't even know about the intruder."

She kept walking, waving over her head. "Thank you, Mr. Ames. We'll be in touch." She should arrest him for cruelty to animals. Talk about giving your poor dog a complex. Minga. What's next? A pit bull named fluffy?

Bradley leaped from the passenger door with the same eagerness as an adolescent boy with his first woody.

She curled her upper lip like poor Buttons back there. "I told you to wait."

"Yeah, but now you're gonna investigate, so you should have backup."

"Whatever." He had a point. Proper protocol dictated to have backup while investigating a report of a suspicious person or a possible burglary in process.

With her Maglite tucked under her gun, she skimmed the heavily wooded areas siding the cabin. "I'll go around back. You take the front. Stay below the windows so you don't get your head blown off."

"Sheriff's Department," Bradley called out as he rushed the front door.

The way he tripped over his work boots reminded her of Barney Fife from the Andy Griffith Show. Not exactly her idea of backup. Unable to watch another second, she hustled into the backyard before Bradley notified everyone in the neighborhood they were there.

"Sheriff's Department!"

Man, he must have missed the part of his training that taught investigators how to enter a residence using exigent circumstances. Announcing yourself is one thing, alerting the suspect is quite another.

When she padded up the stairs, she found the back door ajar. "Sheriff's Department." She stepped inside and had a perfect view of Bradley in the front entranceway. Someone was weeping in the basement. As she raised her hand to gesture to Barney Fife, he took off out the door to chase Buttons, who raced by seconds before. So much for her backup. Frankie kicked the door farther open and tiptoed down the stairs. "Sheriff's Department," she announced, rounding the corner into the basement. The Maglite illuminated a blood pool in the far corner. Something was floating in it.

Behind her, a crushed soda can skittered across the floor.

Frankie whirled around, her weapon trained on the dark corner where the noise originated. "Show yourself."

A squeaky voice said, "Don't shoot. It's me." Sage stepped from the shadows with her hands in the air.

Bradley was clamoring down the stairs, and Frankie gestured for Sage to quickly get out of sight.

"What are you doing?" she asked Bradley, her gun down by

her side. "Clear the rest of the house, you moron. Oh, and thanks for the backup. While you were chasing a dog I could've been shot."

"But I thought the suspect was fleeing." He scanned the basement with his flashlight. "Lookit all that blood. Ooh, what's that recorder doin' there? I bet there's a message on it."

Frankie snapped her fingers in his face. "Watch my lips. Go. Clear. The. House. And while you're at it, clear the front and sides of the yard again too."

Bradley's shoulders drooped in defeat. If he started crying, that would be it. She'd have no choice but to whip him into shape. Literally.

Once he cleared out, she whispered, "Sage?"

Sage showed herself. Her bloodshot eyes sunken in the sockets as though she hadn't slept in days.

"What are you doin' here?"

"Frankie, I…ah…" Her lips quivered, as if ready to bawl.

"Talk to me." Frankie holstered her weapon. "Whose blood is that?"

She shrugged.

"Look. I'm not Niko. Don't lie to me. You're not very good at it."

"Chloe," was all she managed before tears streamed down her cheeks.

"Your twin sister? Why would her blood—" She encircled the object in the blood pool. "Aw, shit. Are you telling me the mutt we're chasing has your sister?"

Sage closed her eyes, dipping her trembling chin to her chest.

"How? Why? Does this have something to do with your assault?"

Her eyes flashed open, and she scowled. "Niko told you?"

"Long story, but yeah. I still don't see how your sister— What an idiot I am. The computer, the calls. It was the killer, huh? He's been contacting you this whole time."

Sage was pacing in circles, rubbing the back of her neck.

"When I press play on that recorder will I hear a message to you?"

Sage froze, twirled back. "You can't tell Niko. Please, Frankie. If there's even a chance Chloe's still alive…"

"I can't cover up a crime scene. Shit. I may not be deputy of the year, but…what you're asking…how would I even… your husband is not a stupid man." She strode to the recorder and slipped on a latex glove. Hovering her finger over the play button she glanced back at Sage, who was biting the knuckle on her forefinger. "I'll tell you what. Let's get you outta here and I'll listen to this later."

She waved praying hands in front of her face. "Thank you so much."

"Don't thank me yet. I can't cover this up, Sage, but depending on what's on that recorder, I might be able to hold off for twenty-four hours to give *you* time to tell Niko."

Sage parted her lips to speak, and Frankie stopped her. "I can't let any more women die. I won't."

"Niko won't talk to me. I've tried."

"Try harder. He's your best shot of finding your sister."

A soft gasp escaped from her open mouth. "You think she's still alive?"

"She's badly injured, that's for sure. I mean, come on, that is her nipple for chrissakes. It is hers, I'm guessing."

Sage stared at the floor.

"I'll say this. Judging by what I saw in the jars at the Thatcher crime scene, I doubt there's enough blood here. Gaines will be able to tell us, though. Besides, the mutt never takes the body. He likes to shock us by displaying his victims. That's my theory, anyway."

"Frankie," Bradley called from the doorway. "I've cleared the property. Can I come down now?"

Why did she agree to let him tag along? "No. Meet me at the vehicle."

"Should I call this in?"

"No!" She took a breath, calmed her tone. "No thanks. I'll talk to Niko when we get back."

"But what about all that blood?"

"Bradley, go wait in the truck, and I'll be there in a minute." *You ever-lovin' pain in my ass.*

Footfalls stomped above their heads. The front door slammed shut.

"You see what I have to deal with? C'mon, let's get you outta here." She took hold of Sage's hand and led her up the stairs and out the backdoor. "The neighbor saw you sneaking around. I can't promise you he won't call the station."

"If Niko doesn't come home, I might need more time."

"You don't *have* any more time. I'm breaking the law as it is by giving you twenty-four hours. Don't worry about Niko. I'll make sure he comes home. Now go. Keep your flashlight covered with your hand and use as little light as possible. If the neighbor calls again, we're both screwed."

Chapter Seventeen

10:00 p.m.

Niko remained at the office. He couldn't go home and face Sage. Not yet. Unreasonable? Perhaps, but that didn't erase the deep sense of betrayal gnawing at his side. The squad room emptied hours ago, with the exception of Ben working diligently at his desk.

He poked his head out his office door. "Why don't you call it a night. I'm here if anything happens."

"You sure, boss? I don't mind stayin'."

"Go home. I'll need you tomorrow bright-eyed and bushy-tailed." Where did that come from? Damn rape. He jabbed his chin. "Have a good one."

On the sofa, he stretched his hands high above his head, releasing a drawn-out yawn. Through the paper-thin walls, he heard Ben say, "I thought you went home? How'd you make out with that call?"

"Where's Niko?" Frankie pressed. "I need to talk to him. Is he still here?"

Shit. Exactly what he didn't need tonight. "I'm in here," he hollered because Ben would tell her anyway.

Frankie swung open the door, took one look at him on the sofa, and crinkled her face. "Whatcha doin'?" she asked as if it wasn't obvious. "Go home. Grow a set and face your wife."

"Don't tell me how to deal with Sage. I don't see a ring on your finger. You know nothing about marriage. Especially *my marriage*."

"You're right. I don't. But I do know Sage. She didn't ask

someone to assault her. You're acting like a child who lost his teddy bear, moping around like this. Be a man, and face your wife."

If anyone but Frankie ever spoke to him this way, he would knock their teeth out. In a flash, he shortened the space between them. His nails bit into his palm as he leaned in real close. "Watch it. You're crossing a line here, Deputy."

She didn't back down or away. "Tell me what happened with Sage."

"You've got a lot of nerve. It's none of your damn business." His spittle flew in her face, but she didn't flinch.

"Fine. Have it your way." She dragged the desk phone across his desk.

"Who are you calling?"

"Sage. I wanna see how she's doin'." She raised the receiver, daring him to stop her. "*You're* not telling me anything, and after yesterday…"

Ooh, that woman knew exactly how to needle under his skin. He unhooked her fingers from the receiver and re-cradled the phone. "We had a fight. Okay? Happy now?"

She punched in the first few digits. "I'll see how she is, then. Why? What's the problem? Unless…"

Chin quivering, he dropped his gaze to the floor. "That bastard ra— He r-r—"

"He raped Sage, like Sophia Lambert," she said in a matter-of-fact tone.

His Adam's apple rose in his throat, confirming with a slight nod.

"I'm so sorry." She rested a supportive hand on his shoulder. "How is she?" Compassion shone in her eyes, and it creeped him right the hell out.

"We've got work to do." As he plodded toward the door, a jangle sounded—Frankie dragging the phone closer. A volcanic blast exploded in his chest, and he whirled around. "What're you doin'? I told you what happened. What more do you want?"

This time Frankie cradled the phone herself. She slid back onto the edge of his desk and steepled her fingers over crossed legs.

"Sit," she ordered, as you would a dog.

Immediately he scooted over to the sofa and sat. Why, he had no idea.

"Your wife, who you love more than life itself, tells you she was raped, and you spend the night in the office. See where I'm goin' with this?"

He hung his head in shame.

"Oh…my…God. You didn't." Her parental tone reminded him of when he was ten years old and his mother caught him flushing G.I. Joes for an underwater combat mission.

He offered a lame half-shrug. "What?"

"You pulled the it's-all-about-me crap. Didn't you?" She jumped off the desk and did a fine imitation of a tough guy with curled muscular arms, her voice baritone, mocking, "No one dares touch my wife and gets away with it." She dropped the act and eyed him keenly. "Let me tell you something, Mr. Wonderful. This ain't about you. I know that might bruise your fragile ego, but it's true. Sage was the one who was raped. *She* was assaulted. Not you. So what, if she didn't tell you. Maybe she was ashamed. Ever think of that, Sherlock?"

From the manner in which she spoke, it seemed as though she'd dealt with rape victims before. Problem was, she never worked in the Special Victims Unit. Colebrook, New Hampshire didn't even have a SVU.

"Rape is ugly. It's dirty. It makes *you* feel dirty. Like *you* did something to deserve it. Pull your head outta your ass." Her face flushed. "Hate to clue you in, partner, but this has nothing to do with you or your wounded pride."

How dare she speak to him like this. On second thought, maybe she had a point. Verbatim, Frankie rattled off what Sage said the other night. Something occurred to him, and he parted his lips to speak.

"And another thing." Now she was pacing back and forth, hands clasped behind her back like she was Perry Mason interrogating a witness on the stand. "Sage knows there's a killer out there." She gestured toward the window. "You told me she saw the crime scene photos. Did you ever think for one minute while you were feeling sorry for yourself that she might be frightened home alone?"

He went to respond, but she beat him to it.

"No. You didn't. Typical man. You ran and hid like a little boy with hurt feelings."

"Now you wait."

He rose halfway, and Frankie shoved him onto the sofa. With a hand on either side, she leaned over him almost nose-to-nose. "Listen to me good. You have a beautiful, talented wife who loves you. You need to beg for her forgiveness. Get down on your knees if you have to, but do not let that woman get away. You'd be lost without her."

He could tell she had to fight to keep her voice even.

"I know I—"

She pulled away, tears wetting her lashes. "Men have no idea what it feels like to have someone violate you so viciously that you never seem to be able to get the stench off your skin. Trust me." Her voice quavered. "You have no idea."

He hardly knew what to say, except, "I'm sorry. I didn't know."

"That's right, you didn't." She ambled toward him, drying her tears with the back of her hand. "Sage went through a terrible trauma," she continued, softer, pain edging her tone. "Now it's happening all over again. She must be frickin' horrified. I can't even imagine what I'd do if—"

Now he was beginning to get the picture. "You okay?" Afraid she might sucker punch him, he hesitated over putting his arm around her.

Frankie gazed out the window—a hollow stare—arms folded on her chest.

Unsure if he should impose, he ran a finger around the inside of his collar. "Umm…when did it happen?"

"When I was seventeen."

"You wanna talk about it?"

Like flicking a switch, she twirled toward him with a fierceness that took him by surprise. "No. I want you to treat your wife like the awesome person she is."

"But she lie—"

"I don't give a rat's ass. She probably knew how you'd react. Can you blame her?" She flung out her hands. "Look at yourself, wallowing in self-pity. It's disgraceful."

Maybe he hadn't thought this through. If Sage told him she was raped…before all the lies…would he have had the same reaction? He never once considered he was the type of man to abandon his wife. So why wasn't he with her now?

He refused to be that man. He'd stood before God and promised to cherish his wife through sickness and in health, good times and bad. Because life threw a curveball, he couldn't break those vows.

Something else occurred to him. He could ask Frankie details about her rape without cringing, but when it came to his own wife, he felt the same dirtiness as she did, as if this ugly truth blackened their marriage. Scarred forever. Marred, like the murdered women. "Maybe it's time for me to go home."

Frankie offered him a halfhearted smile. Probably all she could manage. "I think that's a great idea. C'mon, I'll give ya a lift. I need to talk to you about Joe Longo, anyway. He's got a penchant for bleach."

Chapter Eighteen

11:00 p.m.

On the way home from dropping Niko at his house, Frankie received a call over the radio from the dispatch operator. "Deputy Campanelli," said Doris, "could you please put Sheriff Quintano on the line?"

"I've got his truck. He's home. Why?"

"Copy that. I'll call his cell."

"No, you won't. Tell me what's goin' on."

There was a hesitation in Doris' voice. "We just received a report of a 187 at 3 Forestry Road in Alexandria. Never mind. I should call the Sheriff directly."

"You've gotta be frickin' kidding me? You sure it's on Forestry Road?"

"Positive. A group of kids looking for a place to party found the body. You know how curious teenagers can be. My Brian used to—"

If she had to hear one more Brian story… "Copy that. Ten-four." She hesitated, and then squeezed the talk button again. "You sure it's in Alexandria and not Bristol? There are two Forestry Roads y'know."

"Yes, I'm aware of that. Had you let me finish you would have heard that my Brian used to party in those woods when he was a teenager."

"Crap."

"Sheriff Quintano does not like the use of foul language over the wire."

Frankie took her thumb off the radio and mocked, "Sheriff

Quintano does not like the use of foul language…"

"Deputy Campanelli?"

"Ten-one." It was easier to give her the code for unable to copy than to listen to her crap.

"Can you hear me?"

"Yes, Doris," she droned.

"Sheriff Quintano specifically told me calls of this nature should be forwarded to him. No exceptions."

"Well, Doris, Sheriff Quintano *told me* he didn't want to be disturbed tonight, so I'll handle it."

"But—"

"Don't get your panties in a bunch. Show me responding."

"Deputy Campanelli. You should not speak to me that way. I am only doing as the Sheriff instructed."

"Ten-four."

"But—"

"Ten-four!"

Frankie banged a U-turn, the tires screeching on the pavement as she sped toward Niko's house. Instead of pulling up his road, she kept straight. At the next dirt road, she hung a right down a narrow, winding trail that led through heavily wooded terrain. At the end was a structure begging for someone to put a bullet in its head. Half the roof was caved-in. The other half was hanging on for its life.

Her heels hit the front porch, and the cross boards dipped and pitched like a funhouse bridge that could collapse at any moment under her one-hundred-and-ten-pound weight. This sorry excuse for a porch had better not ruin her favorite boots or someone was springing for a new pair.

Approaching the officer at the entrance, she raised her chin in greeting.

"Hold up." He stuck out his muscular arm, impeding her entry. "You need to sign in first. Sheriff's orders."

Frankie took the clipboard from his strong hands, scrawled her signature, badge number, and passed it back.

They exchanged an awkward glance.

Mm-mm. She'd never seen him before. "So, you new?" She estimated his age at about thirty as she slipped baby blue booties over her ankle boots. Not an easy feat. She once had to go barefoot in booties because her spiked heels kept ripping the material. It was not a good look for her, and one she'd rather not repeat.

"Hebron PD, ma'am." He tipped his hat, and Frankie almost belted him for calling her ma'am.

After that comment, his bronze tan and blond hair would have to sleep alone tonight. "Whatever," she said, flipping her hair behind her shoulder. She strutted into the shack—and her lungs drained of air.

A woman dressed in a fiery-red gown floated below the crossbeams. Eyes and mouth X'd out, blood stained the front of her gown. Her feet bound with zip ties. Crucified, like Jesus on the cross. The nearest window showed an F, bloody drips frozen in time.

Please tell me that isn't Chloe. Hard to tell from this angle.

"Niko coming?"

She jumped, slid her Glock from her back holster, and spun toward the voice. "Ben!" She punched him in his rock-hard chest. My-my, she had no idea muscles hid under that dorky uniform. *I wonder if he has six-pack abs, too.*

What am I sayin'?

"Don't frickin' sneak up on me like that. I almost shot your sorry ass." Ben chuckled under his breath, and she shot him a glare, daring him to relish the moment. "Got somethin' you wanna say, Benny boy?"

"No, ma'…umm…Frankie."

"Good boy. You're learning." She straightened the hem of her raven shirt, fixed the cutouts so her shoulders peeked through. "Let's do this." Head held high, she strode to a wooden box the size of a dorm-sized refrigerator, against the far wall. "Did you open it?"

Like a Saint Bernard spraying saliva, Ben wagged his head side-to-side. "No way. Not without you or Niko here."

"Good. That's good." Shit. Now she had to open the damn

thing. She wiggled her fingers. "Gloves."

"Oh, umm…" He patted his chest pockets, the front pockets of his chinos. Rifled through his jacket pockets and finally withdrew a pair of black surgical gloves. "I knew I had them somewhere." He slapped the gloves in her hand like a nurse would pass a surgeon a scalpel.

"Gimme a little breathing room, will ya?" With gloved hands, she shooed him away and raised the lid. "What the—?" She leaned in. "No friggin' way. That sick muthafucker."

The lid slammed shut, and the bang ricocheted through the empty shack.

Ben cradled his head with both hands. "What it is? What's in there?"

The mutt was sadistic, but this? This was wrong on so many levels.

"Frankie," urged Ben. "Is it a human head? I don't think I can handle seeing a human head."

Pursing her lips, she arched her eyebrows.

"I mean…I'd need a minute to prepare first, that's all. Of course I can *handle it*."

Too easy. "Relax. I didn't expect to see them, is all. Don't worry. It's not a human head." She re-raised the lid and waved him closer. "Go on. Tell me what you see."

Face turned to one side, Ben inched toward the box. You'd think a prison guard was dragging him to his execution the way the toes of his size-twelve boots gripped the wood floor. The color drained from his ruddy cheeks, and he stopped cold. "I'll take your word for it. Just tell me what's in there."

"Cluck, cluck, cluck." She flapped her arms like chicken wings.

"Cut it out. I'm not scared."

"Then look in the box."

"Why can't you tell me what's in there?"

"Okay. If that's the way you want it. The sheriff's job sucks anyway. You're better off staying a deputy." A crack to the ego worked wonders. Wait for it…

"Step aside." He took hold of the lid and peered inside. Within seconds, his eyes got big and round. "What are they?"

"Pick one up," she dared.

Like a good little deputy, Ben did as instructed. If nothing else, the kid sure could take orders. This might be fun without Niko.

Between his hands, Ben squished something that resembled a bloody jellyfish. A shit-eatin' grin arched his full lips, and he tossed it from one hand to the other. "Whatever it is, I like how it feels." He tossed it back and forth. "It kind of reminds me of a—"

"Stop playing with it. That's someone's breast implant, you moron."

The implant sprang from his hands and skidded across the old wooden floor.

"Ben—that's evidence in a homicide investigation!"

"But it's a—"

"Go get it!"

Without another word, he scurried after the implant and returned it to the box.

"If anyone asks, this did not just happen. If the defense discovers…"

When she took a breath, he flashed his palms, yammering, "Okay, okay. Sheesh."

"So we're cool. You're not putting this in your report…right?"

"Yeah. We're cool."

She surveyed the decrepit wooden shack, ensuring everything was in order before anyone who would snitch arrived on scene. "Did you call Gaines yet?" A puff of Aramis slapped her in the face. "Never mind. Hey, Doc. Nice of you to join us."

"Deputy Campanelli." As Gaines neared, he dipped his chin. Close behind, Billy's stubby legs shuffled a mile a minute to keep up with the doctor's long, confident strides.

Ben leaned aside and whispered, "Don't you think we should call Niko now?"

"Probably, but he's dealing with somethin' else. I can handle it."

"But Doris said—"

She grimaced. "Doris better not've called him, or so help me..."

"She didn't. I swear."

The ME and his assistant headed straight for the body. Gaines asked, "Deputy Campanelli, would you mind assisting me in cutting her down?"

"Ben," prompted Frankie, "help the doc."

"What? Why me?"

"Because Billy's photographing the corpse. Ah..." She raised her forefinger at the ME. "Give us a sec." She dragged Ben aside. "Before I got here did you, ah—" she chewed the inside of her cheek— "photograph the scene?"

"Course."

"And scaled?" She held her breath. *Please say yes.*

"Yup."

She relaxed, patted him on the back. "Okay, good. Good job."

"That mean I don't have to touch the body?"

"All right, wuss, I'll handle it."

Arms snaked around the dead woman's legs, she stuck out her tongue at Ben, mouthed, "Pussy."

"Set her here, please." The ME gestured toward a white sheet, sprawled on the floor.

While Gaines examined the body, Frankie studied the victim's facial features. She'd never met Sage's sister, but Niko mentioned they were identical twins. With the stitching over the eyes and mouth, it was hard to say for sure whether this was Chloe.

When Gaines noticed her intently concentrating on the woman's face, she snapped into her self-appointed role as boss of the crime scene. "Got anything for me?"

"No ID. She appears to be in her late thirties to mid-forties. The breasts were removed antemortem and I suspect her eyes were as well. Time of death..." First, he inserted a liver thermometer and read the temperature. Then he measured the ambient temperature around the body and compared the two. "Approximately two to four hours ago. Rigor mortis is beginning to set in. Therefore,

I feel comfortable stating—" he glimpsed his watch— "between seven and nine p.m."

As Frankie scrawled her notes, she said, "I'm assuming she bled out, like the others?"

"That would be correct. Exsanguination. Did you find the blood?"

She swayed her head in a long, drawn out no as she jotted down the time of death and the doctor's other findings. "Not this time. Can you excuse me for a minute?"

Even though everything in her body told her not to, she strode outside to call Niko. Sage answered, her tone weak and quivering from crying. "I'm sorry to interrupt but is Niko there?"

With a breathless sigh, she said, "Hang on."

There was a whisper, rustling, and then Niko came on the line. "This isn't a good time, Frankie."

"I know. If weren't important, I would've never bothered you. There's been another murder. The crime scene's around the corner from your house." From the corner of her eye, she spotted a reporter in a tree snapping photos with a telephoto lens, and hollered, "You—cut that shit out or I'll arrest you for obstruction."

"Who are you talking to?"

"Nobody. Another vulture is all. I took care of him."

"Uh-ha," Niko said, glib, as if for some reason he didn't believe she could handle one measly reporter. "Text me the address."

"What? No. I got this. You should stay with Sage."

Niko became oddly silent.

"I don't think you should leave your wife alone. This is a little too close to home if you know what I mean."

"I agree, but…"

Clearly, he wanted to say something, but couldn't with Sage hovering nearby. Had she told him about the cabin yet?

"You know what, you're right. Keep me in the loop."

"Cool. I won't let you down."

"I know you won't," he said, but there was something other than confidence in his tone.

He was probably upset, and who could blame him? You

couldn't pay her enough to be a fly on that particular wall tonight.

She lifted her thumb to disconnect when Niko called her name. "Yeah?"

"Include Ben. He needs to learn."

Imagine that. For the first time since Ben transferred in, she didn't cringe at the mere mention of his name. "I will. He's with me now."

"Great. Okay then."

"And, Niko?"

"What is it?"

"Thanks."

"You bet."

Frankie returned to the ME, who was squatting beside the body, scrutinizing the victim's chest wounds. Billy was scraping under the dead woman's fingernails with an orangewood stick though Frankie doubted there was any trace. This mutt was way too smart to leave particulates, hair, or DNA. To date, they hadn't found a thing that pointed to a specific suspect. Zip. Zilch. Nada.

Gaines asked, "Is Sheriff Quintano on his way?"

"He left me in charge." Boy, that felt good. In charge. The words rolled off her tongue so smoothly, like fine wine, not like the crap in the box her folks brought to family cookouts. How embarrassing. In charge. Maybe she could be sheriff one day. "There anything else I should know?"

"Not until I have time to do a proper autopsy."

Billy didn't make a peep, his lips smoothed to a straight line. After he royally screwed up at the Thatcher crime scene, he was better off staying mute. For a moment, she almost felt sorry for him.

Nah. No need to go all mushy.

Toward the front of the shack Ben was marking, photographing, and bagging evidence. With her newfound power, she sauntered over. "Find anything interesting?"

"Umm." His face wrinkled like a Shar Pei Chance Rocco once fostered. "Yeah. This." He raised an evidence bag with a gold butane lighter inside.

She snatched it from his grasp. "I know whose this is. Where's the evidence log from the last crime scene?"

"At the house. Why?"

"I've gotta go." She jiggled the evidence bag. "I'll log this in." Halfway out the shack she stopped, asked Ben, "Will you be all right here by yourself for a little while?"

Ben scratched his cheek.

"Earth to Ben." She snapped her fingers. "Did you hear me?"

"Huh?"

"Will you be all right here? I need to run back to the house."

"I'm fine."

That was debatable. "What's wrong? You still freaked about before?"

"Huh? Umm, no. I'm fine. Go." He was wearing three pairs of gloves.

Fine, my ass. "All right. Keep doin' what you're doin' and I'll be back ASAP."

At the station house, Frankie double-stepped it up the stairs and sprinted down the hall to the squad room. She picked the lock on Niko's office door and blew on her talented fingers. On his desk, stacks of file folders were in piles. She found the one marked *Thatcher, Karen* and carried it around to the leather desk chair—so much more comfortable than she imagined. Reclining, she propped her ankles on the desk and flipped through the file for the evidence log. Each piece of evidence was carefully marked with the item number, description, location, date, time, and collection officer's name.

Frankie ran her finger down the list. "Son of a bitch." She straightened. "I knew it."

Chapter Nineteen

Friday, July 21, 2006 6:00 a.m.

I awoke with Niko by my side. Last night we talked for hours, raised our voices, argued, yelled, cried, and ended the evening embraced in each other's arms, I-love-yous whispered in the ear. I confessed everything. Almost everything. Chloe's abduction, the memoir, the calls, cleared my conscience and asked for help. The phenomenal make-up sex that ensued was wonderful, magical. I hadn't felt this close to my husband in years.

In the kitchen, I got the coffee made, scrambled eggs, and was frying bacon when Niko traipsed downstairs.

"Good morning, my love." Without warning, he dipped me and planted a big, wet kiss on my lips. Before I got my bearings back, he said, "Something smells good" and lifted the edge of stacked paper towels I had laid over a paper plate, stealing a piece of bacon.

I tapped his hand. "Good things come to those who wait."

He crunched the bacon between his teeth, smiling like a young boy who'd gotten away with stealing an Oreo from the cookie jar. I'd missed him. Missed us.

He sat at the table, blowing steam off his scalding hot coffee. "So, I was thinking…maybe we should play the game again."

Every pore on my body opened, skin tingling with delight. From the day I received the first phone call, I'd longed to hear those words. "You mean it, pup?"

"I do."

"Oh, Niko," I swooned.

Wiggling his fingers in front of his mouth, pretending to smoke a big stogie, he joked, "That's what she said," doing his best Groucho Marx impression.

I tittered, blushing like a virgin on her wedding night.

"Whaddaya say, after we eat, we try to figure this case out together?"

"Deal." The smell of burning bacon cut short our conversation, and I waved my hand over the pan, wafting the smoke away from Niko's nose. "Not today," I murmured, forking the bacon from the grease and onto a fresh set of paper towels. As a special treat, I arranged the eggs and bacon in a smiley face on his plate. Grinning, I served breakfast, though having my marriage back was nourishment enough.

After shoveling food in his mouth for a full five minutes, his hand disappeared under the table, slipping Ruger a piece of bacon.

"You know I don't want him eating from the—" In the grand scheme of things this was minor. "Never mind." I broke off a piece for Colt. He clasped it gently in his lips and trotted into the living room to savor the hickory flavor. Ruger took Colt's spot next to me and opened his mouth as he did for his pain meds. "Okay. Only a tiny one, though." I set the bacon on his tongue. It disappeared in a millisecond and he reopened his mouth. This time I opened his Rimadyl bottle.

As he chomped the pain cookie into small bits, he glared at me as if to say, "Hey, that wasn't bacon."

I kissed his furry forehead. "Go lie down, baby. Rest your leggies."

Party over, he hung his head and lumbered to his doggy bed. Within seconds, he honked a loud snore.

"He's out." Niko chuckled. His smile dropped. "He's getting old, Sage."

I flashed a flat hand. "He still has quality of life."

"I know. I'm not saying we need to have 'the talk', but I'm afraid we will soon, as much as it pains me."

I forked the eggs around my plate. "I can't think about that. He's fine. He's happy."

"I love him too. I'm just sayin'. I don't want him to ever suffer."

"You almost done?" I cleared my plate, eager to get my hands on the case files and to end this conversation about Ruger. After all, he was my baby. The day I had to live without him would be the day I lost another piece of my heart.

Niko sighed. "I'll get my briefcase."

When he returned to the table, he had four case files that he spread across the tablecloth, separated by crime scene. "You're lucky I made copies to take home."

"You little sneak. You knew last night we were going to play our game."

He grinned. "I plead the fifth, Your Honor." He opened the first case file. "This is the Sophia Lambert case. The homicide that happened in July 2003." His eyes tilted downward. "That's how I found out you were—"

"Did you say July 2003? In Boston?"

"Kingston, New Hampshire. It was brutal. I guess he did follow—" Foreigner's "Cold as Ice" broke into his words. "Seriously?"

I gave him a one-sided shrug. "I was mad at you."

"Clearly." He answered the call.

The newspaper I found in the library mentioned a victim's name. Was it Lambert? Or were there two murders matching the MO in the months before my attack? So many emotions bubbled to the surface, but if I allowed the tears to flow, Niko would stop sharing. On the other hand, if I stayed quiet much longer, my newly formed ulcers would start bleeding. I gripped the seat of my chair, my head throbbing, pulsing.

Niko said, "He's dead?"

The room turned deadly quiet.

I held my breath.

"Thanks for letting me know, Detective." He shot me a strange look I didn't understand. "Babe, I need to tell you something. The man who r-r-assaulted you is named Robert Benson. He was arrested for sexually assaulting his girlfriend."

"How do you know?"

"He left a partial print on our upstairs sliders. When he was arrested, they ran his prints against the partial. They matched."

"You've known his name this entire time?"

"No. I swear I didn't. That was the lead detective on the case. They were trying to get Benson to turn state's evidence on a powerful mob enforcer and they were keeping his arrest on the DL till they had a deal in place." He sipped his coffee. Set his mug on the placement and seemed to try to summon enough courage to continue. "There's more. While at the infirmary another inmate shanked Benson. He's dead. He can never hurt you again."

"Then why do you look like—?" I gasped. "When did they incarcerate him?"

"Six months ago."

"Then who's—?"

"I don't know, but I promise you, I intend to find out. We will bring Chloe home safe." His voice had such conviction I desperately wanted to believe.

"Cold as Ice" broke the silence.

"You need to change this ringtone, I mean it." He checked the caller ID. "One second, babe. Yes, Frankie. What is it?" When he paused, the excitement in her voice resonated from the earpiece. "I'm on my way. Don't do anything till I get there." He stuffed his cell in the pocket of his suit jacket. "Babe—"

"I know. You've gotta go."

"To be continued?"

"Absolutely."

Niko left the house, and nervous laughter took hold. These last few days…harrowing, thinking my rapist returned to finish what he started. Turns out, that wasn't true. A completely new danger was out there—one more menacing and frightening than the past because he was unknown. Faceless. He could be my neighbor, the mailman, or the young man who bagged my groceries. That to me was more terrifying than the monster I'd already met.

Chapter Twenty

8:00 a.m.

The elevator doors slid open.

In the hall, Frankie was pacing back and forth, holding an extra-large coffee from Dunkin' Donuts in each hand. She looked like she'd downed eight cups already. Her hands jittered, her green eyes bulging from her skull.

He barely had one foot out the door before she said, "We gotta go," and scooted into the elevator. "Comin'?"

He didn't dare say no. "You mind telling me where?"

"We need a warrant." She thumbed the first floor button. "I know who we're looking for." She explained what she'd found at the crime scenes—the cherry tobacco, gold lighter, and Joe Longo's nervous habit.

"Why didn't you tell me this on the phone?"

"I did. I told you I had a lead."

"A lead. Not a—" He waved his comment away. "Court isn't even in session yet. We'd have to drive to Judge Milligan's house. Even then, he could be on his way to the courthouse while we're chasing him around town."

"So we'll wait at the courthouse. Get him to sign it before he goes in." Her heels tapped across the elevator floor, which gave him an uneasy feeling in the pit of his stomach. "I broke the case. Me."

Frankie was not an outwardly happy person by nature, and that was fine. He'd gotten used to her brooding, but this, a new improved version of Frankie Campanelli? It was not an understatement to say most men would run for cover, and he was no exception. "Don't get too excited," he said. "Judge Milligan could deny our request."

"Not with all the evidence to back it up, he won't. We got him, partner. We got him by the balls."

The evil glimmer in her eye sent shivers up and down his arms.

During the ride to the courthouse, Frankie hummed along to the stereo. More and more, he worried about what would happen if she had this wrong. He hadn't seen the evidence himself. Not that he didn't trust Frankie's instincts. She was a fine detective, but what if she hadn't put the pieces together right? Yesterday she pulled an eighteen-hour shift.

Granted, the tobacco and lighter seemed to favor Joe Longo, but it also fit a bit too perfectly. This mutt didn't make mistakes, and he certainly wasn't careless enough to leave his lighter behind. He'd gone to extreme lengths to ensure he never left a print, fiber, DNA, or anything else that could trace back to him. All of a sudden he left his lighter? Doubtful. Of course, there was no way in hell he was gonna tell her that. Instead, he said, "Why are *you* driving, anyway?"

"Shush. Relax and enjoy the music. I got this."

Easy for her to say. She wasn't the one bouncing off the passenger door at every turn.

Frankie pulled into the courthouse parking lot and sprang from the driver seat with the excitement of a bride on her wedding day. They should have taken separate vehicles.

"There he is." Full force, she charged the judge.

Niko closed the gap between them and hooked her arm. "If you want this warrant signed, you need to play it cool. Tackling him on the courthouse steps is not the way."

"Very funny." She grimaced. "What do you suggest, then?"

"First of all, take a breath and calm down. Then, politely ask if he'll give you a moment of his time. When he does, make your case."

Talking to her was like talking to a teenager. She yes'd him to death and then bolted after the judge. Not quite running, more of a speed walk, bent arms propelling her faster. When she was a good three yards away, she called, "Judge."

Here we go again. In a soft tone he corrected, "Your Honor, not judge. And be nice."

"Yeah, yeah."

Yammering or not, at least he recognized this woman about to collide with the judge on the courthouse steps.

"Your Honor," she said, her breath labored. Her eyes shifted to Niko and she paused as if remembering his advice. "Could you spare a few minutes of your time? Please. It's urgent."

The judge glimpsed his watch. "I have court in ten minutes. Can you come back at noon when court's in recess?"

Frankie's lips smoothed to a straight line. "I can't. I need a warrant signed. It should only take a sec. I wouldn't ask if it weren't an emergency." She fished around the inside pocket of her sheriff's jacket and withdrew the evidence log.

That's why she was wearing the jacket. Now it made sense why she allowed Sheriff's Department attire to cramp her style.

"I have the evidence to back up my request. See here?" She stuck the log in Judge Milligan's face, forcing him to read. "We've got a suspect in the recent string of homicides. See where it says we found a gold lighter and cherry pipe tobacco? Our suspect had this very same lighter when I questioned him about his wife's disappearance. He smokes a pipe. I saw it with my own eyes. It's him, Your Honor."

Deep creases in his forehead and silver strands in his hair announced his time on the bench. He'd seen his fair share of cases during his twenty-year career, and Niko admitted he was a decent looking man. A sharp dresser with a black-and-white-pinstriped suit tailored to fit. It hung nicely on his tall, thin frame. What was truly impressive was his stance. Powerful, dominant, he demanded respect.

"I'm going to expand this warrant to cover anything on the property—cars, garage, shed. Let's get this wrapped up." As he scrawled an illegible signature, his diamond pinky ring caught the sunlight and shot a beam straight into Niko's eyes, momentarily blinding him. "Nice job, deputy."

Blinking, Niko regained his vision. *Did she take credit for cracking the case?*

"Thank you, Your Honor." She bowed her head, laying it on thick as she backed away from the judge. When she turned toward Niko, she was positively beaming, and she bounced all the way down the courthouse steps. At the bottom, she shed her coat, "Sheriff's Department" swinging over her shoulder as she sauntered back to the SUV with a spring in her stride.

Niko met her at the vehicle. He got inside and pulled the passenger door closed. "Nicely done." He faced front, waiting for her to pull out.

"Can you call Ben and Bradley and have them meet us at Longo's place?"

"What, you're giving *me* orders now?"

She shrugged. "I'm driving."

"Yeah, about that."

"Shush."

The Sheriff of Grafton County did not like being shushed. She was lucky she chose today to push her luck. After last night's lovefest, nothing could ruin his mood. Almost nothing. "All right. You win. I'll play deputy." He called the station and told Ben to meet him at 190 Bear Mountain Road in Bristol, with Bradley and Childs.

Frankie hit a pothole, and Niko's head slammed into the top window frame. "Oops." She offered him a wan grin. "My bad."

At this rate, it would be a miracle if he arrived at the Longo residence in one piece.

Periodic mailboxes tucked between tall pines fringed the sides of the road, houses nestled back out-of-view. Up ahead, a coal-black hawk feasted on a patch of pinecones and something that resembled mashed raspberries. As they neared, he flapped his impressive wings and soared into the air. His talons clutched a branch at the top of a one-hundred-foot conifer. Niko studied the bird as they drove past. Once they were far enough down the road, the hawk swooped down and continued right where he left off without missing a beat.

Niko pointed to a milky-white, split-level home on his right, and Frankie pulled curbside and parked. When he exited the SUV, horse manure seeped into his nostrils and he pursed his lips, waving his hand in front of his nose, skimming the neighborhood.

Frankie pointed at a black stallion, a chestnut mare, and a dark-chocolate yearling in a clearing at the end of the road. A wooden rail fence ran the length of at least three acres around a red barn. Bales of hay stacked against one side, a weathervane swiveling side-to-side on the peak. "Too bad we aren't going there. I'd love to ride that stallion."

A smile lurked beneath his straight face. "I bet you would."

"Ha, ha."

"Get your game face on. People don't like being accused of murder." As soon as the words left his lips, he waited for her usual line.

"No shit, Sherlock."

There it was.

He raised a fist to knock on the front door. The door swung open, and Joe Longo ushered them inside. "Come in, come in. Any news on my wife?"

Niko gave Frankie a slight nod, and she passed Mr. Longo the warrant.

"Sorry, Gordo," she said, a bite to her tone. "We need to search your house." With a sweep of her arm, she shoved Joe aside and marched into the living room. She asked Niko, "Up or down?"

"Hey, I'm playing deputy. That's your call."

Clearly, she liked the sound of that. "I'll take the kitchen. You can start upstairs while we wait for the others."

Outside the master suite upstairs, he rolled a latex glove over his bandaged hand.

Frankie remarked, "Take a seat, Gordo. We'll be awhile."

This was proving to be a never-ending day already, the role reversal game evidently massaging her ego.

He stripped the bed, flipped the mattresses, and emptied the drawers in the nightstand and bureaus. Found nothing. He strode to the walk-in closet and swung the hanging clothes to one side, and emptied storage boxes on the top shelf.

Nothing.

Everyone had a favorite hiding spot, and most used common places. Areas they could get to easily.

Kneeling, he checked Joe Longo's shoes—size ten, the same size found at the crime scenes—and bagged a pair of work boots, not Columbia but with a similar tread pattern. He peeked inside each pair of shoes. First the husband's. Then the wife's.

Mrs. Longo was a shoe-aholic. Niko had never seen so many pairs in one woman's closet. High heels, low heels, spiked heels, wrap-around the ankle heels, flats, open-toe flats, sandals, high and low, some with strings that laced up the leg. She owned boots that crawled over the knee, ankle boots, shoe boots.

This was ridiculous. How could one woman wear all these shoes?

Thankfully, Sage was a simple woman with a passion for household goods, especially anything that emanated a scent. If he bought her a new tart burner or Yankee Candle, he'd guarantee himself a wild night of romance. Flowers worked, too. He loved that about her. If she had been like Mrs. Longo—shoe, shoes, and more shoes—he would have gone berserk years ago.

Inside the closet, handbags hung from hooks on every wall. Neat and tidy, but so many. At least thirty. One-by-one he searched inside pockets and zippered compartments, outside pockets, snapped pouches, and hidden flaps. Some had built-in cardholders. Some had places for a cell phone. Some even had makeup kits in a separate section of the bag.

This was tedious, mind-numbing work better suited for a member of his team. Why did he agree to play deputy today of all days?

As he slid each piece of clothing aside, he checked in pockets, under collars, and inside cuffs. Aimed his flashlight across the carpet.

Clean.

He knocked on the closet floorboards, on the back and side walls and on the ceiling.

No loose floorboards or hollow spots.

At the bed area, he scoured the carpet. Freshly vacuumed.

In the bathroom, he lifted the lid on the toilet tank.

Found nothing.

He yanked the shower curtain aside.

Empty bathtub.

He opened the linen closet and dragged out every bath towel, hand towel, washcloth, and bed sheet. Found nothing. He checked under the vanity and inside drawers, knocking on the sides and bottom.

No hidden compartments anywhere.

He scratched his cheek.

Vanilla emanated from a plug-in air freshener, and the aroma reminded him of Sage—vanilla and blueberry two of her favorite scents.

He opened the medicine cabinet and drew a finger across several pill bottles, reading the labels. Gloria Longo took many meds. That alone could cause problems in their marriage and possibly provoke Joe to murder his wife. Years ago, he worked with a detective who had a bipolar wife. The extreme highs and lows were enough to make a gentle man snap. Cheating, drugs, booze, that woman was up for anything, anytime, anywhere.

To be thorough, he emptied the medicine cabinet in the sink—Vaseline, Vicks vapor rub, hydrogen peroxide, rubbing alcohol, Band-Aids, Tums, nose hair scissors, razors, pill bottles, tweezers, nail file, gauze, bacitracin, hemorrhoid pads, tampons, and panty shields—and rapped his knuckles on the back wall.

Solid.

Damn.

As he loaded the contents into the medicine cabinet, there was a faint squeaking under his right foot. He shifted his weight from one leg to the other.

Squeak, squeak, squeak.

Cobalt blue and white ceramic tiles formed a checkerboard pattern over the floor, only much larger squares. On his hands and knees, he tossed aside a blue shag bath mat. Wedging his fingers between the tiles caused the grout to crumble into dust. In the crap from inside the medicine cabinet, he found a pair of tweezers and bent the two ends apart. Jiggled one end under the tile and popped it loose.

The tile next to it flipped over to reveal a wooden floorboard with two circles drilled out like you'd see in a bowling ball. He stuck his fingers in the holes and lifted the cover. Inside a lined wooden compartment was a rolled-up bloody towel. Before removing the evidence, he snapped a photo with his cell phone. Between the folds was a pointed spoon with a serrated edge. A perfect instrument to carve an eyeball from a skull.

Why this and not the knife? Did he have a duplicate set of weapons stashed elsewhere?

He dropped the spoon and towel into two separate evidence bags, sealed, dated, and signed the strip.

With both rooms now cleared, he headed down the hall to the spare room as Ben, Bradley, and Childs busted through the front door. Bradley called, "Search warrant" and the three stooges fell into the living room on top of each other.

That's quite an entrance.

Before Niko could comment, Frankie bustled to the pig pile of deputies and loomed over them, a closed fist planted on her hip. "Uh, boys," she said. "Get up. You're an embarrassment to the badge."

A few feet from the disgraced deputies Mr. Longo's jaw went slack as he stared at Niko's crew, seemingly in awe of their dramatic entrance. "I'm calling my lawyer. This is ridiculous. You're ridiculous." He aimed the last remark at Frankie.

Niko closed his eyes. *Please don't deck a murder suspect.*

Bristling, Frankie said, "If I'm so ridiculous, then what's this?" She dangled an evidence bag in front of his face. Inside, a bag of cherry tobacco fell to one side. "Once we match this to the tobacco found at one of the crime scenes, you're fucked, pal."

Niko winced at her choice of words.

"You're going down." She soldiered into the kitchen.

Niko clambered down the stairs, and by the time he caught

up with her, she was smelling the air around the kitchen island. "What're you doing?"

She swept her hands toward her face. "You don't smell that?" She waved gloved hands toward Niko, trying to get the odor to reach him. "It's bleach."

"Call CSU. Tell them to get over here now."

Still holding the evidence bag, she fumbled to unbutton her front pocket to get to her cell.

Niko yanked the bag from her grasp. "Now try it."

"This is Frankie Campanelli." Along with her badge number, she gave CSU Longo's address, and explained the urgency.

When she disconnected, Niko asked, "How long?"

"We lucked out. They're still at the last crime scene, so they're sending someone right over."

"Excellent. In the meantime, why don't you collect the computers and search the garage while I prep the kitchen."

The muscles in her jaw tensed. "But I thought I was running the search."

He didn't have time to argue with her. Not after he connected Longo to the homicides. With a clipped tone he warned, "Frankie."

"It's because I told Longo he was fucked, huh?"

"Yes. That's part of it."

"Balls," she muttered as she stormed out the kitchen, acting like a two-year-old who wasn't getting her way.

With his neck already stiff from this case, he resisted the urge to shake his head. Before she slammed the back door, he called, "Have Ben search the vehicles." So his men couldn't contaminate the scene, he cordoned off the area with the strongest concentration of bleach, lowered the blinds, and drew the curtains on the sliders and windows. If there were any traces of blood here, they'd find it.

Frankie burst through the back door, breathing out a lot more than in. "Niko, you gotta see this."

He darted around the island and followed her outside.

As she sprinted into the garage, she tossed over her shoulder, "We got him."

It was amazing how fast she could run in those heels.

A large cardboard box hid below a woodworking bench. Above the bench was a pegboard with black marker outlines showing where each tool belonged. On the left, baby food jars containing nails, screws, nuts, and bolts hung under a natural wood shelf like icicles dripping from a New England winter roof, the lids rubber cemented to the wood.

An empty outline of a handsaw eroded Niko's gut.

"Should I slide it back out, or should I photograph it first?"

He shot her a knowing glare.

"Right. Scratch that."

Inside the box were three hard-plastic wheels and a thick cable-laid rope with unwound strands. Two of the wheels had snapped in half, and one had a chunk missing from the side.

"These must be what he practiced with," offered Niko. "When it couldn't support the weight of a full-grown woman, he switched to nylon rope. They look like the same wheels in the pulley system, though. I wonder why he didn't switch to hard rubber."

"Don't know, don't care." Her gaze found Niko's scowl. "I mean…no clue. Maybe these were defective or something."

"Bag and tag this stuff." He told her what he'd found upstairs. "I think it's time I read Mr. Longo his rights."

"Awesome. Gimme some." Frankie raised a closed fist. Niko bumped it and laughed. She always did know how to turn a grisly situation light.

"Actually," he relented, "you wanna do the honors?"

"Does Pinocchio have a wooden—?"

"Thank you, Deputy."

"What? I was gonna say nose." A vixen grin followed a wink. "Get your mind outta the gutter."

"Uh-ha," he said, glib.

"You got this?" Meaning the box.

"I got it. Go. And be professional. Please."

With a snap of her wrist and a click of her heels, she saluted him. "Yes, sir." A smile arched her lips. "Thanks, Niko."

"Yeah, yeah. Go."

Niko was searching the rest of the garage when a dark blue

SUV pulled in the driveway and a short, stocky redheaded woman got out wearing a navy windbreaker with CSU printed above the breast pocket. Her waist-long chestnut hair caught the wind, feathering strands across her face. Not a beautiful woman by anyone's standard, but she had an allure, a way about her, a *je ne sais quoi.* "Where do you want me?" Shockingly, her voice was deeper than his.

A tall, straggly-haired man hopped from the passenger seat wearing a matching windbreaker. His shoulder-length blond hair covered half his face, a honker of a nose peeking through. Why there wasn't a dress code for forensic personnel in this area was a mystery to Niko. The kid walked like a rapper, a bebop in his stride.

"Dude." He gave Niko a jab of the chin as he asked his partner, "Where to?"

Niko extended a hand to the female investigator. "Sheriff Quintano."

"Barbara Manuel. This is Chaz."

"Chaz…?"

"No last name. Just Chaz."

Who did he think he was, a rock star? "This way please." He showed them to the kitchen and explained why he'd cordoned off the area he needed Luminoled. "You don't know my guys. So, do you think it's dark enough in here?"

"Not quite. Chaz, block the windows." Barbara laid her kit on the island and left to retrieve something from the van while Chaz hung dark paper over the glass to block the sun. She returned minutes later with a tripod, camera, and strobe light. "I don't know if we'll be able to detect blood after someone washed everything down with bleach. Contrary to what many believe, Luminol makes bleach glow, too." She took a clear plastic spray bottle from her kit that held about a quart of liquid and set it on the counter.

Once Chaz finished darkening the room, Barbara set the tripod ten feet away from the designated area and, with a roll of electrical tape, wrapped the front of the strobe light. In the top right-hand corner, she taped half the face diagonally, half vertically, leaving only a small triangle in the bottom-left corner exposed.

Niko read the brand. Vivitar Strobe Model 51. The same make and model used by Boston forensics.

Barbara withdrew a tape measure and measured from the Luminol area to the tripod. "I need twenty-six feet," she told Chaz, who was holding the end of the measuring tape as she slid the tripod backward. When her partner moved out of the way, she adjusted the F-stop on her camera to control the amount of exposure.

During his thirty-year career, he'd seen Luminol testing done many times, but never quite like this. "Why'd you tape up the strobe light?"

"My, my," she said with a fake country twang. "I heard the sheriff was a city boy. You've never seen this technique? Why, it's the only sure fire way to shoot Luminol patterns, I reckon."

"Very funny."

"You ready to watch magic happen, Sheriff? Chaz, kill the lights."

In seconds, the room darkened to inky black. Using the Luminol, Barbara squirted the kitchen island, the floor behind it, and the fronts of the cabinets, saturating an entire eight-foot section of the kitchen. Almost instantly streaks, wipe marks, and shoe prints luminesced a blue-white.

Next to what appeared to be a blood pool Niko zeroed in on one perfect handprint, and his mind journeyed back to when he was in kindergarten and had made an imprint of his tiny hand in cement for his dad on Father's Day. He presented the plaque to his father, who'd swept him up in his strong arms, swooning over how much he adored the gift.

The following Christmas Eve, Mario, Niko's father, was on his way home from buying his wife a last minute present. A high-powered exec left his Christmas party after having one too many spiked eggnogs. Wasted, he passed out behind the wheel and veered into oncoming traffic, striking Mario's vehicle head-on, killing him on impact. The EMTs found a card and a diamond tennis bracelet in Mario's jacket pocket, the price tag dangling off the end.

His mother never recovered, and Niko grew up blaming himself. If he hadn't delayed his father that night, begging him not to go, he might still be alive today. Reminiscing about the past, an overwhelming sadness took hold.

For a few months, he had a son. A son whom he'd never met, seen, or held. The animal who raped his wife stole his one chance at fatherhood. The one chance of feeling that bond between father and son again. The chance to teach him right from wrong, and maybe one day he would have gotten a handprint of his own on Father's Day. If only Benson hadn't died in prison. The satisfaction of putting a bullet between his eyes almost seemed like a fair trade-off. Almost.

"I see some spots the bleach coulda missed," Barbara said, startling Niko. "I'm sure they're probably comprised, but I'll swab 'em anyway. Sorry I don't have better news, Sheriff."

"Do the best you can. I appreciate it."

Hours later—Joe Longo cuffed in the back of Ben's SUV—Niko left Bear Mountain Road and headed home. Frankie could handle things from here. He had to see Sage. Perhaps she'd unearthed something that could help. At the very least, he could change into his sweats and work from home. After all the long hours lately, he deserved a break. He and Sage needed time to heal, and to process Chloe's abduction together.

Unless something else happened while he was gone.

Chapter Twenty-One

6:00 p.m.

Because of the fight with Jess and then with Niko, I'd forgotten about Sandy, the woman in the SUV who identified the mysterious man in the baseball cap as Gay. At my computer, I typed in Alexandria property records.

None listed with the name Gay.

Typing in names that closely matched, I found a Gaynor Madville, who owned one acre with a contemporary home and a lake view. He paid an extra fee for the pleasure of waterfront property. Around here, if you could admire the lake or a mountain landscape the town charged you big bucks for that gratification.

In addition to Alexandria, I searched the surrounding towns of Bristol, Bridgewater, and Hebron. In Bristol, Gaylord Seville owned ten acres with a mobile home. In Bridgewater, Guy Petrovic owned a horse farm with thirty acres and a twenty-five-hundred-square-foot newly-renovated farmhouse. In Alexandria, Guy and Cindy Lemeux owned a two-acre house lot without a structure on the land. Not one recorded with the town, anyway.

Alexandria had no zoning laws. Someone could easily erect a house without the town discovering its existence unless the census bureau paid a visit, but that only occurred once every two or three years and often they skipped properties without structures. In our short time here, I heard rumors of five homes that went unnoticed, the owners paying taxes on only the parcel. If the surrounding areas had the same ordinances, I could be searching for a property that did not exist on paper.

Next, I punched in Ashland, a rural community three towns

over. Gaylon and Gloria Skeeter owned thirty-three acres with a one-thousand-square-foot log cabin on the land. I needed a way to narrow my search. Without more information, I could be at this all day.

Out of nowhere, Colt belted a howl that raised the tiny hairs on the back of my neck. "What is it, buddy?"

He bolted toward the living room window, overlooking the side yard. Ruger's head popped up from crossed paws and he trotted after Colt.

Someone was outside.

Hunched low, I scrambled to the window. Ramrod straight, I pressed my back against the wall. The boys chirped barks back and forth. I craned my neck around the side of the window frame. As a full moon rose over Mt. Cardigan, the sun bowed its head in a lavender dusk sky. Tall maple and ash trees shadowed areas of the yard—perfect shield for an intruder—their branches waving furiously for me to stay out of sight.

Against the wall, my heart jackhammered in my chest.

Colt twirled in circles, barking wildly and fiercely. Ruger flexed his muscles, lip curled, baring his teeth—a low, thunderous rumble deep in his larynx.

The kitchen door clicked open. Footsteps hit the tile.

I froze.

The dogs quieted.

I stared in horror at the archway separating the living room and kitchen. The dogs remained transfixed on the window.

Why weren't they concerned about an intruder inside the house?

"Babe, I'm home." Head down, Niko crossed into the living room, hands shuffling through a stack of mail. "Babe?" He stopped cold, dropped the mail, and unwrapped the bandage on his hand. Drew his 9mm from his shoulder holster and sprinted into the kitchen.

The door clicked shut.

I peered through the window. In the side yard, Niko clipped a thin Maglite to the top of his gun and scanned the area. Arms triangled in front of him, left hand supporting his right, he kicked open the door to his shed. The beam of his flashlight searched high and low.

He sprinted up the walkway, and I dashed to a window on the other side of the room. Watched. Waited as Niko aimed his Maglite inside my Ford Edge and searched for someone hiding out. He got down on all fours and checked underneath. Then signaled it was clear.

He rounded the corner to the front of the house. I darted to another window, the kids on my heels—grunting, noses twitching in the air.

In front of our home, widespread flower gardens dominated three tiers of grass. On the mid-level, a large boulder edged a pond, which bullfrogs used for sunbathing during the blistering summer heat. Beyond the pond was the lower tier. A massive rock border, some boulders taller than me, had mangled magenta vines slithering in, out, and over the top—tangled webs veiling stone faces. From this window, I could barely make out the top of Niko's head as he scoured the lower level. He glanced back at the house, jogged up to the next tier, and vanished.

Someone pounded on the living room door—and my equanimity shattered.

Rap, rap, rap. "Sage, it's me."

I unlocked the deadbolt and spun the center lock in the knob.

Niko forced his way inside, panting like Colt after he chased his ball down a hill. Without a word, he holstered his weapon and folded me into his chest. Held me, stroking my hair. "It's okay. No one's out there. You're safe. I'm not going anywhere." He pressed his lips to the top of my head, uttered a muffled, "Babe?"

Tear flooding my throat, my shoulders bounced up and down.

He pulled me away, and his forehead rutted. "Sweetheart," he soothed, drying my tears with his thumb. "No one's ever gonna hurt you again. I'm so sorry." Voice crackling with pain, he tucked me into his chest. "I should've gotten to you sooner. I should've known he'd come after you."

My gaze found his watery eyes. "It's not your fault, pup. You couldn't have known what he'd do to me. No one could."

"I was the lead detective on the case. It was my job to anticipate his moves." Choking back tears, his words quavered. "You're my wife. The most precious person in my life. In the world, really. I should've protected you." He regained control of his emotions. "Hang on. I've got an idea."

Over the mantel, he removed a painting of a black bear. Built into the wall underneath was a safe I never knew existed. He dialed in the combination. "I've got good news. We caught him. His name is Joe Longo. He reported his wife missing…if you can believe that. When we—"

I jerked my head. "Where'd that come from?"

"This?"

"Yes, that. Why didn't I know we had a wall safe?"

He smirked a cat's grin. "I have no idea why you didn't know." After he had dialed in the last digit, a click sounded and a steel-lined door popped open. "I had it installed before we moved in," he said as if I should have known. "You know how much I've always wanted one."

"I'm still not grasping why you didn't share this with me."

While he fished around in the safe, he explained, "You were so depressed. I didn't wanna bother you."

"How would a wall safe bother me?"

He faced me—a gun in each hand. "Do we need to go into this now?"

"You're right. It threw me to see a wall safe in our living room. Forget it…I guess."

"You sure? Because I can give you all the details if it's gonna keep you from concentrating on what I'm suggesting we do next."

I couldn't tell if he was cracking wise or being serious, but his expression made me assume the latter. "Back up. Did you say Joe Longo?"

He removed an ankle holster from the safe, strapped it on his leg, and slid in one of the weapons. "Yeah. Why?"

"From this area?"

To conceal the weapon Niko adjusted his pant leg. "No. He

and his wife just moved here. Why?"

"He's the married man Chloe's dating. The guy who caused the rift between us."

"You sure?"

"That Chloe's dating him? She was. I don't know if she still is if that's what you mean."

"Joe Longo. You're positive that's the guy."

"Yes. Why all of a sudden would he move here, of all places? He must have tracked us using that hospital bill. Remember when I told you not to leave this number?" I told Niko about calling Chloe's home and Joe answering. "Why didn't I see this before? Why didn't I recognize his voice? I never thought I'd forget that voice."

"You're forgetting more than that."

"I am?"

"Robert Benson assaulted you, not Longo. And he's dead now, so…"

Something wasn't adding up. I was so certain Longo was responsible. What was I missing? "Did you connect Longo to the recent murders? What am I saying, you must have." I wandered away, rubbing the back of my neck, speaking aloud but not necessarily to him. "So if he committed the murders around here, then who's been calling me? Unless…"

Hanging on my every word, he urged, "Unless what?"

The last piece of this jigsaw puzzle fell into place, and the truth revealed itself. "Unless there are two separate killers. Two separate, unrelated events. My attack, Chloe's abduction. A warped cosmic joke. If Longo had Chloe, perhaps he forced her to give him the details from that night. Which would account for how he knew what Benson whispered in my ear when he ra—" The word *rape* held so much power. Too much power. Time to take control of my life. "When Benson raped me."

The muscles in Niko's face cascaded with shifting emotions, and he transformed from hurt to angry to confused and lastly, elated. "Then we've got nothing to worry about, babe. Benson's dead and Longo's locked up."

"Then why don't I feel safe? We're missing something. I can feel it." I pointed to the dogs both curled in their doggy beds, staring straight at us. "Someone was outside. You should have seen their reaction."

"Shit. You're right. Y'know, I had a hunch this wasn't over. Frankie kept trying to reassure me, but my gut said otherwise." He took hold of my hand. "C'mon. We're going on a little field trip."

As he tugged me out the living room, I called over my shoulder, "Bye, kids. We'll be back soon. Watch the house."

* * *

Five minutes down the road, we veered onto a mile-long dirt driveway through the woods, to a small gun range at the end. While writing, I'd heard gunshots many times during the day. I presumed we had a range somewhere nearby, but not this close. Seemed like a rinky-dink operation—obviously not an approved range—but so as not to ruin this for Niko I kept my opinion to myself.

"I can't believe I didn't think of this sooner." He glided the shifter into park. Before he opened his door, he swiveled toward me, excitement radiating off him. "Are you ready?"

I sighed, gave a one-sided shrug. "You sure about this? You know I don't like firearms."

He held both my hands. "You need to know how to defend yourself, babe. If you had a weapon that night…I never want you to feel like a victim again. We should have done this years ago. That's on me." He opened the driver door. "Firing a weapon is very empowering. Who knows, maybe you'll even enjoy yourself."

I remained unconvinced.

Reluctant but trusting my husband, I gripped the armrest on the door and eased out, feeling for the running board with my toe. The sheriff's vehicle was much higher than what I was used to. At five-foot-two, getting in and out was a challenge.

With a big smile, Niko remarked, "My vertically-challenged cutie."

Funny, I didn't feel cute.

As we entered the range, nerves fired in my belly, uncertain about my husband's brainstorm to teach me how to shoot. I'd never held a gun before and wasn't keen on starting now, though if I had one the night of the attack, the outcome might have turned in my favor.

Sunshine-yellow signs entitled Range Rules plastered every wall inside the lobby area. Next to the title, huge bright-red exclamation points immediately drew my attention. I suppose that was the point.

Niko passed me a pair of clear safety glasses and ear protection that reminded me of stereo headphones when I was a teenager. Once we were suited-up, as he called it, he guided me through a steel door, into the range, and a man I'd never seen before flashed three fingers at us. My husband greeted him as though he knew him.

Was he a regular here?

"We're on three," Niko said as if that was supposed to make sense. Halfway down a narrow aisle, he led me to a partitioned area. As we passed other shooters, all in individual cubby-like sections, I couldn't help but wonder if any were criminals. If they ever raped a woman at gunpoint, or robbed a convenience store with their weapon of choice.

My senses heightened—mind on high alert—gaze bouncing left and right.

The range walls, painted a putty gray, had the same gun-safety posters sporadically spaced throughout. Bulletproof glass partitions hugged the sides of each cubby and supported a hard plastic counter. In the distance, paper targets lined the back wall, suspended on an automated pulley system. Even with ear protection, the shots were deafeningly loud, vibrating through my core. Gunpowder and sweat mixed with stifling air, and Niko acted like this place was paradise.

Seemed more like hell to me.

Niko startled me. I offered him a warm smile and didn't let on that learning how to shoot a gun was low on my bucket list.

"First thing I need to teach you is gun safety."

I had a terrible feeling we'd spend hours here.

"There are four basic rules. If you always follow them, you

and the people around you at the range will stay safe.

"Number one, always keep the muzzle of your weapon pointed toward your target, even when it's empty.

"Number two, firearms should always be unloaded when not in use.

"Three, don't rely on the safety switch.

"And four, physically check to make sure the barrel is empty. Not having the magazine in the weapon is not enough. I'll show you how to do that in a minute. How ya doin' so far?"

"I'm okay," I lied.

When he smiled, the familiarity of his face helped me to relax. "First, I'll show you how to properly load a weapon. I usually keep a magazine loaded in the safe, but you should still know how. Here. Take the magazine in your hand and set the end on the countertop. Then take a bullet and push it down and to the rear, under these two ridges. These are called feed lips."

To show I understood I nodded, even though vomiting would be a more accurate response to what I was feeling.

"Now you try."

I loaded the first bullet the way Niko explained. Continuing in the same manner, I loaded the entire magazine and slid the end into the handle of the gun.

He stopped me. "Keep the weapon pointed down range. Hold the gun in your right hand and with your left insert the magazine—not clip as they say on TV— into the magazine well."

And so I did.

"Good. Now, bang the bottom of the magazine to make sure it's in there tight. Then take your left hand and, with your thumb facing you, pull the top slide toward you."

I did as he instructed and a click sounded.

Before I had a chance to question why he explained, "What that did was to strip the top cartridge and insert it into the chamber. Now, point the weapon at the target."

As an avid fan of the series *Castle*, I locked my arms and aimed for the paper silhouette.

"Stop, stop, stop. Let's back up here a minute. You need a

proper stance. Put your feet square to the target, aligned with your shoulders. Put your major foot slightly forward for more balance and control. They call this the isosceles/modified stance. The name taken from the isosceles triangle. A triangle with two sides that are equal in length."

"I know what a triangle is, Niko."

"In shooting," he continued, oblivious to my trivializing his instructions, "the isosceles is referring to the shooter's arms, held straight making them the same length. Of course, you know that a slightly bent arm is better. Right?"

"Right." Did he mention my arms? He was throwing so much information at me, I could barely keep up. Per his instructions, I got into a shooting position.

"Good. Now arms. Don't lock your elbows," he said, not realizing that only seconds earlier he asked me about this. "Even a compact handgun has some recoil. What you want is a slight bend to your arms to absorb that recoil. Keep your shoulders square to the target. This allows your upper body to move a hundred and eighty degrees." He helped me gain the proper stance. "Good. Now let's talk about how you're holding that weapon."

I giggled. "Emulating Detective Beckett isn't working, I take it?"

"Ah…no." He took the Glock 27 from my hands. "See how I keep my index finger straight along the slide of the weapon, away from the trigger? You try." He passed me the weapon. "Keeping that finger straight, wrap your other three fingers and thumb around the grip. Then take your left hand and wrap your fingers around your right, marrying your thumbs."

With an eyebrow cocked I jeered, "Marrying my thumbs? Seriously?"

"Meaning—" he dipped his chin, pausing for effect— "both thumbs should be side-by-side. Not interlocked."

I gripped the firearm the way he suggested. "Actually, that does feel better."

"Because that's the proper way to hold a weapon. Now, aim down range by looking through your front sight. That's the sight closest to the muzzle end. Keep it evenly spaced with your rear sight and make sure it's level at the top of the rear sight. The target will appear fuzzy. That's normal."

I took aim.

"Don't shoot yet."

Rather than tell him he was a pain in the ass, I sighed loud enough to make my point.

"After three shots, I want you to bring your elbows back to the sides of your ribcage. That's called a low ready. You actually can fire in that position too, but until you learn to fire the regular way, I don't recommend it. Ready?"

"Yes." I almost added, "I've been ready for hours."

"After you fire, set the target back in your front scope. You never know if your opponent will need more than one shot to knock 'em down. So get used to aiming immediately after firing."

Again, I took aim.

"And remember to breathe."

"You stopped me to tell me to breathe? Isn't that kind of a natural thing?"

"Not necessarily. When you're defending yourself, you can't concentrate on your breathing. Here at the range you can. Actually, during a gunfight it's best to practice slow, deep breaths similar to the way you breathe in mediation."

"Okay, fine. I get it." I set the target in my front sight.

"Breathing is so important. Holding your breath will deprive your muscles of oxygen. It can cause you to lose focus, get shaky…a number of issues. So let's avoid all of that by breathing. Okay?"

I'd had enough of these never-ending lessons. "Can I fire the damn gun already?"

"All right, all right. In one fluid motion, I want you to squeeze the trigger. Don't hesitate or you'll miss fire. Let the shot surprise you."

I held my aim, waiting for him to give me the go-ahead.

"You ready?"

"I've been ready."

"Fire."

I squeezed the trigger.

The shot fired.

Even with ear protection, it sounded so much louder than I expected. I took my finger off the trigger and laid it along the slide.

"What're you doing? Line up your next shot."

"But I thought you said when I wasn't firing my finger should always be on the slide."

"You *are* firing, though." He took a deep breath. "It's okay. Set your finger back on the trigger and this time use the tip of your finger. Don't go past the first knuckle. Stay in the middle of the trigger. Even pressure. Got it?"

"I think so." I lined up my shot. Fired. Re-aimed. Fired. Then lowered my elbows to my ribcage and squinted down range. "I can't tell how I did."

Niko thumbed a button on the side wall of our cubby and the target zipped toward us. As it neared, I lifted my eyebrows. I had hit the target two out of three times.

Impressed, he said, "Not bad. Let me shoot a few rounds." He replaced the paper silhouette and got into position. Re-explained every…single…step…and then fired in rapid succession. When the target zipped toward us, I could not believe his accuracy. He hit center mass with every shot—and with fractured knuckles, too.

"Wow, pup. You're a fantastic shot."

A wide grin blossomed on his face. "Thanks. Did you notice how I shot? My position and trigger control?"

"Yes," I fibbed. When he was firing, I was staring at the target, not at his stance, but I didn't see any reason to crush his spirits. "I can do it now." We had always been a bit competitive. Tonight, he had a clear advantage. Once a new target was in place, I fired my shots. After four bullets, I stopped and lowered my elbows to a low ready.

A man yelled, "Cease fire!"

My gaze snapped toward Niko, knuckles turning white from a death grip around the firearm.

In an unruffled voice, he said, "Don't panic. Anyone can call a cease fire for any number of reasons. Even something minor like someone reaching under the counter in their booth, or not properly observing the safety rules."

All of my training, Niko's long-winded explanations, flew right out of my head when I heard that man holler. I didn't dare relinquish my weapon. Deadly scenarios swarmed my brain. A man pulled a gun on another shooter, or accidentally shot a bystander. Masked intruders invaded the range, demanding money and jewelry. In moments, they would make their way to us.

In a closed fist, I gripped the Gemini charm. It wasn't worth much—silver and turquoise rarely in high demand—but this necklace symbolized our sisterhood. I couldn't allow some jerk, high on drugs or drunk with power, to rip it off my neck. Especially not now.

Niko eyed my shaky hands. "Babe, you need to lower your weapon."

"No. How do we know we're not in danger?"

"Babe, trust me. Cease fires happen all the time."

"But—"

"Release the magazine by sliding this button toward you." He pointed at the magazine release. "Then clear the barrel and set the weapon on the counter with the open slide facing up. The range officer will wanna see that it's empty."

Sliding the bullet out the chamber, I fumbled, and Niko set his hands on mine. "Let me."

Chapter Twenty-Two

10:30 p.m.

As we strolled through the kitchen door, the answering machine was flashing a red dot, signaling a message. Earlier, Niko and I left the house in such a rush that I forgot to forward the landline to my cell.

Gnawing on my bottom lip, I twirled my hair around my finger. John Doe. I missed his call. With jerky steps, I backed away from the answering machine. Will someone die because of my lackadaisical response? What if it's my husband?

Niko asked, "Aren't you gonna see who called?"

I zipped the Gemini charm across the chain—eyes wide, staring at the blinking light.

He draped his arm around my shoulders. "Talk to me. What's goin' on?"

"Chloe's k-killer," I stammered. "He said t-to answer b-by the s-second r-ring." I snaked my arms around his waist, buried my face in his chest. "If anything happens to you, I'll never forgive myself."

"Why do I get the feeling there's more you're not telling me?"

I raised my head, my gaze searching for a safe place to land. "I made him wait. John Doe. Last time he called, I didn't answer till the start of the third ring. He warned me, Niko. Then I found her blood. Chloe's dead." I wailed and fell into his chest.

With his palm, he caressed my back in large, circular motions. "Babe, you need to calm down. You didn't actually see her body, so you don't *know* for a fact she's dead. Besides, Gaines feels there wasn't enough blood at the scene to constitute exsanguination.

There's no reason to believe the mutt veered away from his usual MO. Unless…"

In his arms, my whole body tensed.

"Let's stay positive." He patted my back, signaling for me to release him, but that was not on my agenda. "Anyone could've left that message. Don't assume the worst." He wiggled loose from my death grip around his waist and aimed a finger at the answering machine play button.

I flung out my hands. "Don't!"

"This is silly, Sage." He punched play.

Jess' voice resonated over the speaker. "Sage, I owe you an apology. I shouldn't have pushed you the other day. I should have been more sensitive to what you were going through. We can still do what I mentioned." She hesitated, not wanting to reveal our plan in case Niko was listening. "Umm. Call me back. It's ten o'clock. I'll be up for another hour."

"What's she talkin' about?"

I stumbled backward and collapsed in the kitchen chair. "Gimme a sec," I slurred, fear slacking my jaw.

He sat next to me at the table.

I took a few deep breaths. "Remember when I called you at work and told you about the strange caller?"

He nodded.

"That was part of Jess' plan."

"You faked that? How could you— No. I'm not buyin' it. You were terrified. You can't fake that kinda thing."

"I didn't fake anything. I *was* terrified. Everything I told you was true. Jess thought…look, I thought he was listening to me. I thought he bugged the house. So Jess came up with a plan to call you at work so it would look like I'd lost control. As long as I didn't mention Chloe we figured she'd stay safe."

"Lemme get this straight. You thought by sending me on a wild goose chase with your computer, you'd keep Chloe safe?"

"Yes. No. You're not hearing me. He actually did hack my email. It looked better if he thought I was frazzled, though. And I was. Hell, I still am. The whole point was to have you take over, but then I chickened out. If you heard John Doe on the phone… Anyway, when I wouldn't let you start a case file, Jess and I came up with a plan B."

"Which was?"

"We planned to go to a store in Tilton where they sell all sorts of surveillance equipment. Jess wanted to put a tracker in the ransom money and then follow it to where he was holding Chloe, but then we got in a fight over something stupid and she drove off before we could go. Now, it's too late. I already dropped the money at the park. I found where he was holding her, anyway, only when I got there…well, you know the rest."

"How much money we talkin' about?"

"Fifty grand. Don't worry. I borrowed it from Jess."

"Sage, Sage, Sage." He palmed his forehead. "Why didn't you come to me? Talk to me. Instead of pretending—"

"I couldn't. He told me he'd kill her if I did."

Eyelids closed, he massaged his temples with his fingertips.

When he became quiet, a fluttering flipped my stomach. Yelling and screaming, I could handle. Silence? No. Anything but that. "Tell me I screwed up. That I almost got my sister killed because I didn't make the right move. Say something. Anything. *Please.*"

As though I was a criminal sitting across from him during an interrogation, he studied me. "Why are you looking at me like that?"

His face softened, but not enough to warrant comfort. I was exposed as if I'd been caught in a lie.

"I'm trying to figure out when it was you stopped trusting me."

"Don't say that." I clutched my heart, a red-hot poker searing my soul. "I trust you, pup. You're the only one I do trust… completely."

"Obviously you don't." He crossed into the living room, removed the black bear painting, and loaded the guns and ammo into the safe.

I hurried after him. "Please don't be like this. I was in an impossible position. If I told you about Chloe, he'd kill her. That's what he said."

Niko locked the safe and rehung the painting. When he faced me, he still had a cool demeanor, and I knew the words that followed would hurt deeply. "I'm your husband, for chrissakes. If you can't come to me when things get rough, then what are we doin'?"

"Don't say that. We have a good marriage. A great one, actually. I did what I thought was best. Please try to understand. Please, pup." I waved him closer, but he backed away. "Fine. It's late anyway. Let's call it a night."

"But I thought you wanted to play our game?"

Excitement soared through me, lifting my spirits. "You mean it? Now?"

He folded me in his arms, and all the fear, self-doubt, and sorrow I'd been holding released in an instant. "I don't blame you for not coming to me right away. If I was in your shoes, I probably would've done the same thing." Softly his lips touched mine. "You sure you're up for this? You've been through a lot lately."

I wiggled out of his arms and cocked back my elbow, revving my arm like a motor. "Oh, yeah. Let's get this bastard."

From under the coffee table, Niko dragged out his briefcase and headed into the kitchen. "I'm still not convinced Longo didn't have a hand in all this. There's too much evidence linking him to the crime scenes."

At the kitchen table, I sat across from him with my chin resting in weaved hands. "What does your gut tell you?"

"That maybe it was a little too easy to connect him." He laid out four murder books, took the crime scene photos from each folder and set them on top.

"And that means?" I stared at the bloody letters at each crime scene. *H-H-N-F.* They must stand for something. The question was what. As I listened to Niko, I repeated *H-H-N-F* over and over, trying to decipher the code.

"That Longo's someone's patsy." He fished another file from his briefcase. "This is the Sophia Lambert file. The one I started tellin' you about. As far as we know, she's the first victim. Because mutts often make mistakes with their first kills, let's include her."

I studied the photographs, the injuries, and the blood spatter. I wasn't sure whether or not to share the Gemini constellation yet. If I did, he'd know the killer was after me as well as Chloe, and I wasn't willing to allow my husband to imprison me at home. As it was, I'd done that to myself for far too long.

Niko asked, "Victim or killer?"

"Killer."

"Really? But you always wanna play the victim. Remember where some of our cases would lead?" He winked, recalling the game nights that ended in bed.

"I'm done being a victim." I sat straighter, taller, my soul stronger than it had been in years.

He gave me a knowing grin. "You're no victim, Sage Quintano. You're a vibrant, beautiful, talented woman who can shoot the tail off a woodpecker."

"Ooh." I pursed my lips. "Bad metaphor."

"Sorry, that didn't come out right. Let's scratch that and say you're a decent shot."

I rose with a photograph in my hands—a close-up of the victim's wounds—and concentrated on the bloody H. "Maybe *I should* play the victim, but only because you know more about how he committed the crime than I do. My previous statement still stands."

"Great." He snatched the photo and leaned it against the salt and pepper shakers so it faced us. "First, he struck her over the head to incapacitate her." He motioned as though he was striking me with the butt of a gun.

"Wait. Where am I?"

"You're probably leaving your house or a place you regularly frequent. You're alone and it's dark."

Whistling happily, I slung my pocketbook over my shoulder and strolled into the living room to demonstrate the victim was totally unaware of any danger looming nearby. Even though rationally I understood it was my husband who would attack, I still braced myself. This was the first time we'd played this game since the rape. It was not an understatement to say I was a tad on edge.

Niko snuck up behind me and tapped the top of my head with a closed fist. I dramatically slumped to the floor, but left one eye cracked open to watch what he'd do next. He slid an arm under my legs, an arm under my neck, and carried me to the sofa.

"I've got you in my vehicle." He loosely handcuffed my hands behind my back and pretended to bind my feet, whispering, "Those too tight, honey?"

This was not the first time he'd ruined the suspense by asking if he was hurting me. Although sweet, we needed this to be as realistic as possible. From the corner of my mouth I said, "I'm unconscious, remember?"

"Now we're at the old schoolhouse in Kingston." He swept me back into his arms and carried me around the room. Then he set me on the sofa. While he pretended to punch a hole in the ceiling, he kept a close eye on me in case I attempted an escape.

Acting as though I was regaining consciousness, confusion and terror laced my voice. "Where am I? What are you doing? Please, don't hurt me." Even for me the words sounded a bit too realistic.

Niko's face whipped toward me, eyes saddening. "Maybe we shouldn't play—"

"Stop it," I reprimanded. "We need to know how he did this. Get back into character."

"Shut your mouth."

For a moment, I wasn't sure if he was acting or serious. Until he tore open my blouse. His strong fingers caressed my breasts.

"What are you doing? He's not making love to her."

"Right. Sorry." Clearing his throat, he shook his head ever so slightly. "Umm."

Jolting upright, I echoed, "Umm? Are you kidding me?"

His arms dropped to his side. "This isn't as easy as it used to be."

"Pup, if we keep living in the past, we'll never have a future."

"Nice quote."

"Thanks." I flipped my hair. "It's mine."

"You are so cute." Our gazes locked, and I envisioned Pepe Le Pew smothering his love with kisses, tiny red hearts floating from his eyes.

Niko broke eye contact first. "Let's start with the injuries. I have you on the floor because there's nothing else in the room. I rip off your shirt and then—" He stopped to think.

I helped him. "You probably strip off all my clothes. You want me in that gown, right?"

"Right. But first, I take your breasts and eyes, because the only blood on the gown is from the wounds leaking. So, using an upward motion I saw off your breasts." He acted it out as he explained. "You're hemorrhaging blood, so I need to stitch you up." He motioned, drawing a needle through my skin, marring my breasts with Xs. "Now I take your eyes. By pressing my finger in the corner, I should be able to pop out your eyeball enough to grab hold of the optic nerve. Oh, hang on. Scratch that. I found a serrated spoon."

In lavish detail, he explained what he'd found in Longo's bathroom. "Obviously I won't do this, but lemme…" With his fingertips, he applied light pressure to the skin between my temple and eye. "I cut the optic nerve and then do the same on the other side. You're bleeding again, so I stitch you up." Again, he drew a fake needle and motioned an X over each eye. "Now the mouth." He repeated the motion.

With a heavy sigh, he fell back on the Lay-Z-Boy, arms opened wide. "I don't get it. What's the significance? I mean… strangling, stabbing, even shooting I can understand. It makes you feel powerful to look your victim in the eye while their life drains out. But this? This doesn't make any sense at all."

I sat upright. "The eyes are windows to the soul. Agreed? So maybe he knew them and can't deal with them watching what he's doing. I think he probably started with the eyes and mouth. And then, removed the breasts."

"Where's my head? You're right. The blood spatter proved that."

I knew exactly where his head was—on my rape and not concentrating on this deadly sport of ours. All it took was one raised eyebrow for me to get my point across.

"I know. I don't have my head in the game." He stood, shaking himself out, rolling his neck. "Okay. Let's start over."

I laid back on the sofa and closed my eyes.

"First, I sew your mouth, so I don't hear your screams. Then I take your eyes and sew those, too." He raised me to my feet—I kept my body limp for realism—and held me by my upper arms. "I like to face you while I take your breasts." He shoved me against the wall, bracing me with his knee. The top half of my body folded over my waist.

Holding one of my breasts in his left hand, he fumbled to keep me upright with his elbow, but he was not having an easy time pinning me to the wall. With his right hand, he sawed upward until the breast detached from my body. "Now I do the other side." He repeated the same sloppy motion. "Now I lay you back down and sew…would I do it while you're standing?"

"What'd the blood show?"

"That he never laid her back down. But how can I sew the wound closed while you're standing?" He paused, thinking. An evil little glimmer shone in his eye. "There are two of them. One holds the victim while the other does the deed."

"Excellent. Now we're getting somewhere."

"This makes much more sense. My partner's holding you while I rig up the pulley, or vice versa. That's why there's a blood pool where the breasts were removed. Okay." He clapped and rubbed his palms, the evil little glimmer returning. "The pulley is rigged up, so I…shoot, I forgot to nail your hands to the board. Lemme start over."

Scratching his five o'clock shadow, his tongue played with the inside of his cheek.

As I waited for him to theorize the MO, I admired a few distinguished strands of silver at his temples. My husband was not a vain man by any means, but I still thought it best not to point out the aging process subtleties in his physique—the belly that wasn't as firm as it once was, the receding hairline, and the crow's feet tipping the outside edges of his warm, bedroom eyes.

I wouldn't change a thing. In my eyes, he was the most handsome man on the planet.

Niko caught me mentally undressing him, and blushed. "If you're gonna keep looking at me that way, this game is gonna lead somewhere else entirely."

"Sorry." Heat flushed my cheeks. "You were saying?"

"You're already cuffed when I transport you. First, I nail your hands to the board, and you start to regain consciousness. That's when I strike you again, giving us the blood spatter. My partner holds you while I remove your eyes and breasts and do all the stitching. Except with Karen Thatcher when we had a box to lie her on. That would account for the second blood pool. The first when I nail your hands, the second when I remove your breasts."

With his hands he sided my face, planting a wet kiss on my lips. "Mwah. I knew it. I do like to face you while I saw off those sweet breasts of yours. Together we string you up on the pulley. It takes both of us to position you right. Why didn't I think of this before?"

I smiled. He knew the answer. That's why this game worked and over the years had solved even the most complex homicide cases. By acting out the crime, Niko could see what was possible and what wasn't. Sharp as he was, he always listened to my theories, which I don't mind saying usually resulted in my husband cracking the case, or so I let him believe.

"Before I string you up, I need to wash the blood off your face and neck and dress you in the gown. That definitely took two people." Eyebrows wrinkled, he gazed at the ceiling. "Did I bring a bucket with me? I must have. When did I drain your blood?"

I had to step in. "You probably did that once I was on the pulley system. That's just a matter of using an embalming needle and sticking the end into a jug of some sort. I would think the directionality would aid in exsanguination. Meaning, having her higher than the jug. Gravity and all."

"That's right. Gaines found needle marks in the femoral artery and we found glass jars at the Thatcher crime scene. At the time, it struck me as odd. Why go to all the trouble of exsanguinating someone and then leave the jars behind?"

I parted my lips to speak.

He wasn't finished. "Unless they got interrupted. Still, the jars were in the same wooden box they mutilated her on."

"Maybe they had to hide the blood fast and planned to come back."

"That makes sense. If the homeless man didn't look up, they could've easily returned."

I took a breath before answering, one breath too long.

"If he hadn't rushed to the next door neighbor to use the phone, they would've killed him, too, for sure."

I waited for a sign that he was done. Niko gave me a tight nod, and I presumed that meant it was my turn. "I agree. Seeing that corpse saved his life."

"Where are the crime scene photos?" Without waiting for a response, he dashed into the kitchen and returned moments later, head down, studying the photograph. "Okay, we're missing the cigarette burns and…what else?"

Now was a good time to share what I'd learned. "The burns are easy. They obviously did that once she was suspended. I need to show you something else, though." As I slipped my arms into my blouse, I carried the crime scene photos over to my computer and typed in the constellation Gemini. "I noticed this the night you didn't come home. Look." I held the picture of the mysterious blood spatter next to the screen. "It's the same pattern."

A smile built on his lips, and then faded. His mouth opened and closed, but no words escaped, and the coloring in his face washed away like finger paints on a bathtub wall.

I rested my hand on the outside of his arm. "Pup, you okay?"

He was falling backward, hands furiously searching for a chair.

I rose and gave him mine. "Sit," I urged. "What's wrong? You look like you saw a ghost."

"Gemini," he said, intoned. "Twins."

"Yeah. So?"

"You and Chloe. All this happened…four women lost their lives…all so they could get to you and Chloe." Niko shuddered as if someone pushed over his gravestone. "They're practicing for—" he gulped— "the twins."

The tendons in my neck stiffened, tugging at my scar. I couldn't fall apart; my husband needed me now more than ever. When we were first married, we made a deal. Only one of us could come unglued at a time. "I'm fine. I'm right here."

With a vacant stare, his head rotated like a possessed doll. He blinked. Blinked again.

"I'm okay, pup." I shook him, and his spine seemed to turn to Jell-O, his body completely limp. "Look at me. I'm fine."

Whatever had a hold on him let go and he sprang to his feet, bustling to the coffee table to examine the Lambert crime scene. "Oh, no. Same blood spatter."

"Let me see." I snatched the photo from his grasp and turned my back so he couldn't see the devastation on my face. "Doesn't make sense. If this was about me and Chloe, then why did they wait three years to—" I twirled toward him. "Did you tell me Longo reported his wife missing?"

"Yeah. Why?"

"What exactly did you find in his house?"

"Same tobacco as at one crime scene, broken pulley system, serrated spoon, work boots that matched the tread patterns, a bleached area in the—"

"Bleach?"

"Yeah. Why? What're you thinkin'?"

"Since the Sophia Lambert case happened three years ago, let's put it aside for now. They started over. Watch." I lined up the most recent crime scene photos, specifically the four windows with the lettering. "H-H-N-F."

I smirked a Cheshire cat's grin. "You said it seemed too easy. That's because it is. H-H-N-F, Hell Hath No Fury…like a woman scorned. Joe Longo was a dog in heat. He couldn't keep it in his pants. I bet if you look into the victims' love life, you'll find they were all his lovers. And what better way to get rid of your cheating spouse? Set him up for murder. It's almost the perfect crime. Almost. What's her name, Joe's wife?" I ambled to the computer and showed him the property records.

Niko checked his notes. "Gloria."

"Bingo. I have a Gloria and Gaylon Skeeter, who own thirty-three acres in Ashland. There's a log cabin on the land." I double-stepped it up the loft stairs. Threw open my closet door and yanked a sweatshirt off the hanger. Within seconds, I was back in the living room, making a beeline for the kitchen. Niko was still staring at the property records, hands clenched around the arms of his chair. "You coming?"

"Where're we goin'?"

"Don't you get it? Chloe and I aren't the twins. They are. Gloria and Gaylon." I darted over to the computer and printed the page. "Let's go check it out."

"I don't know, Sage. Maybe I should call Frankie. I can't risk anything happening to you."

As I was trying to convince him he might need me at the cabin, the phone rang, interrupting my flow. "Who the hell is calling at this hour?" I glimpsed the antique grandfather clock in the corner, beside the sofa. "It's almost midnight." I bustled into the kitchen, calling over my shoulder, "I bet it's Frankie. I don't even know why I'm answering. Hello?"

"Sage?"

"Chloe?"

Chapter Twenty-Three

Saturday, July 22, 2006 12:01 a.m.

"Where are you, Chlo?" I said loud enough for Niko to hear. "Are you safe?"

"That's enough." John Doe broke us apart. "As you can see she's still alive. I know you found the cabin, Sage." He tsked his tongue. "Naughty girl. That wasn't part of the plan."

Was he watching me? Had I missed my sister by mere seconds? "What do you want from me? You got your money."

"Let's see...what about my memoir? You probably haven't written a word."

"We both know you could care less about that. You just wanted to keep me busy so I wouldn't come looking for my sister."

"My, haven't we gotten brave. You're forgetting one thing, Sage. I still have her. So if I were you, I'd lose the 'tude."

Enough. I couldn't listen to any more of his antics. "Fuck you," slipped from my mouth. Where it came from, I had no idea.

With his cell phone to his ear, Niko appeared in the archway, and mouthed, "Keep him on the line."

"I didn't mean that, John. I'm sorry. Please don't hurt her. I'll do anything you want."

Silence knotted my insides, and I feared I'd blown our one chance of saving Chloe.

Eerily calm, he said, "No, Sage. Fuck...*you*."

The line died, and my body melted down the wall—my skeleton rotting into the soil of an unmarked grave. The phone slipped from my grasp and crashed on the tiles. Dropping my face in my hands, an unbearable tormenting pain engulfed every inch of my being. "I just killed my sister," I wailed.

Niko crouched beside me. "No, you didn't. They called back for a reason. Do you actually think they kept Chloe alive this long to throw it away now? These two are planners. They have an end game, and apparently, it involves you. C'mon, we don't have much time." With one hand, he yanked me to my feet.

"What if they call back?"

"What'd you do before, forward the landline?"

I nodded.

"Then do that. But hurry. I'll go start the SUV."

* * *

We traveled an unlit trail through a thick forest. Driving up a steep incline, we jounced, the tires climbing over ledge and rock. Mud coated the windshield and side windows. With a hand on the J-strap, the other on the dash, my stomach flipped and flopped as we struck rocks and tree stumps. Each strike forced us down the hill a few feet. Niko flipped on the four-wheel drive and gunned the gas.

The tires spun and spun.

"Crap. We're stuck." He got out and slammed the door. Marched toward the back of the SUV, and then disappeared.

I undid my seatbelt and sprang to my knees to peer out the rear windshield. I couldn't see him anywhere. An overcast sky allowed no stars or moonlight. Abandoning the idea, I faced front. A silhouette raced through the high beams. A streak of black in a golden smolder. "Niko!"

No answer.

"Niko!"

Silence.

I leaped from the passenger door and landed up to my ankles in mud. A *squish-squash* as I lifted each foot, plodding to the rear bumper. Like a dog burying a bone, Niko was on his knees dragging mud between his legs from in front of the tires. He rose and wiped his hands on his suit pants and for a split-second, a ridiculous question crossed my mind. *How am I ever going to get that stain out?*

From the rear door, he dragged two wooden boards with metal angles on the ends.

"What are you doing? We don't have time for this."

"Whaddaya think I'm doing, Sage? I'm trying to get us out of this frickin' mud, but all I have are these ramps. They'll have to do." He set one board in front of each tire, the angles gripping the mud like fingers of a grim reaper. "Get behind the wheel. Step on the gas when I tell you."

I jumped into the driver seat, eagle eyes on Niko in the side mirror.

He bent over and did something I couldn't see. "Now!" Grunting, he heaved the two-ton vehicle with both hands, shoulders and arms flexing with his thrust.

I couldn't keep the wheel steady. The tires kept falling off the sides of the ramp.

"Dammit." Niko opened the driver door. "Scoot over." He reversed the truck a few inches, enough room to reposition the ramps. "This time, keep the wheel straight. I'll tell you when I'm ready."

"Hurry."

He disappeared from view, presumably setting the ramps in front of the tires. I waited an eternity of minutes. The twins could be killing Chloe while we're stuck in the mud. Not to mention, I had no idea who, or what, was out here with us.

Niko startled me when he hollered, "Now!"

I gripped the wheel with fisted hands. No way would I allow it to get away from me this time. The SUV rolled out of the mud and onto the boards.

Niko appeared at the driver door. "C'mon. Scoot over before it rolls off the ramps."

I crawled over the console, into the passenger seat. Niko engaged the four-wheel drive and drove off the ends of the boards, then hopped out and loaded the mud-covered ramps in the back.

"That sucked," he said, sliding the shifter into gear. "My friggin' knuckles are killin' me."

"You should have never removed that bandage."

"I need to be able to shoot. We have no idea what we'll be walking into."

We chugged up the steep incline to a clearing in the woods with a dirt road to the left and another to the right. Six wooden arrows. Three read *campers, cabins, canoes* to the right. Three read *private property, keep out, violators will die* to the left.

Niko and I exchanged a heedful glanced, and said in stereo, "Left."

"If Gaylon and Gloria Skeeter are from this area," I said, "then it's an awfully big coincidence that we moved to Alexandria, a few towns over."

"Maybe, maybe not. Who suggested this area to you?"

When we were debating where to move, I discussed it with one person. "Chloe. She and Joe used to come up for weekends… went on and on about how beautiful and peaceful it was. The perfect place to start over."

"There you go. So it didn't matter if I left our new number with the hospital or not. They already knew we were coming because Chloe told them."

"Hey, that's my twin you're so blatantly accusing."

Niko flashed a flat hand. "I'm not saying she had anything to do with this. I'm sure it was all very innocent pillow talk. Still, there's not a doubt in my mind, she told them we were here."

As much as I hated to agree, he was probably right. My sister never could keep her trap shut, and I'd give anything to bawl her out for it. If only we could have the chance to squabble again.

"Look." He pointed to a cabin in the distance. "I'm gonna pull over here. We'll have to hoof it the rest of the way."

As I was about to get out, I hesitated. "Ah…" I told him what I'd seen in the headlights. "Are you sure we're safe?"

He withdrew a Glock 27 from his ankle holster, an extra flashlight from the glove, and handed them to me. "I brought us insurance." He grinned, drawing his 9mm from his shoulder holster. "Remember what I taught you. Aim, shoot, re-aim. Keep shooting until the threat is neutralized."

Though I understood the words, actually pulling the trigger

on another human being was a whole other matter. Instead of voicing my concern, I remained positive, confident. *I will bring my sister home safe* became my mantra. I repeated the phrase over and over, as we trudged through leaves, muck, over broken limbs and fallen trees, through picker bushes and streams, my feet sloshing in my sneakers.

A steady hoot-hoot coiled through the darkness from a nearby owl. Scavengers scattered, leaves crunching under tiny feet. Coy dogs bayed, calling their pack. Larger prey breezed through tall pine, birch, and maple trees, branches swaying in the wake of their escape. Sap, soil, and musk rode the warm night air—nature's scent in God's country.

We crept to the side of the cabin and peeked through a window.

A bald man about six-foot-four, if not more, was wearing a black plastic apron and knee-high rubber boots, soldiering toward a door on the far end of a cathedral-high living room, a razor-sharp blade in his hand. Mounted heads of black bear, moose, and deer hung on knotty pine walls. A massive dark-cherry-and-hunter rope rug lounged across wide-pine floors, glossed to a heavy shine.

Cherry toss pillows sat on a tan tweed sofa and matching recliner. Beige-and-ivory-plaid curtains decorated oversized windows, and a chocolate floor vase held burgundy and hunter-green dried flowers.

The spacious living room decorated to perfection. So stylish it belonged on the cover of *Better Homes and Gardens*.

A woman with raven hair and bisque-white skin entered the room. After dragging over a ladder, she rigged two pulley systems from the cross beams. Like her brother, she too was tall and husky, with thick black hair on her arms.

I slapped a hand over my mouth. Those arms. I saw them at the park.

Gloria had a hardened face that showed a lifetime of pain, but Gaylon had a curious innocence. An expression not unlike a mentally challenged person.

She must be the mastermind behind the murders. I tugged

on Niko's shirtsleeve. "What do we do now?"

"I'll go around back. You take the front. Do not come in till you hear my voice. Frankie's meeting us here. I called her while you were on the phone."

The tendons in my neck eased. "Good. I thought it was only you and me. Is she coming alone?"

"No. She's grabbing Ben on the way. You sure you can handle this?"

I wasn't. "I'm sure."

"Stay below the windows. Remember. Don't come inside till you hear my voice."

"Got it." Hunched low, I sprinted toward the front of the cabin, kept my rigid spine against the log exterior, and inched toward the front bay window. So many things coursed through my mind in the span of a few minutes. Nothing I could pinpoint. Madness and chaos dueled for first place.

"Sheriff's department." Niko emerged from a back room and burst into the living room.

Gaylon appeared in the same doorway he left through and Gloria dove off the ladder, lunging at Niko. Everything happened so fast. I aimed through the window.

The gun fired, and the bullet struck Gloria in the back of the arm and spun her around. She fell face first into a bookshelf. I kicked open the front door and barreled inside, but Gaylon grabbed me from behind, pinning my arms to my chest.

Niko hollered at him to let go.

He loosened his grip, and I elbowed him in the gut. Twirled, and slammed an uppercut to his nose with the butt of my hand—exactly as I'd learned in self-defense class. He folded to the floor, cupping his broken nose, blood leaking through massive fingers.

That's when I noticed his eyes—black like Gloria's, only shiny, almost mirror-like, reflecting my image. It must have caught Niko off guard too, because the next thing I knew Gloria dove on his back, clawing his face with blood-red nails.

I summoned my mind to slow. Focus. Checked my stance, feet squared with my shoulders, arms bent, and aimed through the front sight. "Get off him, Gloria."

Latched to Niko's back, she kept clawing at his face—entangled bodies whirling round and round.

I couldn't fire. What if I hit my husband?

"Shoot her! Get this bitch off me!"

Circling and circling, elbows and heads blurred in chaos.

I checked on Gaylon.

He was on the floor, knees hiked to his chest. Lips sealed with paper-thin skin, he groaned and moaned, trying to communicate. Blood streamed from his nostrils, a hand on his temple, head swaying in circles. Black eyes—big and round, as though this was never supposed to happen.

I faced Gloria and Niko. They spun and spun, twirled and twirled. Peering through the front sight I aimed the gun left, right, higher, lower.

Niko was yelling, "Shoot her!" Gloria was screaming something unintelligible. Gaylon's heavy, quick stride pounded behind me.

I pivoted. Squeezed the trigger.

A gunshot echoed in the cabin. With splayed hands, Gaylon clutched his stomach and stumbled backward.

I aimed again. He retreated, no longer a threat.

"Shoot…this…bitch!"

My attention returned to Niko.

He slammed Gloria in the face with his Maglite, and she fell backward, slamming her head on the floor. Niko straddled her hips, cuffed her hands behind her back. Like a flounder on a hook, she squirmed and flopped.

"What do I do? Should I fire?" This woman took my sister. Her and her brother terrorized my family, not to mention caused problems in my marriage. With that gun in my hand, my skin tingled all over, more alive than I felt in years. "If ever there was someone who deserves to die."

Palms up, Niko inched toward me. "Babe, gimme the gun."

Hot tears slipped down my cheeks, and I took aim at Gloria. "Where's Chloe?"

She threw her head back and laughed. "You'll never see her again."

"I hate you. Where's my sister, dammit?" My trigger finger twitched, daring me to pull.

Niko blocked my sight line and gestured for the gun.

"Move. *Please.*" The tears came heavy and fierce. "I need to end this once and for all."

"It's over."

"No. They're still alive. It won't end. It will never end."

"It's all right. Gimme the gun."

"But she knows where Chloe is." I leaned around Niko and pointed the gun at Gloria. "Tell me where she is."

Enjoying my torment, Gloria cackled, reveling in her control. "Let me go, or you'll never find her."

"I'll kill you." I stomped my foot. "Damn you, tell me where she is."

"Ha, ha, ha. You don't have the balls to shoot me."

I took a deep breath, steadied my hands, and set Gloria's skull in my front sight. A pulse pounded on the side of my neck.

"Sage, don't." Niko blocked my path, splayed hands extended toward me. "Gimme the gun."

I sighed and let the weapon swing down on my finger. As I was passing Niko the Glock, I pulled back at the last second and took aim at Gaylon. "What about him? He knows where Chloe is."

"Holster your weapon dammit, and let me do my job."

Because I didn't have a holster, I held the gun muzzle down at my side.

Hands fiddling behind her back, Gloria was yelling profanities, her arms flapping like wings. She glowered at us and let out a shrill, a high-pitched, bleating cry. "You fucking bastard! I'll kill you *and* your bitch wife!" Her eyes narrowed to slits and then widened. Narrowed, widened, over and over.

She reminded me of a possessed wind-up doll. Pull the string and the eyes bulged, let go and the devil inside took over. A shiver ran up and down my body as though tiny chiggers were chewing on my skin, laying their larvae in my pores. As the image took hold, I scratched my arms bloody.

Niko jerked Gaylon's arms behind his back and bound them with zip ties. Fitting. Now he could get a taste of what his victims experienced.

Without warning Gloria wiggled out of her cuffs, scrambled to her feet and plowed head first toward Niko—a crazed bull charging his fallen rider.

I raised my weapon. Took aim.

Fired.

Time wound down. The milieu turned surreal like in a terrible dream. A piercing hum inside my head blocked my hearing. I could see lips moving, but couldn't understand the words.

Absorbing the shot, Gloria buckled in half. Stumbled. Her arms swung wide—like her victims—and she fell backward. Arched back, opened hands to break her fall. The glimmer in her demonic eyes dimmed—a bullet hole in her forehead. Trickling blood cleaved the bridge of her nose and her body crashed to the floor, feet and hands left twitching.

I lowered my gaze to the Glock. Smoke billowed out the barrel.

Gaylon squealed as if I chopped off his limb with an axe. The paper-thin skin stretched to a slash of white, and I waited for his lips to burst apart. His eyelids hooded as though he was trying to absorb the loss, the pain. Experience it. Own it.

I recognized the sacrifice. When I found Chloe's blood in the cabin, I had the same piercing ache in my soul. And I knew—part of me would be lost forever. No matter how much pain they caused, I had to avert my gaze, unwilling to rejoice in his suffering.

Like blowflies to a corpse, two pulleys captured my attention. Outlined in pencil above the rope was Hell Hath No Fury… Like a Woman Scorned. My sister and I were the duo's ultimate denouement. A grand finale. The couple's final act of vengeance.

Gemini, the twins. Stand-ins for Gloria and Gaylon.

No doubt, Chloe's affair with Longo set this in motion and inspired a macabre climax. Twin corpses in matching long, flowing gowns suspended mid-air—ghostly pale faces marred with black

X's over the eyes and mouth.

The mental image quaked my knees.

A few things still puzzled me. Where was Chloe? Where were the gowns? The eyes? The breasts? The blood?

Niko darted in and out of each room downstairs yelling, "Clear!" He hustled up the stairs. A door slammed open and a few moments later, he hollered, "Clear!"

I raced to the doorway where Gaylon appeared—a set of narrow, steep stairs descended into darkness—and called out, "Chloe?"

Silence.

I slid the Maglite from my back pocket and leveled it under the Glock, and crept down the stairs. The temperature dropped ten degrees. Ceilings hung low. Dim lighting. A single light bulb at the end of a loose wire swung back and forth…someone had run past. A steady *drip, drip, drip* from a pipe leaked rusty water over a dank cement floor.

"Chloe, you down here?" I swept the flashlight left and right.

Nothing.

From upstairs, Niko called, "Babe, in here," and I followed his voice to the main level, to what I assumed was an office, off the living room.

A steel hydraulic table—an embalming table—had an elaborate setup of clear plastic tubing and two IV bags, sucked dry of crimson fluid. A large glass canister sat underneath with a bloody line of demarcation around the top.

"Why aren't you looking for my sister?"

"What do you think I'm doing, Sage? I'm hoping I'll find something here that'll tell us where she is. By the way…" He dropped a duffel bag at my feet. "Give Jess back her money."

"Where'd you find it?"

"Upstairs in the master bedroom. Looks like it's all there."

"Then why ask for a ransom? I don't get it. Unless…" I stopped, unwilling to share my theory. Which was, the trip to the park was indeed a trap. Gloria probably counted on me hanging around. What she didn't account for was that I had enough sense to hide in the wooded lot at the back of the park. Had I not argued with Jess, I might have stayed in the vehicle on the side street. In which case, she might have abducted both of us.

"What the hell is this contraption for?" I said. "Don't tell me they were embalming people, too."

Niko shuffled through a stack of pamphlets. "From what I gather, you're looking at a homemade blood transfusion kit."

I slapped one of the IV bags. "That's disgusting. Who does that?" More and more, I feared I'd never find my sister alive.

"Instead of smacking shit around, why don't you help me look through all this stuff." He stepped aside to reveal a pine table piled high with literature on various topics—breast cancer, health, age defying tricks and tips, a rare eye disease I couldn't pronounce, and a how-to booklet on home blood transfusions. Protruding from under a medical report was a chocolate leather-bound book about half the size of a hardcover novel with a brass buckle left unlatched.

I swiped it off the table.

"I found a hospital bill for Gloria," he said. "She had a double mastectomy. That explains why she sliced the breasts off her husband's lovers. It probably infuriated her to see perfect, youthful tits."

As I was about to flip to the first page, Niko theorized, "Gaylon was born with a rare eye disease. So in Gloria's warped mind she probably thought she could fix him."

"Unless she's a skilled ophthalmologist that wouldn't even be in the realm of possibility. Even if she was…"

"Hey, I never said she was sane. Clearly, her brother's a mute. So maybe he's mentally challenged too. Gloria, being the sick fuck that she was, probably wanted to make him feel better by giving him eyes to play with." He swatted his hand. "Ah, who the hell knows?"

"Actually, in a creepy sort of way that makes sense. Who was the blood for, do you know?"

"That was for Gloria. I saw something on that earlier." He flipped through a stack of papers. "Here it is. Experimental treatment for cancer. Something about new blood increasing the white count…blah, blah, blah…to help fight the disease. I don't know. Sounds like nonsense. If this was possible, every cancer patient in the world would be getting transfusions."

"What's her blood type?"

He ran his finger down Gloria's medical record. "AB positive."

"Universal recipient. She was able to receive almost any type of blood. That explains why she chose her husband's lovers rather than targeting a specific group of people with matching blood types. She could get retribution and try to heal herself. Two birds. One stone. So to speak."

"Does that mean Gaylon has the same blood type? Are yours and Chloe's the same?"

"We do, yes, but that's because we're identical twins. We came from the same egg. Gloria and Gaylon are fraternal twins, so they could easily have different blood types. One egg didn't split, creating two babies. Two separate eggs were fertilized. Now that I think about it, I did read something once about rare mutations occurring in one percent of multiples. Perhaps Gaylon was that one percent."

"I guess we'll never know…unless they kept literature on it. He certainly isn't gonna tell us after you killed his sister."

"Hey."

"You know what I mean." He set down the paperwork and rubbed the sides of my arms, gazing into my eyes. "You did the right thing. That crazy bitch left you no choice."

"I still killed another human being. I'm not sure how to deal with that."

"I know, babe. I wish I could tell you it'd be—"

"Sheriff's department," Frankie called out as she crashed through the front door.

I stuffed the leather-bound book in my waistband, concealed with the hem of my blouse, and hustled to the doorway. "We're in here."

Weapon drawn, Frankie swept her hands across the living room. Ben kept his back to her, surveying the front yard.

A proud grin emerged on my lips as I drew myself up tall. Look how well my husband trained these fine deputies.

Frankie asked, “That it, only two?”

“Isn’t that enough?” With darting glances at Gloria’s corpse, I said, “Frankie, I…I…”

Niko laced his fingers with mine. “She was advancing. I had no choice.” His Adam’s apple rose and fell. “Honest. Ask Sage. It’s a clean shoot.”

“It’s cool. I don’t need to check your story.”

My husband couldn’t lie his way out of a parking ticket with the sheriff’s vehicle. A split-second after his false confession, Frankie winked at me, surmising I killed Gloria. Defending myself felt damn good too. Nothing I did could change the past, but I refused to remain a casualty of rape. Sadly, it took losing my sister and taking a life to open my eyes. Now I had to deal with that. With Niko by my side, redemption and acceptance almost seemed possible.

Below my feet a slight whimper creeped through the floorboards.

“Everyone, quiet.” I tracked the sound to the basement doorway, where I’d been minutes before. Hands cupped around my mouth, I called, “Chloe?” My voice carried into an endless pit of darkness, bounced off hollow walls, and boomeranged back to me.

Another whimper floated up the stairs. Then a soft groan.

“I’m here! I’m coming!” With Niko’s spare flashlight in my back pocket, I flew down the stairs, my hands running the railing. “Where are you?” Heart thrashing against my ribcage, I shined the light on the walls, the floor, the ceiling.

I couldn’t find my sister anywhere.

I got on my hands and knees and crawled around the outside edge of the basement, searching for a hidden door.

Niko hollered down the stairs, “Did you find her?”

“No.”

“I’ll check the kitchen for a trap door. Frankie, take Ben and search the perimeter of the property.”

“What if we can’t find her?” I cried out. “Chloe, where are

you?" I stuck the flashlight between my teeth and brushed my fingers up and down the north wall.

Found nothing.

I bolted to the south wall and ran my hands high and low. Tiny balls of grit coated my palms and I wiped them on my jeans and tried again.

Found nothing.

I hustled to the east wall and knocked up, down, left, right.

Found nothing.

"Chloe, say something. Help me."

On the west wall, I continued in the same manner. First, running my hands over the wall, then knocking from one side to the other. "Chloe?"

In the far corner, my fingernail dug into a crevice and followed it around a doorway recessed into the wall. "Chloe, you in there?"

A soft moan seeped through the cracks and stole my breath. I pounded on the doorway, tears flooding my eyes, my throat.

"Son of a bitch, how do I get inside?" I threw punches and kicks, slammed my shoulder against the door.

It wouldn't budge.

No doorknob, no latch, no handle of any kind.

I bolted up the stairs, called, "Niko."

No answer.

"What the hell is going on?" I bounded over to the window. Niko, Frankie, and Ben were nowhere in sight.

"You!" I shoved the Glock in Gaylon's face—a raging inferno in my gut. "Tell me how to get inside that room."

His watery eyes tilted downward toward at his apron pocket.

"What's in there?"

Refusing to help, he whipped his face away.

I wasn't sure if he had a blade that could slice my finger, or what awaited me. With the toe of my sneaker, I brushed across his lap. A rectangular shape jutted the apron. Holding my aim on Gaylon's face, I slipped my left hand into the pocket and withdrew a remote control.

In record time, I was in the basement aiming the remote at the secret doorway.

The wall opened to reveal a tiny room with Chloe slumped in the corner. A rank odor of decay struck me in the face, and I covered my nose with the crook of my arm.

In a puddle of blood, contusions and abrasions scarred Chloe's bare legs. Her head had fallen forward. Stringy, wet hair shielded her face.

As I swept the bloody strands aside…my blood chilled to ice.

Crimson oozed from needle holes at the top and bottom of Xs over her eyes and mouth. In an ace-black gown with a sweetheart neckline and short, pleated sleeves, purplish bruises littered her arms. Used insulin needles scattered around her bare feet, cigarette burns on the soles. Above her head, a hanger held a matching gown that teetered on an iron spike.

Unable to trust my eyes, I clawed my hair back and blinked. Hands clasped around the base of my neck, my vision tunneled on her injuries. Desperation strangled my voice as I fell to my knees, and slurred, "Dear God, no… My beautiful sister. What'd those animals do to you?"

With the back of my hand, I gently stroked her cheek. If only I could soothe her with my touch, erase the horrors she endured.

Chloe let out a pained moan, and her body crumbled to the cold cement. I tucked my flashlight in my back pocket and slid my arms under her legs and neck. Bending my knees for leverage, I struggled to lift her.

She was too heavy. "Niko!"

No answer.

I pivoted, dragged her arms over my shoulders, and pushed off the floor with my feet. Dead weight on my back, I stuck out my right foot…then the left. An exaggerated stride as I attempted to carry my twin to the staircase. "Help me, Chloe." I dug in my heels. One foot. Then the other. I needed to find the strength to save her.

One foot. Then the other. I neared the bottom stair.

"Niko!"

Silence.

Clasping Chloe's wrists with one hand, I gripped the railing and dragged us up one tread at a time. *Bang, bang, bang* pounded the wooden stairs as I plodded to the top landing.

I fell into the living room, and Chloe rolled off my back and landed face-up.

I cried, "Niko."

All three converged in seconds. Each storming through a different entrance.

A mournful expression crossed my husband's face, and he scooped Chloe into his strong arms. "Frankie, call a bus," he urged, laying Chloe's limp body on the tweed sofa.

"We don't have time. She's dying," I wailed. "We have to take her ourselves. Please. Let's go."

Red drool escaped the corner of Chloe's bluing lips, a rivulet of blood to her chin.

I pinched Niko's sleeve, tugging, pulling. "Please, we've got to go."

"Go," insisted Frankie. "I'll take care of these two and meet you at the hospital."

"Toss Sage your keys," said Niko. "My truck's back a ways."

Frankie lobbed the keyring. "Which hospital you goin' to?"

"Speare." I shoved Niko out the door. As he ran, Chloe's head bobbed up and down, her legs dangling over his arm. I opened the back passenger door and climbed inside. "I'll stay with her. You drive." Cradling Chloe's head in my lap, I urged him to pass me something to cut the wire with, and he handed me the Swiss Army knife Frankie kept in the glove compartment.

Between the arthritis in my hands and the adrenaline coursing through my veins, I couldn't open the damn thing. I held it over the front seat. "Pull out the scissors for me."

Niko plowed over downed trees and rocks. "Sage, little busy here." He veered right, spun the wheel to the left, attempted to steady the truck.

"I can't keep her stitched up. *Please.*"

He slowed the SUV and steered with his knee while he

extended the scissor arm on the knife. "It's not the sharpest. Oh, here." He tossed an evidence bag over the seat. "We need to preserve the evidence."

"I could care less about your stupid evidence, Sheriff." The scissors trembled at Chloe's right eye. The vehicle was rocking so severely I didn't dare make the cut.

"That's not fair. I know you're emotional, but that's no reason to destroy evidence in a homicide investigation."

"Whatever. Fine. I'll put it in the damn bag. Leave me alone. I need to concentrate." Lowering to her mouth, I pressed the bottom edge of the scissors to her lips and snipped from corner to corner. With my fingertips, I gently tugged on the wire. *This isn't wire. It's thread. Thick thread.*

Next, I moved to her eyes. I required a steady hand, and Niko hitting every bump and divot in the road was not helping. "Keep it steady. I can't cause her any more pain."

"Why don't you wait till we hit paved road. There's nothing I can do about it. You saw how crappy the road is, and we're coming up on that mud. Hang in there a little longer. I'm doin' the best I can."

I swept my sister's wet hair from her face and dabbed beads of sweat off her brow with my shirt tail. "You're safe now, Chlo. Please don't leave me." I kissed her cheek. "Love you to the moon, 'round the world, and back again. I'm so sorry about what I said. It wasn't fair to make you choose between me and the man you loved." I neglected to mention Joe's wife did this to her, so she wouldn't think that was my way of saying, "I told you so."

To estimate how much longer until the tires hit tar, I peered out the passenger window. Nailed to a tree were six wooden arrows. Smooth surface would soon follow. Niko flipped on the siren, deafeningly loud inside the SUV.

I rolled my head to relax and prayed for the courage and skill to pull this off. Once we hit the asphalt, I lowered the scissors to Chloe's left eye, snipped the bottom two legs of the X. Cut the top two arms, and gently tugged the thread.

Without incident, it slipped out of the holes. I transferred the scissors to her right eye.

Crusted blood gripped the thread like the ghostly fingers of Gloria Skeeter.

I whispered, “I’m sorry,” and smoothed the skin above her lashes. With her eyelid taut, I wiggled and maneuvered the thread out the hole. “Oh, thank God. Are you all right? Did I hurt you?”

No response.

I lowered my cheek to her chest. The siren drowned out every noise. I could barely hear myself think, never mind hear her heartbeat.

Tears blurred my vision as I leaned over her face, searching for some small semblance of my sister. Blood wept from needle marks around her eyes and lips. Her skin was pallid, clammy.

“We’re five minutes away.” Niko adjusted the rear view mirror to see in the backseat. “How is she?”

I touched two fingers to the side of her neck. A faint pulse. “She’s very weak. Hurry.” Wetness moistened my lap, and I rolled her onto her side.

Blood.

I inhaled a quick intake of air. As I exhaled through my mouth, I chanced a peek under the sweetheart neckline. “Sweet Jesus.”

Chapter Twenty-Four

7:00 a.m.

After staying at the cabin for hours, Frankie careened into the hospital parking lot. Earlier Niko called and told her Chloe would likely be admitted to ICU post-op. The unknown—no confirmation from anyone that she'd made it through surgery—drove her to work harder, faster.

As much as she yearned to be with Sage, someone needed to hang around while the ME took his sweet time to arrive, process the scene, and wait for the ambulance to transfer Gaylon Skeeter to the hospital. She had to hand it to Ben. If it weren't for his quick thinking to call in Childs to accompany the prisoner, she'd still be at the cabin waiting for CSU. He actually might make a fine sheriff one day. Fine with her. No way could Frankie kiss the mayor's ass. Not without her stomach protesting.

No time to wait for the elevator. She took the stairs two at a time and burst through the side entrance to the ICU. Then slowed her pace and bustled to the nurses' station, flashing her badge. "I'm Deputy Sheriff Campanelli. Are Sheriff Quintano and his wife…let me start over."

Frankie straightened the hem on her leopard-print top, allowing herself a moment to regroup. "Chloe Phillips was brought in earlier tonight, severely mutilated and near death. Sheriff Quintano is her brother-in-law. He called and told me she was still in surgery as of…" she checked her watch, "two hours ago. Is she still in surgery, or…?"

"I will look." A nurse with sandy-blonde hair knotted in a tight bun ran her finger down the computer screen.

How many patients could this unit possibly hold? Eight, ten tops? Didn't seem like there was another side to this section of the hospital, so why didn't this broad know the patients' names by heart?

"It looks like she is still in surgery," the nurse said as she stood and leaned over the top of a high, curved desk, pointing to the right. "Through those doors you will find a waiting room. Please have a seat in there. You are welcome to check back with me in an hour or so."

I'm welcome? Someone thinks her shit don't stink. Frankie held a tight smile and headed toward the double doors. Peering through a strip of glass in the waiting room door, she searched for Niko and Sage. At the far end of the room, they huddled in kitty-cornered chairs, Niko with his arm around his wife, her head resting on his shoulder as he lightly caressed her arm with his fingertips.

If only Frankie could find a love that strong. Once things quieted down, Gunther, her Saint Bernard, should have a check-up. He'd enjoy seeing Chance again. Maybe she'd luck out and find him still single.

Three other couples were inside the ICU waiting room. Their foreheads rutted, heads down, staring at their shoes. No one spoke. The room was so quiet, even the air conditioner didn't dare hiss. To respect their peace, Frankie padded toward Niko and Sage and lowered into a plastic-sealed chair next to Sage. The seat released a Whoopee Cushion noise, and everyone in the room grimaced at Frankie—a slow, disappointed shaking of six heads.

Waving her arms, she mouthed, "Sorry." She shot an icy glare at anyone who had the audacity to hold her gaze and leaned aside to Sage. "Any word?"

When Sage turned, she had dark circles under red-rimmed, puffy eyes, her pale skin mottled with blotches of rose, and streaks of tears through smudges of her sister's dried blood.

Without making eye contact with anyone or anything in particular, Frankie sat in silence, picking at her chipped scarlet nail polish. Forty-five minutes later, Niko leaned around Sage to Frankie. "Would you mind seeing what's going on? I should stay here." For his reason why, he slightly nudged his head toward Sage.

"Me?" She touched an open hand to her chest. "Umm…" No friggin' way. What if the nurse told her Chloe didn't survive surgery? She couldn't face Sage and tell her that her twin sister was dead. "I can stay with Sage. I don't think it's my place, not being family and all."

Sage piped up. "Frankie," she said in a tone that warranted her full attention, "you *are* family. Please. I can't stand the waiting. It's tearing me up inside." A lone tear fell from her eye.

Frankie's heart twisted into knots. Patting Sage's knee, she relented. "If that's what you want."

Out in the hall, she peeked through the glass in the door. Sage buried her face in Niko's chest, her back rising and falling as though she'd broken down. An invisible strike to the gut forced Frankie to look away, and she ambled toward the nurses' station. The nurse who told her where to wait was still behind the desk. "Excuse me, Nurse…" She waited for her to fill in the blank.

"Peters."

"Nurse Peters, Sheriff Quintano and his wife have been waiting for hours. They've asked me to find out the status of Chloe's condition."

"Full name, please."

She'd spoken with this woman less than an hour an ago. Even a preschooler could remember someone's name for forty-five friggin' minutes. Before responding, she took a moment to calm the wave of adrenaline, on the verge of spiking into torrents. "Chloe Phillips."

Nurse Peters ran her finger down the screen. By the end of her shift, Frankie doubted Peters' co-workers could make out the patients' names through all the smudged prints, and she couldn't imagine this made her too popular, wiping her grimy paws on everything.

"The doctor will be out to speak with you momentarily."

"We both know that's a non-answer, Peters. Listen, Ms. Phillips is the victim of a brutal assault. Vicious…you can't even imagine. Her family doesn't need any more torment. So, please.

I need an update, and I'd appreciate a straight answer this time."

The nurse ignored her and shuffled papers around the desk, similar to Niko's MO.

Instead of her usual brazen approach, she appealed to her compassionate side. With any luck, she had one. "Please, Peters. Have a heart. Gimme something I can share with the family."

"I'm not supposed to—"

Frankie slapped the desktop much harder than she intended. "Tell me how she is, dammit."

The nurse smoothed back a loose strand of hair that had fallen from her bun. "She's in critical condition. Any more than that you will have to get from her doctor."

"Where's he? I want to speak with him."

"He'll be out—"

Frankie leaned over the desk, and calmly said, "Don't you dare say 'shortly' or 'momentarily' or anything like that, or I'll shove that phone down your throat. I'll ask you one…more… time. Where's the doctor?"

Shifting in her seat, Peters fidgeted with her collar. "He's in the lounge. It was a long surgery."

Frankie leaned even closer. Through gritted teeth—her jaw clenched so tight she could barely form words—she gave one last warning. "Get. Him. Now."

Twice the phone slipped from her grasp. "Dr. Monahan, there's a law enforcement officer who'd like to speak with you about Chloe Phillips. She is very insistent. What should I tell her?"

On her best behavior, Frankie controlled the urge to rip the receiver out of the nurse's hand and beat her over the head with it.

"I'll tell her. Thank you, Doctor." Acting as though she were Queen Shit, Nurse Peters rested clasped hands on the desk. "The doctor will come speak with you."

If only Niko wouldn't get pissed if she clocked this bitch. She tossed her one last spiteful glare and paced in front of the desk, peeling her nails until the doctor decided to grace her with his presence.

Through a side door, a brawny man in scrubs entered the hall, and Frankie nearly tackled him, bunching his shirt in balled fists. "Are you Chloe Phillips' doctor?"

"Yes. Doctor Monahan." He paused to glance at her hands, and she straightened the wrinkles in his shirt by pawing long swipes. With two fingers, he removed her hands from his chest. "Are you family, miss…?"

She stuck her badge in his face. *Where's your smug look now, buddy?* "Deputy Sheriff Campanelli."

"Pardon me." He shook her hand. "I would be happy to speak with the family directly."

I thought that might work. "After you." She swung her arm toward the waiting room. Thank God, she didn't have to break the news herself.

Hands clasped loosely behind his back, Dr. Monahan walked with exaggerated, confident strides, as if waters should part in his presence. Outside the waiting room, shoes scuffing against the linoleum made Frankie take notice.

"Doctor—" Nurse Peters was waving a chart.

Nice. How brain-dead does a doctor have to be to forget his own patient's chart?

They entered the waiting room, and Niko rose with his wife still locked in his arms. "How is she?"

Dr. Monahan suggested, "Please, have a seat."

Frankie wrung her hands. *That's never a good sign.*

Niko slumped into the chair, shoulders curving over his stomach. Sage clasped her hands in her lap, eyes tilted toward the floor.

They must be preparing themselves for bad news.

"As you know," Dr. Monahan said, "your sister suffered severe physical as well as emotional trauma. The optic nerve in the right eye was badly damaged and the left was completely removed. We called in an ophthalmologist to repair the damage. However, there was a lot of swelling. As of yet, we simply do not know the outcome."

A spark of pride shone in the doctor's amber eyes, and Frankie glimpsed Niko and Sage to see if they noticed. "We were able to repair some of the breast tissue, though she will still need to undergo plastic surgery for esthetic purposes. They do amazing work with implants these days. Of course, she will never be able to breastfeed a child. If she does decide to get implants, she will also need to have nipples tattooed. Which is a lot easier than rebuilding a pair."

The doctor paused to read the chart.

The nurse said he completed Chloe's surgery moments earlier, so why did he need to read the chart? Maybe he was letting the news sink in. Mighty white of him.

"We cleaned and stitched a small incision in her torso and gave her a blood transfusion." He raised his eyes to Sage. "That's why we asked you to donate. Being her identical twin made you a perfect match." Again, he reviewed the chart. "Ms. Phillips suffered abrasions and contusions to several parts of her body and broke two ribs. One of the ribs punctured her right lung causing ARDS."

Frankie leaned forward to gauge how the Quintanos were taking the news. Sage was rocking back and forth, her hands clenched into fists, an audible sigh escaping her lips like air from a balloon. Niko stared out the window behind Frankie, grinding his jaw, tears pooling in his eyes. Neither fully understood the magnitude of what Dr. Monahan was saying. *Guess it's up to her to ask.* "What is ARDS and how do you treat it?"

Eyes closing, Sage gave her a gentle nod and Niko mimicked the behavior—each thanking her for what they couldn't ask themselves. Frankie gripped the armrest of her chair, bracing herself for the answer.

"What that means is the fractured rib punctured her lung wall. In layman's terms, think of it this way. When you breathe, the lung expands in the same manner as a balloon if someone was blowing it up. When you exhale, the muscles relax and, like a balloon, the lung springs back. However, if the air escapes the lung, and into the area around the lung, the lung can collapse inside the chest. When the fractured rib struck the lung, it punctured a hole. Thus allowing air to escape."

"So that's what ARDS is," countered Frankie, "a collapsed lung?"

"No. Sorry. Let me rephrase. Once the injury occurred, it caused the lung to become inflamed and its small capillaries, or vessels, leaked too much fluid into the lung's air alveoli, or sacs. This kept the lung from filling with air, which caused the respiratory system to fail. Acute Respiratory Distress Syndrome or ARDS."

He grinned, seemingly proud of himself for explaining this in terms they could understand. Frankie grinned too, but not for the same reason. She envisioned herself smacking the smile off his arrogant face, pummeling him until he showed some freakin' compassion for two people she would kill to protect.

"ARDS is a severe form of ALI—excuse me, Acute Lung Injury—and occurs between one to three days after injury."

Not amused. Or impressed. Because neither Niko nor Sage could ask the hard questions, that particular nightmare fell on her shoulders. "Are you telling us Chloe could die?"

"ARDS can be life threatening, yes. However, I believe if Ms. Phillips makes it through the next twenty-four hours, her chances of survival are about…instead of giving you a percentage, let me preface my statement with…I remain hopeful, as I think you should."

This dancing around every question routine had to go. "Whattaya doin' to help her? Anything? Or are you just—" Frankie flashed air quotes— "hopeful?"

Exhaling through his nostrils, he pursed his lips. "We placed—" he checked the chart— "Chloe on a ventilator and—"

Frankie leaped from her chair. "You don't even know her first name? What kind of doctor are you?" She flung out her hands. "Un-freakin' believable."

When her gaze met Niko's glower, she clamped her mouth closed and lowered to her seat. "Tell us exactly what's going on. Exactly. And don't leave anything out this time. These people are suffering." Her gaze strayed to Niko, and this time she found redemption.

"As I was saying, Mr. and Mrs...."

Frankie leaned in, accentuated, "*Quintano.*"

"Right. Pardon me. As I was saying, Mr. and Mrs. Quintano, the ventilator will help Ms. Phillips—ah, Chloe—breathe until she is able to breathe on her own. If after a few days...let's cross that bridge when we get to it. We have also supplied nutrition, fluids, and antibiotics through an IV drip. This combined with PEEPS should help."

"PEEPS, Doctor?" Frankie prodded, so damn tired of his vast vocabulary and acronyms she didn't even have the strength to raise her voice.

"PEEPS stands for Positive End Expiratory Pressure. Basically, what that means is *the way* we distribute the oxygen into her lungs. In small amounts rather than a heavy flow. I assure you, Mr. and Mrs. Quintano, your loved one is being carefully monitored."

Sage and Niko each glanced at Frankie, as if to say, "Satisfied?" Acknowledging she'd remain quiet, Frankie dipped her chin.

In a hoarse voice Sage asked, "Can we see her, Dr..." she paused.

Frankie chuckled under her breath. Touché, tossing Dr. High and Mighty's callousness in his face.

"What I mean is, is my sister awake?"

"I apologize. I thought you knew. Your sister slipped into a diabetic coma."

Frankie shot to her feet. "A coma? You didn't lead with that?"

Niko reached around his wife and patted Frankie's arm. "It's okay, Frankie."

"She's got a point, Niko," murmured Sage.

"Can they see her or not?"

Dr. Monahan's gaze raced across their faces and landed on Niko, the calmest of the three. "You can visit with her for a few minutes. Be advised though, she will not be aware of your presence."

Niko held a flat hand up to Frankie—code for, don't say it—as he thanked the doctor for his time and asked for her room number.

Dr. Monahan checked the chart. "Room two. Take a left at the nurses' station, second door on your left. I feel I must warn you. The ventilator and equipment, combined with the injuries she sustained, might make your loved one look…for lack of a better word…scary."

That was his first heartfelt response. Finally, a glimmer of a human being. About time. Silently, Frankie gasped. What the hell did he mean by "scary"?

Chapter Twenty-Five

8:45 a.m.

As the three of us strode down the hall, I clung to Niko, my arms curled around his to postpone my imminent collapse. My sister needed the strength I found at the cabin, not a blubbering mess. "Give me a minute," I told Niko and veered into the ladies' room.

In the mirror above the sinks, I stared at my reflection—cheeks sallow, coloring pasty white. *Get ahold of yourself. You can do this.*

I rummaged through my bag for a barrette. Clipped my hair back and splashed cold water on my face. Leaning on the sink, a fractured version of myself stared back. I needed a way to feel stronger. True strength, not my usual false facade. First, undue stressors had to go. I called Jess. "Hi, it's me. We found Chloe. She's in the hospital."

"Oh…my…God. Is she all right?"

"She's critical, but we're…hopeful. Listen, I'm so sorry about the other day. I should never have spoken to you that way."

"Stop. Didn't you get my message? We both said things we regret. How about we start over?"

Relief emerged like a burst of cold air on a hot summer day. "That would be nice."

"What hospital is she in?"

"Speare. In Plymouth. But if you're thinking of driving up, don't. She can't have visitors yet, anyway. They're allowing Niko and me to see her for a minute, and then, even we have to leave." I explained the details of Chloe's condition. "Mainly I wanted to hear your voice and tell you that I have your money."

"You do?" she said, surprised. "How?"

"It was still in the duffel bag when we found them." I briefly explained who and why this all happened. "I've got to run. I'll call you when we know more."

"Keep your chin up. I'll plan to drive up tomorrow, if not for Chloe than for you."

"That sounds nice. See you then." As I dropped my cell in my bag, knotted muscles in my neck and shoulders released a tiny amount of tension, but my head still throbbed with a vicious headache, a splitting migraine that had manifested the moment I saw my sister's injuries.

I removed the barrette and brushed my hair, straightened my wrinkled, bloody clothes, and ambled into the hall. Should I call Mr. Chen, too? Nah. He probably already knew about Chloe from the wind or a stray bird. Either that or he heard my heart sing when I'd discovered my twin was still alive.

How Mr. Chen knew the things he did was one of the great unknowns in my life, but somehow he was always with me, if not in body then in spirit. Perhaps he knew how to astral project with control and a destination in mind.

I had always considered myself spiritual, but his spirituality went way beyond most people's comprehension, including mine. Once this nightmare ended, I would have to ask him to teach me how to reach that second plane of existence. What a great way to check on family and loved ones.

I'm a terrible person. My mind should be on Chloe's recovery. What if she dies? What if I never get to tell her how sorry I am? Praying hands held close to my chin, I gazed toward the heavens, tears trailing over my lips and down my neck.

Dear God, please help her. I promise to never say a harsh word or to think a bad thought. I'll pray every day, go to church on Sunday, and study my bible. Worship you the way you deserve instead of being the lapsed Catholic I've become. Please let my sister survive. Please.

I dried my tears and met up with Niko and Frankie. Interlocking my fingers with my husband's, I entered the hospital room. The image of Chloe in that basement repeated in my mind, and the air grew heavy, my body wilting as if rebelling against the act of standing.

My husband gave me a gentle nudge toward the bed. "It's okay. Talk to her. I bet she can hear you."

When I focused on my twin, breath writhed in my chest. I hovered my hand over her arm, and then abandoned the idea.

Chloe lay supine, her hair swept away from her face. A large vent tube ran down her throat, the end stuck between her teeth. Next to her bed, the ventilator expanded and deflated like an accordion, and each time a loud hiss sounded as if a rattlesnake was hiding in the nightstand, ready to strike if I got too close.

In addition to the holes from X's, stitches also marred her right eyelid, left cheekbone, and above her right wrist. Purplish-black bruises marked her arms, forehead, and around her neck—fingers squeezing, strangling, imprinting her skin. A strong antiseptic overpowered the private room but did nothing to hide the sense of impending death.

My chest constricted, and it was near impossible to catch my breath. My carbon copy was in that bed. If Gloria and Gaylon had been successful, I could easily be lying beside her. Or worse, hanging in that cabin undiscovered for days.

Niko had a distant stare as though he'd envisioned me lying there, too. His dull, wet eyes slid toward me, and he offered me a quivery smile.

I stuck out my hand to touch her. She looked like a monster, not my beautiful sister. Resting my hand on hers, her skin was clammy and cool as if this was an empty shell, and her soul was somewhere else.

Did she astral project? Had her soul escaped the confines of this body, free and light, soaring through the clouds waiting to return? Or was she undecided whether to keep flying toward heaven and not look back? If she was, I couldn't blame her. Those animals brutalized her body, a physique Chloe worked hard to maintain.

As I sat vigil at her bedside, a nagging question haunted me.

Could she live with these disabilities, emotional as well as physical? With someone who was used to being the brightest star in the room, the center of attention, scars could diminish her inner light.

If she survived, she'd require help to heal. I'd make up the spare room and take her home with us rather than let her return to her one-bedroom Cambridge apartment. We could reminisce about our childhood, laugh at the foolish twins playing dress up, clomping around in our mother's heels.

My lust for revenge needed to end. Benson was dead. The Skeeters were no longer a threat. It was time to thank those who had helped me cope, and pay it forward. I'd hung on to negative emotions for far too long. Now I needed to concentrate on the future, a future filled with joy, surrounded by loved ones and friends. Chloe's ordeal put many things into perspective.

If my sister survived, I would stay by her side and tend to her every need. If she survived, I promised to let her lead her own life without judgment from me. If she survived, I would tell her every day how much she meant to me, how I'd always envied her free spirit and yearned to be more like her. If she survived, I'd do everything in my power to help her forget the evil acts committed against her. This would not emotionally cripple her as my rape did to me. I wouldn't allow her ordeal to swallow her whole.

If she survived…

As we exited her room alarms blazed, machines beeped, and two nurses raced by us, knocking me into the door frame. I banged a U-turn and hustled toward Chloe's bed, where the nurses were performing CPR. Within moments, Dr. Monahan sprinted into the room, shouting orders at the nurses.

"What's going on?" I cried. "You have to save her."

"Get her out of here," the doctor demanded.

Niko put his arm around my waist and dragged me away from the bed. Unwilling to leave my sister alone with strangers, I rolled out of his grasp.

Frankie bolted into the room, and Niko hollered at her to help him remove me.

With volcanic eyes, I spun toward her. "Don't you dare touch me."

"Sage, don't make me do this." Arms out, she inched toward me, ready to tackle me if that's what it took.

"Chloe's dying. I can't leave. Please, Frankie, don't make me leave."

"Get her out of here," the doctor shouted.

In a cool tone, Frankie said, "You need to let them do their job."

Before I could respond, Niko had me in a bear hug, pushing me out the door.

My world shattered into a million pieces, and I collapsed in the hall, wailing, missing my sister already. Niko held me as I sobbed into his chest, two of us huddled on the floor.

Chloe's room was in total chaos, crash carts rolling in, medical professionals darting in and out, the doctor yelling orders. Overwhelmed with so many emotions, too many emotions, I could barely breathe, tears trailing my cheeks, over my lips, down my neck. I gasped for air, my chest heaving, the drab hallway spinning, and I thought for sure I'd pass out.

Everything stopped in an instant, and the room turned deadly quiet, except for one long flat line, a hum that signaled the end of my sister's life.

"Time of death…8:59 a.m."

Chapter Twenty-Six

April 19, 2007 Thursday, 3:30 a.m.

"Ouch. Your nails." Niko lifted his pajama top and checked for blood. "Geesh. All right, all right. I'm awake."

A fist on her hip, Sage waddled around to his side of the bed. "It's time."

"Time? Time for what?" His gaze traveled to a small, hard-shell suitcase in her hand, and he whipped off the covers. "It's time." He leaped from the bed and framed her belly with his hands. "Hey there, little man, you ready to meet your daddy?" He gave his unborn child a peck and then palmed his precious wife's face. "My beautiful Mommy, are you ready to meet your son?"

"Let's go—now."

Okay, so maybe now wasn't the best time to get overly sentimental. He couldn't help it. He thought this day would never come. Somehow they'd gotten a second chance—a miracle—and this time, nothing could stop them from becoming a family. "Let me throw my pants on and we'll go."

With two hands Sage held her belly, puckered her lips, and breathed out short, staccato breaths. "Hurry. This baby is coming whether you have pants on or not."

"Please calm down. Stressing isn't good for you or the baby." Arms flying, he tossed clothes out of his dresser. What should he wear to meet his son? Sage closed in, and he didn't dare turn around. If he didn't get moving, he'd have claw marks down his back, too.

Not green. Blue? There's probably enough blue in the

hospital. He couldn't fade into the background. Black? No, he might look mean or angry in black.

Ah ha, got it.

He pulled a maroon Polo shirt over his head and slipped into a pair of jeans, combing his hair with his fingertips. Patting his front jeans pocket, he grinned as he hustled out the loft, making it halfway down the stairs before he remembered he'd left the mother of his child in the bedroom.

Oops.

He peeked over his shoulder. Sage was on the top landing, breathing out a lot more than in, holding her belly, glaring at Niko. "Ooh, honey." He jogged up to meet her and offered his hand. "Sorry. Lost my head. Guess I'm a little excited. Won't happen again."

"You can't have this baby without me, you know." She winked, showing she wasn't as angry as she appeared. How could she be? They had always dreamed of this day.

Niko draped one arm around her back and held her hand across her belly—the waltz position—assisting her down the stairs. "Easy." Even though she looked so adorable waddling, he kept that to himself. Pregnant or no, a smart husband never commented on his wife's weight. About four weeks ago, he learned that little tidbit the hard way.

Sage was positively beaming this morning, her mood light and fun like it'd been throughout the entire pregnancy. Their marriage had never been stronger. Once they discovered their makeup sex—the night after he unearthed that soul-crushing secret—resulted in this precious gift, Niko bought every book he could find on parenting and pregnancy. He accompanied her to each doctor visit—the ultrasounds his favorite—and leaned more on Frankie to take up the slack in his absence at work.

Downstairs, his gaze roamed from one side of the living room to the other. He scuttled into the kitchen and checked by the door. Huh? Where did he leave—?

"Looking for these?"

From his peripheral vision, he caught his wife's silhouette, his shoes dangling off two fingers. Not wanting to upset her, he gently unhooked them from her grasp. "Where were they?"

"Next to your briefcase in the living room, right where you left them."

He offered her a wan grin. "Thank you, dear." He slid one foot into his loafer, but before he had a chance to put his foot in the other one, Colt zipped by, snatched it in his teeth, and ran to the bottom of the stairs. Head down on front paws, his rear end shot in the air and his stubby tail wagged like a metronome on speed. "Colt, not now buddy."

Colt's hips waved side-to-side, his head mimicking a bobble doll on a station wagon's dash. His I-wanna-play gambit.

With an awkward grin, Niko's gaze slid to Sage, and she grimaced. He opened his arms wide and shrugged. "Don't blame me. It's his fault."

Sage waddled over to Colt and with one pointed finger ordered, "Drop it." On cue, the little traitor dropped the nutmeg loafer, and she leaned over, scooping it with one hand.

"Was that so difficult? Seriously, Niko. We've got to go, or I'm going to have this baby right here." Pain from another contraction registered in her eyes and her grip tightened on the shoe.

Niko inched closer, gently tugged the loafer from her grasp, and slipped it over his white sock. Searching left and right, he patted his pockets.

"Your keys are on the rack in the kitchen. Honestly." She shook her head, lumbering toward the door. From behind, her walk sort of reminded him of Ruger, but again, he kept that to himself.

He held open the door for Sage and told the kids, "Next time you see us, we'll have your baby brother. Uncle Ben will stop by in a few hours to let you out. Watch the house."

From his doggy bed, Ruger groaned his acceptance. Head drooped, Colt sulked in the kitchen, his tail perfectly still. Neither of the kids looked happy about this.

* * *

Friday, May 11, 2007 11:00 a.m.

I laid Noah Philip Quintano in my bed and surrounded him with pillows. Interlocked my fingers and stretched high above my head, releasing a drawn-out yawn. I crawled next to Noah and propped my head on an open hand. The doctor advised not taking naps with a newborn, but I couldn't resist lying next to him while he slept.

My eyelids became weighted, and I struggled to stay awake, the rhythm of my son's chest lulling me into tranquility. Like his Daddy, his tiny nose whistled light snores, billowing through the loft.

Somewhere between admiring my perfect child and fighting the need for sleep, I must have drifted off, because my legs jerked me awake and I rolled off the side of the bed. Tan Berber carpeting cushioned my fall, but my head hit the nightstand on the way down. My ears rang with a loud buzz as if I'd stuck my face in a beehive. I wiped the back of my skull and checked my palm for blood.

I sprang to my knees and peered over the pillow at Noah. Sound asleep, Noah suckled, his pink tongue darting in and out of wet, puckered lips.

Exhaling, I sat back on folded legs. The house was dead silent. Soft tap, tap, taps of Colt's nails on the ceramic tiles announced he was scheming for a way inside the cookie jar, out of reach on the kitchen counter. Normally I'd holler down to him. Today, I didn't have the energy.

Setting one hand on the mattress, I hoisted myself to my feet when a separation between the mattress and box spring drew my attention. Unbidden, my mind replayed the day I lost Chloe, that awful day in the hospital when she succumbed to her injuries, the day her soul chose heaven over dealing with an imperfect life. Because she had never regained consciousness, I feared her last memories might be of Gaylon and not of me, in that basement.

When Niko and I returned home, I plodded upstairs to change my clothes, saturated with my sister's blood. As I slipped off my jeans, the leather-bound book dropped to the floor. Not wanting a reminder of Gloria's wrath, I stuffed it under the mattress with the intention of perusing the contents after we'd buried Chloe.

Time got away from me.

I discovered we were pregnant. Niko and I converted the guest room into a nursery and redesigned the lower section of the loft, added an antique padded rocker, second crib, and changing table, for when Noah came home from the hospital.

Now, as my child slept, I slid my hand under the mattress and withdrew the book, unbuckled the front, and flipped to page one.

This was no book. It was a diary. Gloria's diary.

I skimmed through the pages, some with bloodstains, drips as if Gloria was writing while hooked to the IV. She listed each victim's name, where they lived, worked, what places they frequented. Times and dates meticulously detailed as though she and Gaylon were outside, watching, waiting for the perfect time to strike.

I thumbed through the diary for Chloe's name.

Toward the back of the book, my heart sunk to my gut.

Chloe Phillips. 1419 E. Meadow Place, Apartment 9B, Cambridge, Massachusetts. Interior design. Call for appointment.

Heat jagged up my chest as I read and reread what followed.

Gloria met Chloe and hired her to redesign the cabin. Once Gloria gained Chloe's trust—my sister returned day after day during the course of her work there—it didn't take much to abduct a woman in her own home. Her intention was to display the two of us at the cabin on Partridge Way, but apparently, the neighbor's German Shepherd ruined the plan. Gloria was afraid his barking would alert the authorities before they were ready.

She was right, of course. A dog named Buttons destroyed my chances of saving Chloe and his owner called Gloria to let her know about the intruder. But by that time the Skeeters no longer owned the cabin. Months before, they sold the property to a developer who planned to tear it down the following month, which is why their name didn't come up when Frankie ran a background check on the owner of record.

I read farther.

The pencil marks above the two pulleys were a stencil. Gloria intended to scrawl the message in my and Chloe's blood. Then take her brother and disappear to Aruba where, according to her notes, there was no extradition. Clipped to the diary's back cover were reservations and tickets.

Odd that they choose the same place Niko and I honeymooned.

I flipped back a few pages.

Gloria used a computer to generate the man's voice that haunted my phone. Most of the stories she told me were true, except for the meshing of her and brother's experiences. In her warped mind, they were one person. Gaylon had the girlfriend and went to the masseuse, but it was Gloria who'd killed them, defending her brother's honor.

They beat and tortured Chloe as payback for sleeping with Joe. When Gloria pressed my sister about her twin, Chloe begged her to leave me alone because I'd already been through enough. But hearing that I'd had a violent past intrigued Gloria and she demanded the details of my assault. When Chloe resisted, which she did several times, they took a body part—first the left breast, then the right, and then they moved on to her eyes.

Jaw clenched, I ran my fingers over the Gemini charm. How long did it take my sister to reveal the truth? Even after my lecture about dating a married man, she never once stopped loving me. She protected me until she had nothing left but an outer shell of herself.

Granted, the Skeeters gave her insulin now and then, but the high sugar levels in her blood forced her into a diabetic coma. That, combined with the pneumothorax, and her body just couldn't handle any more. Before her system shut down my sister endured excruciating pain. No wonder she told them what Benson whispered in my ear that night in Boston. She was trying to survive.

If only there was a way for me to have prevented her suffering.

The sad part was, no amount of wishing could ever bring my sister back. Moving forward, I could only show Noah how incredible his aunt truly was and tell others about how she sacrificed, how one unselfish act saved an entire family. If it weren't for Chloe, Noah would not be alive, and I promised to never take that for granted.

With the butt of my hand, I wiped my teary eyes dry. Snapped a Kleenex from the cuff of my sleeve, I'd kept for when my emotions bubbled over—a habit I adopted from Judy the day I finally made good on my promise to do a reading—and blew my nose.

My twin left this earth defending what mattered most in this world: family. In my eyes that made her a true hero.

Closing the diary, I startled when Niko entered the loft. "What are you doing home?"

"I missed my family," he said and kissed my cheek. Lowering gently, he perched on the edge of the bed, careful not to wake Noah. "Do I wanna know why you're on the floor?"

"Umm…probably not."

"Whaddaya have there? Wow. The publisher did the first print run of 'Scarred'? That's wonderful, babe. How's it look?"

I parted my lips to speak.

"You did remember to change the names, right? We can't risk a lawsuit."

"Erm…"

He held out his hand. "Lemme take a look. I'm dying to read it. You're always so secretive about your work."

"That was then. This is now."

"No, I know." He wiggled his fingers. "So?"

"This isn't 'Scarred.' It's…"

A grave expression replaced his smile, and he dropped his hand.

"It's Gloria's diary, and before you say anything, I forgot I even had it." I told him about stashing the diary under the mattress. "In all the chaos, I don't recall taking it from the cabin."

"Lemme guess. It's filled with surveillance details on each victim, including what they did to them, and why."

"How'd you know?"

Niko twisted his lips as though that was a stupid question.

"There's a section on Chloe." I hung my head and told him what I read.

He slid down to the floor. "I'm sorry, babe. That must've been hard to read."

"There's only one thing I can't figure. Neither Gloria nor Gaylon had any computer experience. She even talks about being all thumbs when it comes to technology. Her words, not mine. So, who hacked my computer and showed her how to disguise her voice?"

As he stood, he swatted his hand. "Ah, I'm sure it's nothing to worry about," he said, but his eyes betrayed him. "C'mon—" he stuck out his hand to help me up— "let's snuggle with our boy."

Colt bolted up the stairs and dove on the bed, circled round and round, and nested with a heavy sigh, making himself comfortable near the footboard. Ruger crested the top stair, lumbered over, and flopped on the carpet, in front of the nightstand.

As I lay in bed, surrounded by the ones I loved most, I should have felt safe. Niko and I finally had our "dream come true," our fresh start. Instead, a foreboding darkness needled my bones, my mind consumed with deadly images.

What did our future hold? A co-conspirator was still out there, roaming in the shadows, stalking the streets—and free to return whenever the mood strikes.

ABOUT SUE COLETTA

Sue Coletta is a member of Mystery Writers Of America and Sisters In Crime. She lives in northern New Hampshire with her husband and four-legged baby. If you catch her strolling on the beach or roaming the rural backroads don't be surprised if she stops to chat with you about her books or her two beautiful granddaughters. Just don't ever call her Grandma.

GET IN TOUCH WITH SUE

Website
www.suecoletta.com

Facebook
www.facebook.com/SueColetta1
www.facebook.com/SuePhillipsColetta

Twitter
www.twitter.com/SueColetta1

Blog
www.crimewriterblog.com

Goodreads
goodreads.com/SueColetta

Google+
plus.google.com/u/0/+SusanColetta

StumbleUpon
www.stumbleupon.com/stumbler/SueColetta1

Pinterest
www.pinterest.com/suecoletta1/

LinkedIn
www.linkedin.com/pub/sue-coletta/a0/1b9/161

Tirgearr Publishing
www.tirgearrpublishing.com/authors/Coletta_Sue

CPSIA information can be obtained
at www.ICGtesting.com
Printed in the USA
LVOW07s1731101017
551899LV00013B/849/P